EXCHANGE
AT THE
BORDER

Alexandra Goodwin

Everglades Publishing

Exchange at the Border
All Rights Reserved.
Copyright © 2015 Alexandra Goodwin
v4.0

Cover Photo © 2015 thinkstockphotos.com. All rights reserved - used with permission. Rasputin image from conspiraciones.es

Everglades Publishing

ISBN: 978-0-692-39365-9

Library of Congress Control Number: 2015903966

PRINTED IN THE UNITED STATES OF AMERICA

To my mother, Grace Salem
For giving me wings

Acknowledgements

I am fortunate enough to have had an army of teachers, from early childhood all the way through college and beyond, who gave of themselves with love and joy and generously shared their wisdom and knowledge. I am especially grateful to my novel writing teacher Mark Spencer, author of *Trespassers, A Haunted Love Story: The Ghosts of the Allen House,* and *The Masked Demon,* among many others. Mr. Spencer guided me through the magical process of creating something from nothing.

My gratitude goes to Prudy Taylor Board, author of *A Grave Injustice* and *Murder a la Carte,* among many other books, who inspired me to start "one page at a time."

Special thanks to Patricia Gaviria, author of *Volver a Ser Feliz* for her invaluable input and advice.

My early readers: my mother Grace Salem, my son Glenn Goodwin, my husband Craig, fellow writer Laura Cherington, my friends Rossana Wallenburg and Betty Elster: thank you all for your incredible feedback and insightful observations, your honesty, and your support. To my friends Stacey Rowe and Julia Wolfe, thank you for always cheering me on, and to my daughter Sabrina and son-in-law Joshua Dunn for sharing in the enthusiasm of this journey. My eternal gratitude to my father Albert Salem for making it all possible.

Special thanks to my sister Cynthia Semaan for providing me with some of the research used in this book, and for celebrating each milestone with me as the story developed.

Finally, this book could have never been written without the love and support of my mother, Grace Salem, who prompted me to write down all the stories I imagined, especially the crazy ones. She taught me to listen to that voice inside that nags us, and guided me toward the fulfillment of my dream by encouraging me to recreate my world and writing about it.

Last but not least, I thank my husband Craig, for putting up with my seclusion, tantrums, and mood swings during the four years it took to write this novel. As I put my heart and soul into this story, I could not have asked for a better soul mate.

Preface

When I set out to write this book, I had no idea of the journey I was embarking on. Scenes of towns in Mexico and Russia, where I have never been, flashed through my mind at the most unexpected times. Characters, both fictional and historical, began populating these places with increasing frequency, until they became so insistent that I could not continue to ignore them. I could not understand. Where did they come from, and what were they trying to tell me?

It wasn't until they began waking me up in the middle of the night that I decided to acknowledge them. I took a notebook and began to write down these images. Soon that notebook was filled with seemingly disconnected scenes, interspersed with endless notes from research I felt compelled to do on a specific period of Russian history.

Puzzled about what might become of it, I began connecting the dots, and gradually the words shaped up into the book you now hold in your hands.

Because this is a work of fiction, completely imagined except for the historical allusions, I took the literary license to make up the names of certain cities in Mexico and the United States. Any similarity with real places is purely coincidental. The names of places in Mexico are in Spanish, and their meanings are intentional. A brief translation follows:

Las Colinas: The Hills

Ciudad Encantada: Enchanted City
Paso de los Valientes: Passage of the Brave
Valle de las Serpientes: Valley of the Serpents
I hope you enjoy the journey as much as I enjoyed creating it.

Prologue

Ekaterinburg, Russia
July 17, 1918

All is still. Even the doctor, the cook, and the waiters have been shot. I hover above the bodies of my family and members of our royal household. How can I still be thinking? It is hard to see through the curtain of gun smoke. Billowy clouds of gray and a red blotch here and there have turned the basement into a chamber of horrors.

Blood flows in a steady stream from my father's head. They executed him first. Then they shot my mother. Twice. She lies in a puddle of her own blood, still warm, while the cement on the floor soaks up the life she once had. At least she does not have to witness Tatiana's death, or the screams of pain coming from Olga, or my sister Maria as she writhes while losing consciousness. My mother, Czarina Alexandra, bore enough pain to last her a few lifetimes, witnessing my brother, Alexei, endure the curse of hemophilia. She would probably be glad to see that the prince will not be suffering much longer: he bleeds so fast. I hear a whimper. A moan, perhaps? A gunshot. He is quiet now.

It was four o'clock in the morning when the caretaker in the village summoned us out of bed. He said the White Army was coming to rescue us from the Reds and we should wait for them here. "Just sit comfortably in these chairs. It won't be long." We must have waited two hours in the sepulchral silence of this cove, but my nurse realized we were going to be executed when the first guard entered and pointed his gun at us. She used the pillow that she brought down from the upstairs bedroom to shield me from the bullets. She didn't know that my mother had sewn all our diamonds and precious stones to the inside of our gowns. It was hard at first for the bullets to penetrate, but once they did—the guard was relentless—the gems shattered inward. I'm a glittering, bloody wreck.

An invisible force thrusts me back into my body as it twitches, and I gasp for air, almost fainting. The pain is excruciating. I try to move away from my desolation, but my legs won't respond. The intense pain paralyzes me and pins me to the ground. The last of the guards marches out of the room, the sound of boots resonating on the frigid floor. The door behind me opens. Then it shuts.

I hear the sounds of blood dripping and my own fading breath. While my life unravels, Rasputin's image appears.

Rasputin, our beloved friend. What would he think if he saw us lying like this? Would he cast a curse on the Reds? He did say to my mother more than once that the dynasty would only last as long as he was alive. He foresaw our demise with his inner eye, but as powerful as he was, even he could not stop it. Mother should have known our days were numbered when he was assassinated. And although certain sectors of Russian society thought he was the problem in Russia, they weren't content with just getting him out of the way. Their fury extended to my family. To me. What did I do to them?

Now I see that Rasputin's spirit and his influence were

enmeshed in my mother's soul like a hook in a fish's mouth. The people of Russia saw her as a threat to the country. In order to eradicate all the vestiges of Rasputin's debauchery, members of the royal family offered my father, Nicholas, the opportunity to save himself by isolating my mother in a convent like a leper. Nevertheless, he refused; he loved her too much, and he chose that we remain together, believing the lie that we'd be exiled to Europe.

But no country opened their doors to us, and the emerging forces wanted to do away with the monarchy, once and for all. The only way to do that was to eliminate us. Without knowing it, my father went along with the extinction of monarchy, accepting the legacy of violence and destruction that would stain this nation's history for generations to come.

Red Army, royals, and peasants—their anger drowned in a sea of blood.

Chapter 1

T he gunshots did not keep up with him. Porro Camorra climbed the brick wall that separated the hacienda from the world he belonged to and jumped. Now that he was on the other side, he wondered if he would ever see Azucena again.

Only an hour earlier, the lines that had separated society since the Spanish conquest of the New World had blended with their tears, blurring all notions of class, place, and etiquette. Overtaken by happiness, he had kissed Azucena openly, in broad view. He had just finished his shift working at her father's agave farm when she came running.

"Porro, I have something important to tell you," she said.

He looked around to make sure nobody was watching.

"What is it, *mi amor?*" he asked, wiping the sweat from his forehead.

"Um…"

"What?" He thought it odd that she would hesitate.

"I'm pregnant," she blurted out.

A wrecking ball.

"It's not true."

"Yes."

Everything in Porro's field of consciousness turned upside down. The silence between them held unspoken accusations of rape and betrayal, his breath suspended like a kite swiftly disconnected from the string. His senses emerged from the depths of turmoil, doubt, and fear. He weighed the implications this would have in both their lives. Only a moment ago, he was the loyal servant at the Gonzalez Barista estate, the young man who had faithfully served the family since he was thirteen. Only a moment ago, she was one of the heirs to the massive wealth that had blessed the Gonzalez Baristas throughout the generations. Which way would the scales tip this time? Would the force of his love for Azucena prevail over centuries of class and race discrimination?

"I'll talk to your father," he said.

A shadow came over her face. "We'll never be able to marry. My father will never approve!" She burst into tears.

"Don Francisco is a fair man; don't underestimate him. I'll go to my room, take a shower, and dress like a gentleman. I'll go to the main house tonight and ask your father for your hand." Porro managed to smile, his white teeth glistening in the sun against his dark face.

"He'll never go for it, Porro. Not in a million years."

"You'll see. Everything will work out." He gathered his tools and put them away in the shed. "Go to the main house now and wait for me. I'll be back tonight." This could be the beginning of something huge, where the division between classes would blend in the sea of love. Then again, it could indicate the end of life as he had known it. He turned to Azucena once more and kissed her, long and tender, as never before.

Azucena turned around and walked the winding path

laced with roses and cactus in bloom. She passed the gazebo with its iron benches and ornate octagonal walls. Two cement eagles guarded the steps that led to the back porch. She tiptoed inside the house.

"I saw that." Cesar came out from behind the curtains in the library. Startled, she stopped. "Wait until I tell Papá what I saw," he said.

"There's nothing to tell." She hoped he was bluffing.

"You kissing Porro? Father's not going to like that."

"I'm not afraid of you. Go ahead! Tell him. Besides, Porro is coming tonight to talk to Papá."

"About what?"

"None of your business."

"It is my business. You are my little sister, and I'm not going to let an Indian get involved with our family."

"Too late for that, Cesar," she sneered.

Cesar came closer to her. "What do you mean?"

She didn't respond. Instead she walked past him to her room. She had to get ready for dinner and the big moment with Porro. Cesar grabbed her by the arm. "Not so fast."

"Let me go! You're hurting me!"

"Cesar!" Their brother, Carlos, walked in, taking off his working gloves and hat. He had been in the stables supervising the new groomer. "Let her go," he said, freeing her from Cesar's grip. "What's all this about, Azucena?"

"She's a tramp!" Cesar yelled.

Sobbing, Azucena stuttered as she tried to say something, but she couldn't.

"You can tell me. I'm your favorite brother, remember?" Carlos said sweetly.

She lifted her eyes to him. "I…" she began.

"Go on, don't be afraid," Carlos prompted.

"I…am…pregnant."

The world stopped turning and dead silence saturated the room, yet everything whirled around like the eye of a hurricane.

"Who's the father?" Carlos mustered.

Azucena shook her head. If anybody had a right to know, it would be her father.

Carlos pulled Azucena to his chest. "It's okay; you don't have to tell me," he said, stroking her hair. "I'll arrange for you to stay with Aunt Sofía in Ciudad Encantada. The air on the coast will be good for you, and you'll stay there until you have the baby. I'll make up some excuse for Papá."

"No way! I'm marrying Porro!" she gasped. The secret was out. "He's coming here tonight to ask for my hand." She pushed him away.

"Azucena! Papá must never know about this. It will kill him," Carlos said.

"Papá is reasonable. He will come around. Porro will prove to all of you how good he is."

"He doesn't belong with us, Azucena. Don't you understand? He can't possibly blend in. Too much mixed blood."

"I'm going to kill that bastard," said Cesar, taking a rifle from the cupboard. He opened the French doors and ran out.

The estate towered above the valley below. It was one of the biggest pieces of land owned by one of the oldest families during the settlement of the Inquisition. It comprised hundreds of acres flanked by a stream that wound around a forest and clear fields of agave. Porro knew his way around, but he realized he was trapped within the walls that surrounded it. He saw Cesar coming out of the main house with a rifle on his shoulder and began to run. In his haste, he failed to go toward the main entrance, veering instead toward the back of the hacienda, which was closed off by walls without gates. As Cesar ran after Porro, Carlos went after his brother to stop him. They kept a close distance from Porro but were unable to get him. It was getting dark quickly, and there was no moon this night.

Suddenly, Porro tripped on a branch, entangling himself in the brush. The brothers gained on him, panting like wild dogs after their prey. As Porro tried to get up, a hand pushed him down.

"We got you!" said Cesar.

"Let me go!" Porro tried to free himself from Cesar's strong grip.

"No way, amigo. You're dead!" Cesar lifted his rifle to his shoulder, focused, and pressed the trigger. Porro covered himself with his hands, waiting for sure death, but Carlos pushed Cesar's arm away from Porro and into the sky. An owl fell from a branch.

"What's the matter with you? Are you crazy?" Carlos said.

"We need to get rid of him."

"Not like this, Cesar. We wouldn't get away with it no matter what we say, and Azucena would never forgive us."

"I don't care about her forgiveness. Look what she's done to our reputation."

Realizing he was still alive, Porro seized the opportunity

to spring back up and pounce on Cesar, trying to knock him down. But Cesar was stout and immovable like a statue. He grabbed Porro by the neck and pushed him back down.

"Fucking Indian," Cesar said, kicking him in the shin. "We need to do something fast." He turned to Carlos. "If Papá knows about this, he'll force them to marry."

"Papá will never accept him as his son-in-law. All we have to do," Carlos whispered, "is threaten him so he doesn't come back. We'll tell Papá that he found another job somewhere else. I doubt Porro will have the courage to come back if we threaten him."

Cesar's thirst for revenge rose up like vomit. He started kicking Porro's legs.

"Stop!" Carlos said. Then he turned to Porro and pulled him up.

Porro stood up with difficulty. His legs ached, and he had a cut under his knee. It was bleeding. Carlos looked him in the eye. "Now you listen to me, Porro, and listen well. You must leave and never come back, you hear me?"

Porro didn't answer.

"I'm talking to you!" Carlos said. "Did you hear me?"

"I'm not leaving until I talk to Don Francisco," Porro said. "I'm going to propose tonight."

"You're not talking to anybody as long as I'm the eldest brother," said Cesar.

"You can't stop me."

"You lowlife, you need to know your place in the world! You don't belong with us!" Cesar said.

"I love your sister, and I want to marry her."

"You'll never be part of our family, and I'll make sure

my father never finds out about this." Carlos became more forceful.

It had always been that way. He'd be stuck in the role that society had assigned to him since birth. No matter how well he behaved or how smart he was, there was no way out. His only hope was Don Francisco, who was a reasonable man. All he needed was a chance to prove to him that he was worthy of his daughter. The fact that he was willing to assume the responsibilities of a father would show, without a doubt, that his love for her was greater than their class differences.

Cesar aimed his rifle at Porro. Confident that he had cornered him, he gloated in the fear that shone in Porro's eyes and delayed the shooting, counting the seconds marked by the quick breaths coming from Porro and Carlos. Suddenly, Azucena snuck out from behind him and jumped on him. Cesar fell forward, the trigger went off, and Carlos fell backward as Porro sprinted out of the way, disappearing into the night.

Chapter 2

The room was dark and gloomy despite the bright red and yellow walls. An old sofa sat under the window, partially covered by a white lace curtain. In front of it, a vase with fresh cut sunflowers sat on a pine coffee table adorned with Spanish ceramic tiles in bright shades of green, orange, yellow, and blue. Old newspapers lay neatly stacked in a corner of the room. In the kitchen, a pot of beef stew with jalapeños, onions, and garlic had been simmering all day, infusing the house with a spicy aroma.

"Just like that," Celestina repeated, with her hands on her waist.

"It's not so simple, Mamá. I have to leave," said Porro.

"But you have a job, responsibilities, and obligations. You can't leave like that!"

"You would never understand."

"What I don't understand is why now, why so suddenly. One moment you have a job, and the next you are packing to go to America!"

"Mamá, please, don't make me explain," he sighed.

Celestina looked at him. "What have you done, son?" she asked in a low voice, almost afraid of the answer.

"I can't..."

"You are running from the law," she said knowingly.

"It's not the way it seems. I really didn't do anything wrong. You have to believe me, Mamá."

She believed him. He was a man who had been born old, carrying all the streetwise knowledge of somebody who had lived a gruesome life. He had not had a childhood like her other six children, because he had come to this life unexpected, uninvited. There had been no time left for him, for love, or care. He grew like the weeds, wild and everywhere, because of, or despite, the circumstances.

"People die crossing the border," she continued.

"I'll die if I stay."

"So you are running away." She hadn't noticed anything unusual in his behavior lately that could indicate he was in trouble. "Is somebody trying to hurt you, son?"

"It doesn't matter."

"Porro, you need to tell me what's going on."

He did not respond.

"What have you done?" she insisted.

He didn't want to lie to his mother, but how could he explain to her that he had been seeing the daughter of his employer, and got her pregnant at that?

"You'll have to accept this, Mamá." He picked up his backpack from the sofa and headed for the door. Celestina gasped.

"Don't leave, *m'hijo*! Please! I am sure we can find a solution if you would just tell me what happened!" She began to cry.

"Excuse me." He went past her.

She intercepted him. "Don't leave, Porro! I need you! I'll tell you what. Let's go to Father Lozano—"

Porro laughed for the first time that evening, thinking how glad the priest would be if he stopped seeing Azucena. Besides, how would Father Lozano view the fact that she was pregnant?

"No, I can't see Father Lozano," he simply said.

"I still don't see why you have to leave the country. Please, Porro. If not for me, at least do it for Paco—"

"What about Paco? I can't be responsible for my brother. I tried to help whenever I could, but really, it's not my fault he's retarded." A swollen vein, thick and blue, crossed his forehead like lightning. It happened each time he got angry. "You brought him into this world, not me," he went on. He immediately regretted losing his temper, especially when it came to Paco, whom he loved more than life itself.

Celestina dreaded the vein. It'd be better to ignore the comment. Why add to his stress? He had always been considerate with his brother, and he was always reliable. Now if he left, it would all fall on her. Her other children did not help much, having moved on with their lives.

Porro looked at his watch. It was 8:00 p.m. "I must leave now," he said.

"I know." She approached him slowly, the way one approaches a spooked horse, and caressed his cheek. She wished she could take back her words, but his fury was already unleashed. Maybe he would have stayed a little longer. Maybe she would have been able to help.

He limped to the door. The wound in his leg was beginning to swell. As she glanced at him, his skin dipped in chocolate, his hair slick and straight like the feathers of a crow, she thought of his father. Like him, Porro would cross that threshold and never come back. He exuded an animal strength, uncharacteristic for a person who was only five feet tall. He seemed confident, but as his mother, she knew his spirit was trapped in a corner somewhere. He seemed so resolute and yet so vulnerable. He was running away from something fierce, dark, and menacing. What could she do to help him?

She waited for Porro to turn around at the last minute, to have second thoughts, to suddenly realize that he didn't have to leave after all, but he didn't. So she approached him instead.

"Promise me you will take care of yourself. Stay out of trouble, and always pursue the good path. Find a church and a priest to guide you. Will you let me know that you are okay at least?"

"I can't promise you any of that, Mamá. I need to go now."

He opened the front door. The street opened up dark and menacing like the mouth of a monster waiting to engulf him. He had always been afraid of the dark. But now he had no choice.

Taking a deep breath, he put his right foot forward. Facing his biggest fear, he stepped into the night.

The bus ride from Quetzal to Paso de los Valientes took eight hours. He had had to wait a couple of hours for the next available ride. The ride was smooth across the dark country-side dotted with faint, orange lights coming from the windows of the early risers. He was overcome with anxiety mixed with exhaustion. Feelings of sheer happiness for Azucena's pregnancy collided with the more urgent need to stay alive so he could one day reunite with her and marry her. He needed to sleep so he could be fresh and alert for what awaited him, but between being hungry and full of foreboding, he couldn't. The police were probably looking for him already, since Cesar would clearly take this opportunity to enlist the authorities against him, but first they would rush to Carlos's rescue, trying to save his life. By the time the police decided to go after him, he would be long gone. He hoped Carlos was not dead, since he was the nicer of the two brothers. He understood Carlos's position, and he knew that with time, he would earn the approval of Azucena's Spanish family. As far as Cesar, he had been an angry, temperamental man as long as Porro could remember, and he had had his brush with the law. Porro was surprised that Cesar had access to guns, because he knew he was on probation for assaulting a trespasser who turned out to be a contractor.

As soon as he left home, Porro had gone to his friend Alvaro, whom he had known since elementary school. Alvaro was a foreman in a construction company, and he made good money. If anybody could lend him money, it was Alvaro. Porro knew he could count on him for anything, including borrowing the $2,500 it would cost to cross the border. Alvaro put him in touch with a Coyote who was scheduled to guide a group the next day.

"I charge two thousand dollars a head, but you are joining at the last minute, so it will cost you two thousand five hundred," Coyote had said on the telephone.

Although Porro couldn't see the correlation between the two facts, he agreed. He had no choice.

By the time he got to the terminal in Paso de los Valientes, the sun was beginning to rise above the red roofs of the little houses, the dust like a veil of speckles. He could feel the power of the desert already in his veins, beckoning in a sinister, insistent manner. He could almost taste the other side.

He went to the restroom to clean the wound in his leg. The dressing was soaked with blood, so he threw it away. He covered the wound with paper towels, and he splashed cold water on his face. When he stepped out, people were beginning to show up, probably on their way to work. The strong aroma of freshly brewed coffee hit him, but he didn't dare buy anything. Just in case the police got wind that he was leaving the country, he decided to lay low. No witnesses.

The morning dragged on, and it grew increasingly hot. Porro dozed off on one of the benches outside the terminal, waiting for Coyote and his group to gather in the afternoon.

Around four o'clock, after siesta, a man in his early forties counted money in a corner of the bus terminal. He was five feet tall and had a sizable belly and a long, black moustache. He was white. Porro walked over to him.

"Porro?" Coyote guessed.

"Yes."

"You got the money?"

"Yes." Porro dug his hand in one of the inside pockets of his backpack, took out a thick envelope, and gave it to the man.

Coyote turned his back on Porro to count the bills one by one.

"Good!" he said moments later with a smile. "As soon as the whole group is here, we'll begin our journey." Then he motioned to Porro to have a seat on one of the benches. A young man in his twenties was already sitting there, peeling an orange. The peaceful look on his beardless face reflected his innocence. A sheer luster of sweat covered his cappuccino-brown skin, which gave away that he was a mestizo. He carried a khaki backpack that bulged behind him like the shell of a turtle, weighing down his small frame. He gnawed on the orange without bothering to separate the sections. Juice dripped from his chin, slipping down his fingers and arms. He slurped, wiped his hands on his pants, and took out another orange from his backpack.

"Want one?" he offered.

Porro stood by the bench, ignoring him.

"My name is Marco Sanchez," said the young man, extending his hand. When Porro looked away, he simply shrugged. "Where are you headed?"

"Same place you are," Porro scoffed. He bent down, picked up a pebble, and threw it toward the fountain in the center of the street. The pebble landed in the water, making a clean "plop" sound as it hit the surface.

Same place. Porro wondered why others would leave the comforts of home for an unknown destiny. He wondered how many of them were actually running for their lives.

"Where are you from?" Marco went on.

"Chiapas," he lied.

Marco didn't buy it. People from the jungle region of Chiapas were of Mayan descent, peaceful and hardworking. They were also poor. This guy looked like an Aztec warrior.

Marco continued, "Are you traveling alone?"

Porro shifted and sighed. "Yes," he said resigned.

"Me too," said Marco.

Porro considered the situation. He knew it was not easy to cross the border. It wouldn't be a bad idea to make a friend or some kind of connection. Feigning interest, Porro asked, "So, why are you leaving Mexico?"

"I have a sister in America that I haven't seen since I was five."

"You're lucky."

"I suppose," said Marco, looking down at the floor.

"You suppose? You'll have it made!"

"We'll see. I haven't seen her in such a long time; I don't know how it will all work out."

"What's her name?"

"Marena."

"She must be happy to see you."

"Actually, she doesn't know I'm coming."

"Do you know where she lives?"

"When my aunt died, I found the letters my sister had sent me from America in one of my aunt's drawers. My aunt kept them from me. One of them had an address in Hope, Texas."

"Why didn't she want you to know?"

"She was afraid I would run away looking for her."

"What about your parents?"

A shadow came over Marco's features, and his semblance was suddenly somber. "It's your turn, my friend. What's your story?"

Porro hadn't thought about what to say if somebody asked. He had to be careful. He couldn't afford to end up in jail.

"I don't have one," he said, shrugging his shoulders.

Marco laughed. "Like hell you don't."

Porro had to think fast. If he told the truth, he could be caught. If he lied, it could backfire. He decided to bury his past somewhere inside his heart. It was too sacred to share, especially with a stranger. It belonged to Azucena and him only.

"Well, if you insist. My story begins," he pointed north, "in Hope, Texas."

Chapter 3

It was still dark outside since there was no moon. The stars sprayed the sky with a dusty glow as Gwen made her way to the guesthouse in her backyard as she did every morning. Unlike every morning, today she felt uneasy. She was due in two weeks, and she wasn't sure if her hormones were playing games with her head, or if there was something else adding to her uneasiness.

She and Tony had not been getting along lately. "You have an insatiable need for attention," he had told her. And that had been enough for her to shut him out and muddle through the darkness that lurked in her mind. Slowly, she had slipped into a hopeless depression. The doctor had told her not to worry. "Every woman gets depressed during pregnancy. It's because of the hormonal changes," he had said. Still she had reason to be depressed sometimes, although she tried in vain to push those feelings away.

She entered the guesthouse, which had been converted to house chinchillas. Inside, the temperature was permanently set to five degrees Fahrenheit to simulate the frigid climate of the mountains in Peru. A mixture of freshly cut grass and urine smells pervaded the air. She scratched her nose, walked to the closet, and taking out a gray sweater and a pair of work gloves, she put them on. Then she covered her nice sweater with a blue apron, but the ties weren't long enough to go around her pregnant belly. She shivered.

When she approached the cages that lined the wall, the chinchillas skittered forward. Six cages were mounted on a stainless steel shelf, connected by a corridor on the top where the male paced up and down at his leisure. There was only one male for every six females, and the corridor was designed in such a way that he could enter each female's cage whenever he wished. While the females came closer to the front, expecting to be petted, the male squirreled along. It was a good system designed to breed chinchillas. Galileo, the male, was named after the famed astronomer because of his uncanny ability to shine in every show. Gwen had bought him on the spot after he'd won first place for the fifth time in a row. One of Galileo's prized attributes was the rare dark silver of his fur, and his coat was soft, puffy, and silky. He was a third-generation champion, pure pedigree, and was a direct descendant of a chinchilla that had been imported from the mountains in Peru.

Gwen approached the cage where Victoria, her favorite female, was sitting. She pulled the tray under the cage forward and examined the droppings. There was no wax stopper, which meant she had not been impregnated. Gwen was annoyed. "Really, Galileo, I don't get it. She's pretty, and she's young; what more could you ask for? If you don't visit her soon, I'll lock her gate and you'll be out of luck. You continue playing hard to get, and you'll see where that gets you," she said.

As she walked over to the shelf on the opposite wall, where she kept the food pellets in an airtight container, she acknowledged that despite everything, she had a lot to be thankful for. She loved Tony and he loved her, but there was a void

EXCHANGE AT THE BORDER

in her he was unable to fill. This being her third pregnancy, she thought she'd be satisfied. Daniel and Melody kept her busy enough, but when she was alone with her chinchillas, she couldn't ignore the humming of her story begging to be heard. She had been so protected since...but no, she didn't want to think about that now. Old memories haunted her, images that popped up at the most inconvenient times. She couldn't help it. She tried to suppress them, but it became more difficult as time went by. Ever since her mother had died, she had tried to make sense of her pain. Then again, which mother was she grieving? She had put together all the pieces of the puzzle from the papers she'd found hidden in the drawers of Dolly Parker's dresser. It wasn't what she had found there but what she had hoped to find and didn't.

She scooped the dry food with one hand, while she opened the cage with the other, and refilled each container with fresh food. All the feeders were empty, which meant the chinchillas were eating properly. Then she disconnected the water bottles from the ring that held them, washed each one separately in the sink, filled them with distilled water, and replaced them in their respective bottle holders.

Opening the cages one at a time, she removed the "bathtubs," which were rectangular stainless steel containers, but because chinchillas are susceptible to pneumonia, they cannot bathe in water; therefore, they "bathed" in marble powder. This polished the coat, neutralizing the odor-producing bacteria that settled between the skin and their long hair. Gwen refilled the tubs with marble powder, put them back in the cages, and closed each door. She pulled the trays from under the cages and rolled up the newspaper that lined each one. Some of them, soaked in urine, broke before she could reach the trash can. She sprayed disinfectant, wiped them clean, layered them with clean newspaper, and replaced them under the cages. Then she proceeded to clean the room completely: she dusted the exposed walls; wiped the counter, table, and stool; and washed the sink and faucet. By the time she had swept and mopped the floor with disinfectant, she was exhausted.

Suddenly, she saw in the corner of her eye one of the chinchillas lying on its belly, a gray fluff ball curled up in a corner of the cage. Gwen approached it slowly. Chinchillas didn't sleep when there was food and activity around. She opened the cage, but the chinchilla didn't move. Taking the lifeless body in her hands, she noticed another chinchilla breathing with difficulty. Immediately, she put the dead chinchilla back in its cage, took off her apron and gloves, washed her hands, and rushed out the door. Another death. How many more could she endure?

She crossed the backyard in the misty gray morning toward the main house and called the vet.

Gwen was dismayed to find the house so quiet. The kids needed to go to school. Don't tell me he didn't get them up, she thought. This was not the first time he overslept, and it would not be the last.

"Hello? Anybody home?" she asked, looking up from the foot of the staircase.

The grandfather clock in the corner between the staircase and the front door struck seven ten in the morning. The bus would come promptly at seven fifty. She walked to the kitchen, dialed the number for Dr. Sinclair, and left a message with the answering service that he needed to come in right away. Even in the most sterile environments, bacteria spread fast, and if this were a case of pneumonia, as it seemed by the symptoms, it would only take a week to lose most of the animals.

After she hung up the phone, she looked at her watch. What should she do first: wake up the children or prepare their lunches? Lumbering heavily up the stairs, she decided to wake them first. Tony would have to make their lunches while she dressed them for school.

She entered Daniel's room. It was tidy, the bed made, but Daniel was not there. Alarmed, she went into Melody's room and found the same. She ran to the master bedroom and pushed the door open.

"Surprise!" A chorus of beloved voices greeted her from behind the side of her bed. Tony, Daniel, and Melody were cleaned, brushed, and dressed. Melody ran to her and hugged her, holding a "Happy Birthday" balloon, while Daniel and Tony carried a huge box wrapped in lemon and hot pink, her favorite colors. A big white bow was plopped atop the box and held down an envelope with a card inside.

"Happy birthday, Mommy," Daniel said.

"Happy birthday, Queen." Tony kissed her tenderly.

"Thank you, honey!" she said with tears in her eyes. "You are my best gift! You, you, and you!" she said, pointing at each of them.

"We love you, Mommy!" the children chimed in unison.

"I love you too, darlings! What a beautiful surprise! I think I'll open the gift tonight after dinner. What do you think?"

"Good idea, Queen," said Tony. "Kids, go downstairs and get ready for school. I will drive you this morning. We already missed the bus." He ushered the kids toward the stairs. Then he wrapped his arms around Gwen and whispered something in her ear. She blushed and pushed him away, but he did not let her go and began kissing her neck. She shuddered with delight as the spattering noise of broken glass in the kitchen pulled them out of their reverie.

Chapter 4

It was five o'clock on Tuesday afternoon. Two couples, one of them with a seven-year-old boy; a single young woman; and ten men between the ages of fifteen and twenty-five conglomerated near the fountain by the bus terminal. They all carried the bare minimum: Some had a small plastic bag with clothes for a few days, but most of them carried backpacks, except for the couple with the boy. The mother carried three small bags with clothes, a backpack, and a canvas bag with fruit, tortillas, and chili peppers. Despite the weight, she stood upright and strong, while her husband carried three gallon-size bottles of water in each hand and two in his backpack.

Coyote came out of the terminal one last time. Standing in the middle of the square by the fountain in the street, he looked in the direction of the group. The afternoon was fading into the evening. The sky was clear, except for the few clouds that stretched on the horizon, forming a curtain of pinks, oranges, and purples like a blanket for the sun to lie under. The smell of donkey manure enhanced the rancid smell of cheap beer.

"Listen up, people!" Coyote's voice was as dry as the desert.

The group gathered around him.

"We will be traveling at night and during the day, depending on the circumstances. Sometimes the immigration officers patrol the area during the day, in which case we'll have to hide. Now, this is the desert. There aren't many places to hide, but I will be your guide. We'll rest when we can. If we don't make much progress during the day, and it looks safe, we'll trek during the night. There's no moon this week, so it will be a challenge. There will be times when we'll just have to wait it out until it's safe to go on, and this could mean staying in the desert for a few days. This will delay your entry into the United States, and it could take up to a month between walking and waiting. You will need to be quiet—no talking, crying, or moaning, you hear?"

The group nodded.

"You will follow me in single line. If you fall behind, you will be left behind!" He looked around at their faces, seeking a sign that they understood.

The group stirred.

"Are there any questions?" Nobody answered. "You can still turn back if you feel you can't make it." Coyote waited. On the last trip, two women turned around before they had even started. He had to give them most of their money back, although he kept a portion of it for holding their space.

The couple with the seven-year-old boy looked at each other. They could still turn back and stay. They would just have to make the best of what life had laid out for them. The husband sighed. "Are you up for this, Mecha?"

"As long as I am with you, Gordo, I am."

"All right then, let's go!" Coyote turned around, motioning the group to follow him. One by one, the group marched behind him, steady and resolute.

The sun was setting on their left as they headed north. It was the best time of the day, when the heat goes to sleep and leads the way for the night to wear a blanket of ice on the darkening earth. One step, then the next…they made good progress across the diminishing town. An hour later, just as they had been told, they were already in the desert. It was flat for as far as their eyes could see, and so far the vegetation consisted only of thistles and weeds, pushing their way through occasional rocks and cracked soil.

The air became colder as the sun disappeared quickly behind the mountains in the west. As the evening progressed, a thousand shades of green slathered the sky with pink and purple, giving the horizon a sense of eternity. The beauty of the landscape contrasted with the roughness of the earth, tough and unforgiving.

They continued like that for three more hours, without stopping to rest. They reserved their water for the next day when they would have to endure the heat without shade.

By nine o'clock that night, Coyote stopped. "Okay, people, we'll take a break now. Those of you who want to eat can do so. Tonight we'll make good progress since the sky is clear. We have the whole night ahead of us, so if you need to do anything, this is the time to do it."

Porro and Marco sat on a rock. Marco took a package wrapped in white paper from his backpack and opened it.

"Do you want some?" he asked Porro.

Porro took three tortillas, filled them with the mixture of rice and beans, rolled them up, and ate. The rest of the group settled in little clusters. Mecha took two tacos from her bag and gave one of each to Gordo and their son. They would eat the perishable foods first, reserving the fruit and chili peppers for the rest of the trip. They ate in silence.

They rested for a few minutes before Coyote summoned them to resume the march. They continued walking, one step at a time, following the person in front of them. Porro and Marco were behind Mecha and Gordo, not too far from the front or the back. Having done the same journey for ten years now, Coyote knew the terrain like a salmon knows where to spawn, instinctive and certain. He led them in a zigzag across the desert, knowing when to slow down, when to turn right or left, and when to hasten the pace. The stars sprayed a dainty glow on the black sky like miniature diamond studs, turning the desert landscape into a world pregnant with hope and new life.

At 3:00 a.m., Coyote stopped again.

"Time for a break, people. If you need to go to the bathroom, do it now because it will be light in about two hours, and then we'll need to hide. We're very close to an area that has bushes, and that's where we will spend the day. We'll need to be quiet for a long time. It will be boring. It will be tiring." He began to walk along the line of travelers, inspecting them one by one. The only light came from the silvery glow of the stars above. Their eyes had adjusted to it. When he got to Mecha, his features softened imperceptibly. He observed her closely, lingering on her youthful features. She lowered her eyes, embarrassed, as his eyes rested on her cleavage. He licked his thick lips. Gordo stirred. Their eyes locked in a mental confrontation, the aggressor challenging, and the possible victim on guard. Gordo did not move; he did not even blink. Coyote continued with his inspection.

"What is that you're wearing?" he asked, pointing to Marco's chest, where something glinted in the dark.

"Nothing." Marco instinctively covered the object in his hand.

"Don't play stupid with me, boy. What is that you have hanging from your neck?"

"I told you, it's nothing!" Marco said, clasping his fist around his chain.

Coyote shook his head and shrugged. These assholes think they can outsmart me, he thought. He walked over to Porro and continued on to the men behind him. Then, unexpectedly, he turned around fast and threw a punch at Marco's jaw. Everybody gasped. They all had heard stories about unscrupulous Coyotes. You just never knew which kind you were going to get. They were all aware of the perils of crossing, and many times the biggest enemy was Coyote himself. Marco fell to the ground.

"Give it to me," said Coyote, holding out his hand.

Marco stroked his jaw and then spit on Coyote's hand. Coyote wiped his hand on his pants and turned to Porro. "Tell your friend to give me what he has hanging from his neck."

"He's not my friend," said Porro, keeping his eyes on Coyote.

Coyote could hear Porro's breath getting faster and shorter. He sensed an animal energy in Porro's eyes, framed by the emerging vein across his forehead. He knew some of these men were fearless; most of them had nothing to lose. They would kill if they had to, even if that meant sabotaging their goal to get to the other side. But many others were so eager to get to El Norte, they would take abuse as long as they got to the other side. For some reason, Coyote couldn't tell precisely which group Porro belonged to.

For the time being, Coyote decided to leave Marco alone. They had a long journey ahead of them. The farther they went into the desert, the more they would depend on him. This was only the second day. He knew he had the upper hand. Women didn't fight, and the men wouldn't stick their neck out for anybody. Even if they were capable of taking him down, they wouldn't. They needed him to guide them across the desert.

He turned around and walked over to the front of the group. "Okay, people, let's go!"

Porro offered his hand to Marco, but Marco refused. "Fuck off," he said as he shook the dust off his clothes and then stood behind Porro. They looked ahead as they followed one another toward the waning darkness.

Chapter 5

It was close to noon, and the sun beat down on the desert. Despite the warnings, nothing could have prepared them for the merciless heat that awaited them. Some of them weren't even aware of the thorns that stuck to their shoes and pants. Those wearing shorts got stung and had to stop occasionally to pull out the thorns. One snagged Porro's wounded leg, making the gash deeper and painful. Still, the group was upbeat. They were on their way to a better life, and all they had to do was plug along, one step at a time, each passing day bringing them closer to their dream.

Mecha and Gordo were sitting around a creosote bush, with a few acacia trees and tarbush providing a makeshift shelter. They began to weave dreams about El Norte. Lucas, their son, was well behaved. At some point, he wandered off into the brush to explore the surroundings. He imagined being the Lone Ranger on the lookout for Indians as he had seen so many times on TV. He ventured out a little bit more. Mecha took out some apples from her backpack.

"Why don't you invite those two boys over, *mi amor?*" she asked Gordo. "I'll check on Lucas in the meantime."

"Sure."

She disappeared behind some bushes while Gordo walked over to Porro and Marco who were sitting a few feet to the right. "You wanna join us?" he asked.

Marco smiled. Porro hesitated a little before getting up.

"I am Marco," he said.

"And I am Porro."

"Nice to meet you both," he said. "You can sit with us if you'd like. We can eat together."

Soon they were all catching up on their stories.

"I have a sister in Phoenix, Arizona," Gordo started. "She went ten years ago, and she's doing very well. She works for a wealthy family as a housekeeper, and she told us that her employers could use more help. The cook got married, and they asked my sister if she knew anybody that could replace her. She immediately wrote to us. We'll have a place to stay as soon as we get there. I will take care of the yard and household maintenance, and our son will go to school with the gringos. He will be the first one in our family to get an education. He wants to be a doctor." Gordo smiled at the thought.

Porro was about to say something when he spotted Coyote in between some branches in the brush. He got up and snuck toward the bushes. Gordo didn't seem to notice. As he walked over to the spot, Porro heard the stir of leaves and then a muffled whimper. He tiptoed in the direction of the sounds. A few feet from where he was standing, Coyote was forcing himself on Mecha. She struggled, her body pinned to the ground while he thrust with force. Porro thought about his options. If he interfered and tried to save her, he would have to fight Coyote, and he was already a target thanks to Marco. Porro couldn't afford to let anything or anybody get in the way of his reaching America. He needed to stay alive, and going forward toward Hope was his only option.

Mecha groaned, and Porro imagined if that were Azucena,

he would want somebody to come to her rescue. He walked slowly toward Coyote, but Coyote sensed his presence behind him. Just as Porro reached to grab him, Coyote jumped away from her. He pushed Porro, causing him to lose his balance and fall forward. There were small rocks on the ground, and as he hit the ground, a protruding rock stabbed his leg at the wound on his knee, opening a bigger gash that began to bleed profusely. Taking advantage of Porro's vulnerability, Coyote kicked him in the same spot. Porro suppressed a scream, holding his leg. It throbbed and bled. Grabbing him by the collar of his shirt, Coyote then put his hands around his throat and squeezed.

"When are you going to learn to mind your own business?" Coyote whispered. Porro had to close his eyes to avoid being cross-eyed due to Coyote's proximity to his face.

"Bastard!" Porro managed to say as he fought to breathe. The vein on his forehead was blue and swollen.

"C'mon, boy, aren't you gonna hit me?" said Coyote.

Porro was unable to speak as Coyote tightened his grip.

"You didn't see anything," said Coyote.

"Ugh!" was all Porro could manage.

"And you didn't hear anything!" continued Coyote.

Porro's face was turning blue from lack of oxygen. He couldn't free himself from Coyote's grip. Feeling he was going to pass out, he summoned the little strength he had left and instinctively kicked forward with his good leg, hitting Coyote in the groin. Coyote released his grip on Porro and bent forward, holding his breath. Now Porro was face-to-face with Coyote, who managed to stand up straight, still holding his groin. Porro felt the warmth of his blood trickling down his leg, which had begun to swell and burn in an ugly combination of fire and needles. Despite this, he stood like a wild cat ready to pounce, every muscle of his strong arms tight and powerful. He also knew he could beat Coyote to a pulp if he wanted to, but at the same time, he realized he was vulnerable. He had to stay alive and cross over if he ever wanted to see Azucena and their child again. He wasn't familiar with the terrain, and his life was in Coyote's hands. Coyote knew this all too well. He smiled, relieved. He had him. Knowing Porro wouldn't throw the first punch, Coyote tucked his shirt in and buckled his pants. Porro lowered his guard and relaxed, but his leg could barely hold him. At that moment, Mecha got up slowly, fixing her skirt. Her hair was tangled, her face strewn with dust. "Not a word of this to my husband," she warned Porro.

Coyote held his hand out to Porro. An unspoken pact had been sealed in the vastness of the desert.

Chapter 6

Ekaterinburg, 1918

Like a freight train going in reverse, I am thrust inside a long and narrow tunnel. In the dark, my entire life unreels fast and unstoppable. Images flash backward like a deck of cards shuffled before a game of poker. The train slows to a stop as a black dot appears in the frozen ground of Siberia. In the lead gray silence, it moves closer and closer until it gradually takes the shape of a shabby-looking peasant, his elongated black coat over run-down brown boots. His long, grimy hair, parted in the middle, hides a bump on his forehead—a crippled devil's horn—and under a swollen, pockmarked nose, a wispy beard darkens his sunken cheeks. It's our friend Rasputin!

From my bird's-eye view, a scene unfolds before me in a way I never experienced while I was alive. Rasputin confidently enters the palace, as if he has always belonged there. One of the courtiers announces him to my mother, Czarina Alexandra, and escorts him to her study. He bows to her. She is regal, beautiful, and intelligent, her composure an ice curtain that covers her pain, until she speaks. Then she breaks down.

"Grishka, how kind of you to come. Alexei is in his room having one of his attacks. Please help him," she pleads. Rasputin nods and goes to my brother's chambers, followed by my mother. I hate hearing Alexei cry; his wailing is arrhythmic, punctuated by spasmodic degrees of hopelessness and desperation. Maria, the nurse, can't do much to help him, but when our friend Rasputin enters the room, his presence is enchanting. It exudes peace, warmth, and power. Maria lowers her eyes and fiddles with her hands; she looks like a trapped bird desperate to escape. Rasputin walks toward her, knowing his hypnotic gaze paralyzes her.

"Leave us alone, Maria. Rasputin will take it from here," commands the czarina. Maria scurries past them, relieved.

When my mother and Rasputin are finally alone, he walks to my brother's bed, kneels down, and brings his face very close to Alexei.

"Lord Omnipresent, I implore you to have mercy on this soul..." His words dissolve in a sea of muffled pleas, lost somewhere between now and eternity. My brother becomes mesmerized, staring at Rasputin, as his breath slows down and his tears stop flowing down his milky cheeks. Amid his chants, Rasputin's hands hover above Alexei's chest, then rest on his torso, and slide all the way down to his feet, only to come back up. Rasputin is transported into another dimension, electrifying the air. He never touches Alexei, not even once.

The czarina gazes at my brother's transformation in disbelief. Her thin lips curve into a smile, soft and imperceptible, while she revels in complete adoration of the only person capable of helping her son. Standing three feet away from the bed, she watches, afraid to interfere, but as soon as Rasputin gets up, she runs to him.

"Grishka! You are a godsend! How can we ever repay you for what you do?" She is the empress! How can she act that way? Rasputin lowers his head humbly and starts for the door, and she follows him.

"Come again tomorrow."

"Of course, Matiushka. I'll be back." He exits the room, leaving Alexei enveloped in a peaceful sleep, free of pain.

Seen from above, Rasputin looks like a shabby, decrepit peasant, and my mother, the czarina of Russia, has fallen under his spell. I can see now the phony smile when he tells her what she wants to hear. The czar and the czarina don't issue a single decree or make a single decision without first consulting Rasputin. He has gained complete control of my mother's will, she who was thought to be stronger than the czar. Rasputin's word becomes law, carrying the authority of someone who can see the past, the present, and the future, as if he were reading it from a catalog.

Rasputin's influence on my parents causes a stir in the palace among those who don't believe in his special powers. Like my uncle Nicholai Alexander and his cohorts. Rumors circulate around the palace about my mother having intimate relations with Rasputin. The whole atmosphere is infected with the poison of mistrust and intrigue, injecting venom in the minds of the dukes and military men who think it's up to them to rescue the republic from the ineptitude of my father, Czar Nicholas, whom they believe has become a puppet of Alexandra and Rasputin.

The letters she wrote to my father while he was away on official business are placed in front of me. As I read them, I learn that she writes to Nicholas every day and tells him how much she loves him and misses him. She doesn't love Rasputin in a romantic way, only for what he does for my brother. As he bestows relief on Alexei, she relies on Rasputin's guidance and predictions with respect to the political affairs of the state. That's all. I wonder what Rasputin's position toward my family is.

Another scene unravels before me. Rasputin enters an apartment. A half hour later, he leaves accompanied by a woman, who holds his arm as they walk together to the bathhouses. There are other women already in the bath, and Rasputin gets in with them! The women lather his body with soap, and he kisses one, then another. When he gets out, he caresses one of the women, who is naked and writhes with pleasure. I can see he has an insatiable sexual appetite, which he satisfies with prostitutes and women of society alike. They all end up succumbing to his charm.

It's so hard to face reality from where I stand when I can't do anything about it. It hurts to see the total abandon and loss of control of these women, but men are not exempt. They all are in favor of this peasant who furrowed his way into my family, a rat who gained control of one of the most ironclad women in the history of the Romanovs. Did I have to die to see this?

Chapter 7

By the end of the week, life in Las Colinas, Mexico, had begun to roll back into a forced routine, as Carlos recovered in the hospital from the gunshot wound he had suffered during Porro's chase. Cesar enlisted the police in a fruitless search for Porro, not only to ensure he'd be behind bars for a long time but also to distract the investigators from uncovering the truth about the shooting.

When four days passed by with no word from Porro, Azucena descended into depression, and having to hide both her pregnancy and the events of that fateful night from her father didn't help matters at all.

While she wondered what had become of Porro, a group of immigrants was becoming one with nature as they acquired a new respect for the parched land. This forced bonding was pivotal to their survival as they trekked during the night and rested in the day.

"Stay still! Who lives?" Lucas said with his right hand in the shape of a revolver.

Porro raised his hands in the air. "Don't shoot!" he played along.

"I will make you my prisoner," said the boy, smiling. "Finally, I caught one!"

The boy escorted Porro to the spot where his parents were resting, all the while pretending Porro was an Indian. His parents were also supposed to be captive Indians, even though they were engaged in a lively conversation about big homes, clean streets, and grocery stores that smelled of disinfectant instead of juicy fruit.

"Oooh, I want some!" Lucas pointed to the grapes his parents were snacking on.

"What, this?" His mother played along.

"Yes," the boy replied, perplexed that his mother was not eager to share with him.

"Only Indians eat eagle eyes," said the mother, snuggly. Then she put one in her mouth, rolled her eyes, and made a sound of pleasure. "Mmm...so good."

"Ewww!" Lucas jumped up, momentarily grossed out by the thought. But then reality won. "I'll tell you what. You are not Indians anymore. You can be my mommy and daddy again."

"What do you think about that, Gordo?" She winked at her husband.

Just when he was going to answer, somebody screamed in the bushes. Gordo stood up and ran in the direction of the noise as Mecha pulled Lucas to her lap. Gordo saw Coyote coming out of the thicket, wiping his bloody hands on the inside of his shirt. His eyes flashed.

"We are resuming the march," he said, panting.

"What's going on?" challenged Gordo.

"None of your business."

"It is my business," said Gordo, walking past Coyote in the direction of the bushes.

Coyote intercepted him. "No, you don't. Let's go."

"Let me through." Gordo pushed him, but Coyote drew a knife from his back pocket. Gordo froze. Coyote approached

Gordo slowly, grabbed his arm, and twisted it. Gordo clenched his teeth, sweat dripping from his face.

"What are you going to do about it now?" challenged Coyote.

Gordo tried to free himself from Coyote and saw from the corner of his eye somebody lying in the brush. The body wasn't moving. Coyote tightened his grip, and Gordo winced and panted. He didn't want to attract Mecha's attention.

"I will cross you over if you behave," Coyote whispered in Gordo's ear. "The desert is tricky, and without me you don't have a chance. You don't want to jeopardize your family now, do you?"

Gordo knew he was right. As much as he wanted to help the injured man, his family came first. "No," said Gordo, struggling.

"I didn't think so," said Coyote, releasing his arm. Walking past Gordo, he put the knife away, fixed his shirt, and approached the group. "Okay, people, ready?"

"We can't go in this heat," someone protested.

"Then stay here and rot!" Coyote answered. "Those of you who want to get to the other side, follow me."

The sun was a murderous fireball. If they walked in those conditions, they would suffer, but if they stayed, they would perish for sure. Coyote continued, "It's all good with me if you stay. I already got paid."

One by one, the reluctant group of perplexed Indians and mestizos picked up their belongings and followed submissively, too preoccupied to notice that two men were missing from the group.

Chapter 8

Just south of the Texas border, Porro hid as best he could. Marco lay on the ground, a puddle of blood quenching the thirsty earth. Porro had heard the scuffle from the bushes and then nothing. Dead silence. His instinct told him to hide. He knew Marco had been hurt, and he realized he would be next. As for Coyote, he had left in such a hurry that he neglected to do a head count before resuming. In fact, he probably didn't care who made it across. He had already made his money, and fewer people meant easier crossing. Porro concluded that by the time Coyote realized he was missing, the group would be too far ahead to bother coming back for him. Let Coyote assume Porro would not survive the desert alone.

It took about forty-five minutes for the group to disappear from Porro's view. Only when he saw them far in the distance, like black pearls undulating in the heat, did he dare to crawl toward Marco. Dragging his swollen leg, which now oozed with green pus, he approached the body as it lay limp, facing the sun on the reddening earth. Marco was still alive but had lost a lot of blood. Porro figured if he wasn't dead yet, he would be soon. It didn't look like he would survive, and in his condition, he'd be a burden to Porro.

The heat pounded on the body. Three ravens had begun to circle above. Soon they would dive down and begin shredding the flesh. Porro limped toward the area where Marco had left his belongings. He opened the backpack and took the remaining apples and the jug of water.

It had only been four days since he had left home. The police were probably looking for him, and he knew they would never suspect him of leaving the country. They would go on a blind chase, harass his mother, and eventually give up. He thought of Azucena and their unborn child, how he had held her in his arms only days before. They could have been so happy together. What would she do now, alone without him, bearing the fruit of their love? Would she go along with her brothers and let them dictate the fate of her life? Perhaps. No, it would be unlikely that Don Francisco would find out and force her to marry somebody else. But then again, Porro knew it was the only way for her to save her reputation. Would she be able to love someone else the way she had loved him? As Porro pondered these questions, he felt defeated. He loved her and she loved him. They belonged together, even if society thought otherwise. Don Francisco appreciated him as a worker and eventually would come to terms with it. He was sure he would have accepted him as his son-in-law. Now, not only would Porro have to grieve for losing Azucena but he also was forced to run for his life. The brothers illustrated clearly the legacy of hatred and discrimination that began with the arrival of the white man in the New World.

Soon it would be night, and he was alone. He could fathom being chased by monsters, aliens, and wolves. But the dark in the desert? Suddenly, Porro considered turning back. His chances of making it to the border were so slim, especially with his infected leg. If he went back though, it meant sure death. His only recourse would be to turn himself in. He would go to trial, but would the truth about Carlos's shooting come out? Or would Cesar succeed in convincing the court that Porro was guilty? Was it prudent to take that chance? Porro turned toward the south and squinted in the afternoon sun. No, it would be suicidal to trust a system that had always failed him. There was no turning back. All he had to do was focus on reaching the north, where he had heard freedom and equality ruled, and everybody was treated with respect.

He turned back north again. Something glinted on the ground. He walked in the direction of the spark and realized that in his haste, Coyote had failed to take the locket from Marco, the reason for attacking him in the first place. Porro approached Marco's body, which lay still, and kneeled down to unclasp the locket from his neck. He saw with dismay that Marco's chest heaved imperceptibly, or was his mind playing tricks on him? He weighed his options. If Marco was still alive, he soon wouldn't be. It would be impossible to carry him in that state toward the border. Should he wait until Marco died and give him a proper burial? He decided that would be suicidal for him. If he stayed in the desert, he would die of dehydration himself.

No, he would have to leave Marco behind. Slinging the two backpacks on and holding the water in his left hand, he limped north through the burning sun, his fist closed around the silver locket. I'll have to find Marena, he thought.

Chapter 9

G wen was worried. The chinchillas were dying, and the vet couldn't stop the epidemic. Despite being so far along in her pregnancy, she spent most of the day monitoring the animals' behavior and keeping notes in a journal, just as Dr. Sinclair had told her to do. They had inoculated the animals with antibiotics, but some had already contracted pneumonia and it was too late.

She came back from the chinchilla house and started getting dinner ready when the phone rang.

"Gwen," the voice on the other end said when Gwen answered. "Turn on the TV, channel seven."

"What is it, Bebe?"

She had met Bebe in school, and Gwen had been drawn to her from the beginning. Bebe was intrigued by Gwen's dark hair and sparkly eyes, and she found the coffee-and-milk tone of her skin to be unique and exotic. She also never believed Gwen's name was really Gwen. At her insistence, Gwen had told her the story, but first she made her swear she would never, ever tell anyone. They had made a pact that would seal their secret for the rest of their lives.

"Just do as I say," said Bebe.

It was fifteen degrees outside. A fire crackled in the fireplace, rendering a woozy feeling of comfort. Gwen wiped her hands on the kitchen towel while she walked to the living room where Tony and the kids were watching cartoons.

They laughed as an angry swarm of bees chased after the Road Runner. Gwen changed the channel.

"No!" said Daniel as the image of a well-groomed reporter replaced the cartoons.

"Yes, I'll explain later, love," said Gwen, sitting next to them.

"A group of people trying to cross the border at Hope, Texas, was apprehended by the border patrol. According to the authorities, they will be detained at the Immigration Center in Hope and eventually be deported back to their countries of origin."

The voice of the reporter faded as Gwen lowered the volume. She instinctively caressed her belly.

"Imagine leaving your native country for a better life somewhere else and getting caught before you make it," Tony mused.

Gwen's thoughts trailed off back to…

"Mommy, what's a 'mimigrant'?" Daniel brought her back. He was only seven.

"Immigrant, Danny. It's a person that leaves the country of his or her birth to go to another country."

"Are we going to leave this country, Mommy?"

Gwen didn't answer right away. Her mind was somewhere in the desert, some twenty years before.

"Mommy?" Daniel insisted.

"No, honey, this is our home and we have no reason to leave, but a lot of people from other countries want to come here because they think life here is better than back home," Tony explained.

"Daddy, I'm afraid," Melody said, rubbing her eyes. It was past her bedtime.

Gwen looked at Tony, sorry to have listened to Bebe. She didn't need to stir up the internal turmoil that had constantly gnawed at her since she had been rescued and immediately adopted into an American family. Although her life appeared to be nicely tucked into a comfortable routine with a loving husband and kids that kept her busy, the truth was her life could capsize at anytime.

"There's nothing to be afraid of, honey," Tony answered.

Regretting that the kids had heard the news, Gwen changed gears as she had learned to do, pushing away her sadness and feelings of emptiness, and began sniffing like the ogre when he sniffed out Jack and the beanstalk. The children giggled.

"Mmm...I smell something," Gwen said, ignoring her growing anxiety. She tickled both kids under their arms.

"Cookies?" Daniel ventured.

"No."

"Pizza?" offered Melody.

"Nnnope."

"I smell something too!" joined Tony.

"What do you smell, Daddy?" Daniel laughed.

"I smell clean sheets, snuggling under the blankets, and sweet dreams."

"No! I don't want to go to bed!" Melody protested.

"But it's past your bedtime, honey."

"I'm afraid!" She began to cry.

"What are you afraid of, my darling?" Gwen tucked a curl behind Melody's ear.

"I am afraid the bad policeman will come here and take us away too," said Melody between sobs.

"That won't happen, Melody." Gwen cuddled her.

"How do you know?"

"Because we're not doing anything wrong."

"Those people weren't doing anything wrong either. They wanted to have a nice house like ours," said Daniel matter-of-factly.

Gwen gave Tony a look. He cleared his throat. "Who wants hot chocolate?" he said.

"Me!" Daniel jumped up.

Melody suddenly stopped crying.

"Very well, one big hot chocolate coming up for Daniel!" Tony got up from the sofa, glad to get out of the situation. Melody was quiet.

"I'll have one too," said Gwen.

"One for Mommy coming up!" Tony disappeared in the kitchen. Soon he appeared with a tray with two mugs full of frothy, creamy chocolate milk.

"One for my Queen," he said, handing Gwen a cup. "And one for you, young gentleman," he said, giving the other cup to Daniel. He looked at Melody, convinced she would ask for hers. Instead, she pouted and began to cry again.

"I'm afraid!" she said, tears streaming down her cheeks.

Gwen sighed. It was going to be a long night.

Tony had to get up early the next day. He went to bed first, leaving Gwen to contend with Melody and Daniel. After much fussing, lullaby singing, and bedtime stories, the kids finally went to sleep.

Once in her room, Gwen tossed and turned in bed. The image of the group being apprehended at the border played over and over in her mind as she closed her eyes. Frustrated, she turned on the light on her night table hoping not to disturb her husband, who was breathing deeply and steadily.

"Is the baby coming?" Tony said, startled as he sat up on the bed.

"Shhh…go back to sleep. No baby coming."

"What's the matter then? You can't sleep?"

"It's not important. I'm just a little uncomfortable. My belly is getting too big," she said. "Do you mind if I read?"

"You can read downstairs," suggested Tony.

She would much rather stay in the warmth of her bed, next to him, but she understood. The light would disturb him, and he had to meet a new client the next morning to give him an estimate for remodeling their house. Reluctantly, she turned off the light and walked to her closet. She put on her slippers, wrapped herself in a plush robe, and waited a few minutes until her eyes adjusted to the dark. Then she checked on Daniel and Melody, who looked snug and cozy under their blankets.

She went downstairs and made her way to the kitchen. The quarter moon glowed through the organza curtains in the living room. A chill ran through her body as she opened the fridge and took out a plump tomato. After she washed it, she took a bite as if it was an apple, leaning on the sink and letting the juice stream down the sides of her mouth and chin. She reached for the salt, sprinkled some on the open flesh and continued to eat until it was gone. She rinsed her hands and, without drying them, reached for the kettle, which she filled with the water still running from the faucet. Then she turned on the stove. Gwen opened a cabinet and took out a can of black orange pekoe tea leaves, dropped a spoonful in a mug, and waited for the water to boil.

An ominous feeling haunted her as she paced around the house. Flashes of the immigrants followed fleeting visions of her own crossing when she was twelve, images in which her parents were no longer part of the group and she was being dragged by a kind Samaritan who made sure she got to the other side safely. She pressed her head, trying to stop the influx of memories that threatened to bury her in an avalanche of despair.

"The father is dead, but the mother is still alive!" Roca had said to one of the women crossing with the group.

"We'll have to leave the mother then. She won't survive the crossing," the woman had said, taking Marena's hand.

That was all she dared to remember. One day her parents were with her, and the next they had vanished like fog after dawn. Over the years, she had learned to accept her new place in the world, a world that included wealth, opportunity, and a loving environment with her adoptive American parents. But the lack of bonding that comes from blood relatives etched a thirst for attention no love could quench. The memory of Marco, who had been left in Mexico, waned as time went by but mysteriously intensified with each of her pregnancies.

Dolly and Edward Parker had given her a life she never would have had if her parents had remained alive. She had been Marena until the adoption became official.

"Your name is Gwen now," Dolly had said as she braided two ponytails and laced them with red ribbons.

"Why?" she had asked.

"Because you're an American now, and you need an American name."

The kettle whistled. Gwen hurried back to the kitchen.

Steam came out of the spout as she poured the water in the mug and let it steep. Then she transferred the beverage into a clean mug, trapping the leaves in a tea colander. She added two spoonfuls of raw sugar, stirred it, and walked to the living room, settling down in the rocking chair by the window. The moon smiled down at her with its platinum lips. Unable to sit still, she went back to the kitchen, spilled the tea in the sink, and opened the fridge again. The last tomato. Without washing it, she bit into it, and the red juice seeped through her fingers. Salty tears mingled with the juice and fell like raindrops on the memory of a brother and sister separated ages ago.

Chapter 10

P orro walked a few miles before he decided to rest. He drank the water, which had turned warm by now. He didn't feel like eating. He was tired and somewhat worried since he now was alone in the immensity of the desert. He had no choice but to trudge forward in the direction of the north, and since he didn't have a compass, he would use the sun and the stars to guide him.

He lay on the ground and closed his eyes. It was dangerous to abandon his consciousness to sleep. He needed to stay aware of his surroundings, but he also had to be well rested when he resumed his march at nightfall. He wasn't afraid of being alone, but he dreaded darkness. He knew coyotes and other predators hunted at night, and he could become easy prey.

When he woke up five hours later, he appreciated his solitude. He allowed his instinct to guide him. As the desert unfolded before him with each step, his senses sharpened. There was a wild element in him, unknown to him until now.

When the temperature dropped to forty degrees, Porro quickened his pace to keep warm, but his leg made it difficult to make good time. Whatever it was, he kept reminding himself he was on his way to freedom, and each step was one step farther from the police in Mexico and one step closer to staying alive. All he could hear was the in and out of his breathing and the crunch under his feet, which kept him on guard. It was impossible to see if he would be stepping on thorns and thistles, but he had no choice but to go forward. Occasionally, a scurrying noise in the near distance put him on guard, but he assumed any animal would be afraid of him. The desert was his ticket to America, and he acquired a new respect for it. He allowed himself to blend in with the environment. He became one with nature. He was at peace.

He continued like this for four days, sleeping during the day and walking at night. A sliver of the moon had appeared, growing a little bit more each night and making it easier to see. His food supply had dwindled down to a mere apple and two dried-up tortillas. He was down to his last bottle of water too, and he hoped to reach the other side before he completely ran out of it. The pain in his leg, though, increased with each passing day, and it had spread above his knee. It felt hot inside the skin, but he was strong and determined. The heat was brutal during the day, contrasting with the merciless cold that descended at night.

He never saw the group again, but he knew he was on their track when he stumbled upon empty jugs of water, crushed and flattened, littering the arid landscape.

The morning of the ninth day brought with it a view of the fence that separated Mexico from the United States of America. His heart began to race, a wave of excitement running through his body. Perhaps because he saw the end approaching, he became aware of the fire in his body. He felt light-headed, his lips were parched, and his breathing was fast and short. His leg was now turning blue, and he could only lean on his toes as he walked. But the view of the fence brought a whole new perspective to the present and his future, and he could almost taste the other side. Strangely, there were no signs of the group.

He found a rock and sat against it. Was this where Immigration was likely to pop up at any moment? He drank the last drops of water, imagining each was a gallon. He wasn't sweating anymore. All the heat remained trapped in his body. He wondered how he would break the fever without any water but decided not to worry about that for now. He bent down and dug a hole in the ground, burying the empty bottle so nobody could track him. It would be a long day without water.

Before nightfall, Porro prepared for the most dangerous part of the journey. He had decided not to climb the fence during the day. It would be safer to cross at night, just as the moon had begun to shine brightly. He calculated how many steps it would take to reach it, and he guessed it was only a hundred feet from where he was standing.

As night descended, he slung the two backpacks on his back and licked his cracked lips with a stiff and swollen tongue. It was just as well he didn't have any more water since he would need both hands to climb. Taking a deep breath, he began counting off the steps toward a new life.

Chapter 11

He had made it this far, and there was no turning back. He reached the fence, a steel wall rigged with two-by-fours as a makeshift ladder that stretched as far as his eyes could see. He wondered how he would be able to climb it with his injured leg. What awaited him on the other side? Would the desert suddenly become a field of roses? If it did, there would be thorns; there was no beauty without pain and suffering. But he knew life in America was better. It was the land of opportunity, and he would work hard, make good money, and save it. And one day he would return to Mexico a gentleman, defying the destiny that had been forced on him. He would look for Azucena and claim his rightful place as the father of their child. It wouldn't take him too long either, from what he had heard others say. Money was easy and plentiful. He would be able to return in time for his son or daughter to grow up under his guidance. Porro decided right then and there to make that his immediate goal. Nobody other than Azucena and him would raise their child. He would show Don Francisco how capable he was of providing for his daughter. He would buy a big house on a mountain overlooking the Pacific in Ciudad Encantada, where she would settle like a princess away from the past, surrounded only by beauty, wealth, and love.

Here we go, Porro said to himself. He gathered all his strength and hoped his leg wouldn't fail him. The fence was eight feet high. All he had to do was reach the top, cross over, and climb down again, slowly.

Only an occasional scurrying scraped the dead of the night. The stars twinkled like diamonds in the sky, enveloping the bright smile of the moon. Holding on, he began to climb. He had gone over plenty of fences back home when he played hide-and-seek as a child. He considered slinging the two bags over to the other side to free himself of the weight, but he feared immigration would be somewhere close and hear the noise.

He lifted his left foot onto the first post, holding on to the piece of wood above him, and pushed himself up. He tried doing the same for the second step, but his right leg ached and throbbed with such intensity he was unable to rest it on the post. He used the first leg again, barely leaning his weight on the toes of his bad leg to propel himself up. The bags hung heavy on his back. His parched throat became drier with the effort as his arms did most of the work. His bad leg oozed. Keep going, he told himself, you're almost there. It seemed like an eternity, but he finally got to the top. He could now see the new land, faintly illumined by the crescent moon. He held his breath to appreciate the silence. Nothing moved. He was alone in the universe, except for the city of Hope, which awaited him ahead. Standing on his good leg, he slung the injured one over the fence, poking with his foot in search of a post to lean on so he could begin the descent. It didn't take long for him to realize that the other side was smooth. There was nothing on which to anchor his feet. Coyote would have known this, and he would have prepared them for it. Now on his own, his hands became wet with sweat despite the cold.

While he tried to figure out how to get to the other side, he heard a helicopter in the distance, flying south toward him. He could go down again and lay flat on the ground, safe on the Mexican side, but he remembered he had no food or water. It would be suicidal to turn back. He couldn't stay on top of the fence either. Eventually he'd get caught. His heart pounding, he jumped.

He couldn't have seen it; he couldn't even have imagined it was there. As his bad leg hit the boulder, he heard a crack when the bone broke. The few seconds between the fracture and his awareness of it seemed to last hours. Everything was happening so quickly and yet so slowly. Porro lost his balance and hit his head on the ground as his body split in a thousand shards of pain; his thoughts became confused and incoherent. He lost his bearings as he slipped in and out of consciousness, the helicopter spotlight missing him by two feet. The sound of the motor disappeared into the distance as it flew back north, away from him.

As his pain returned with his consciousness, he let out a howl deep from within, loud and full of pain, frustration, and fear. He tried to move, but he was stuck to the ground. His bad leg ached and burned. Realizing he was alive, Porro wasn't sure this was good either. The helicopter had vanished into the night, but he couldn't move. Now he would really be at the mercy of snakes, coyotes, and scorpions. He shivered as the temperature dipped down to thirty-five degrees, and he began to cry. Perhaps he should have let Cesar kill him. Now he wished the authorities had apprehended him. As his awareness drifted, he thought of Azucena and the baby, how futile everything had been if it ended with his death. His mother would never hear from him again. In a few hours, the sun would come up, and he would be stuck to the ground, the heat grilling him. There was no other solution. He heard the voice of his mother telling him to pray. I'm not praying, he thought stubbornly.

He wasn't sure if it was a dream or not. Somebody was shaking a jar of coins. He opened his eyes, but the bright light of the sun blinded him. He closed them quickly. The sun had already risen, but he had no idea what time it was. His body was hot from the inside out. Heat was everywhere—in the air, his head, and his mouth. He tried to moisten his lips with his tongue, but it was stuck to his palate. As he moved it to open his mouth, it felt like the peel of a mango as it separates from the fruit. When his tongue finally touched his lips, it was like sandpaper, dry and rough. He was thirsty and his heart raced.

There was the sound of coins again, this time closer to him. How long had he been lying there unable to move? It felt like several days, but Porro knew that it was impossible to survive the brutality of the desert without water for more than a full day. A body would wilt and die of dehydration under those circumstances, so he concluded this must be the next morning. He wished the immigration patrol would come soon. You want illegals? Here I am! Porro thought. His only aim was to stay alive, whether it was in America or back in Mexico.

The jar shook again. Holding his breath, he turned his head in that direction to discern what it was. He wished the sky were as cloudy as his mind. The rattlesnake slithered over his legs, inching its way across his immobile body. Porro thought his lungs were going to explode and was relieved when the snake, miraculously, continued on its way, sparing him. But it was only a matter of time before the coyotes, the real ones, would come in the night and shred him to pieces.

Night had come again, and with it twenty degrees. He was burning and hurting, but this time he hoped that somebody, something, would take him away from his misery. They need to come tonight, he thought. They must. Where are they?

The worst part was being aware. At least when he lost consciousness, he existed in an ethereal world, where pain and discomfort were nonexistent. His heart, deprived of water, beat feverishly, and his head throbbed. He felt hot inside and cold outside, and there was nothing he could do about it. He thought about Azucena and how he had failed her.

He lost consciousness again. But this time he floated as if suspended from a hot air balloon. Then he became detached from his body. A dark cylinder, like a tube, surrounded him, and he realized he had entered a tunnel. Despite the darkness, he wasn't afraid. He was propelled through it at a high speed until he saw a bright dot at the other end. He felt immediate relief from his physical pain as the light became brighter and closer. Still traveling toward it, he became embraced by it. The sense of peace and love was overwhelming. He was entirely transformed. *America?*

Chapter 12

Heaven, 1987

It's been seventy years since my last life review, a breath in the grand scheme of things. Finally settled in my new home, I gloat in the peace that eluded me on Earth. I've come to terms with the horror of our betrayal, and I have moved on. Today is the seventieth anniversary of the fall of the Romanovs, which ended with our assassinations. They thought that by killing us, they would end social injustice. What a joke.

Because of the jewels sewn into my gown and the pillow that Maria put in front of me, my wounds weren't severe enough to end my life right away. I wavered between life and death, but when I gleaned a piece of Heaven, I wanted to stay. From here, I learned that a lot was said and written about me after my death, especially speculations that I—another joke—did not die after all. Speculators weaved fairy tales about me being alive somewhere, living the good and glamorous life as a socialite in Paris, New York, even Zurich! Believe me, I had a choice, so I chose Heaven. Who wouldn't?

Looking back, I've done a lot of healing, although I don't like to use that word. It's what got my mother in trouble to begin with. "We need to find someone who can heal Alexei," she used to say to my father. Had she not been so involved in my brother's illness, she wouldn't have met Rasputin or obsessed about him as the ultimate man of God, the healer.

It is this obsession, I believe, that caused the rumors about my mother and Rasputin to circulate in the palace, creating discontent and intrigue within the royal family. It was the beginning of the end as Russia dipped itself in an inkwell of red. I learned that when people kill each other, they interfere with the divine plan, and they disrupt the natural flow of events set for that plan.

First, they got rid of Rasputin. Then they gave an ultimatum to the czar that he commit his wife to a convent somewhere in Siberia as a condition for him to continue ruling. But he refused. He loved her too much. The opposition had no choice but to get rid of us, not just him, lest my brother inherit the throne and continue the legacy of inequality and discontent. Our blood tainted the consciousness of the Bolsheviks, soaking up the winter white of Siberia and turning everything red, from the inside out.

I haven't aged and have learned a lot about evil, forgiveness, and love. It was essential for me to understand what happened, and I will say this much: the butterfly effect is in full force here in Heaven too. We make decisions that affect what happens on Earth, but since we are not human, we don't make mistakes. Everything happens according to a plan, and all elements are needed for this plan to work.

"Anastasia, Anastasia!"

"Tatiana?"

"We have a visitor."

"Who?"

"The elders won't tell us. They are calling the whole population of Heaven to a symposium."

"Is it mandatory?"

"Yes. A visitor has asked for a special audience in presenting his case."

"Anastasia, Tatiana?" The usher bows to us. "This way, please."

I look at my sister, but here in Heaven you have the ability to know without hearing, to see without eyes, to talk without words. We make our way through the crowded auditorium and take our seats in the first row. I did not know we were royalty in Heaven too!

The elders enter in a procession and take their places in front of the audience, each one occupying a seat at the half-moon ivory table. The audience grows silent.

"We are gathered today because we need your help." The voice of Main Elder echoes through the echelons of this court. "Two angels came up from the lower courts with a very special request." He cleared his throat. "We have been asked to consider giving a second chance to a soul that dwells in Purgatory. This particular soul claims he needs a chance. He says he has had to work with what he's been given and insists the DNA of his spirit is admittedly flawed. He has a fervent desire to purge himself from the negative aspects of his soul, but for this he needs to go back to Earth. It's only through us that he will be able to access the road to a new lifetime in which he will be given new challenges to overcome and redeem himself."

"Allow me to add something, Main Elder, please," interrupts Julius Elder. "All of us here are part of the Divine Soul, and though imperfect and stained with our own impurities, we have the ability to correct these deficiencies. The soul in question has a very different makeup." He looks down and takes a deep breath. After a long pause, he looks around. The auditorium is filled all the way up to the ten-thousandth floor. He whispers something to the elder next to him. Then he nods, clears his throat, takes another deep breath, and continues. "As I was saying, this particular soul is made of the forces of evil, and he does not have the ability to rehabilitate himself."

Someone in the audience raises her hand.

"Yes?" says the Main Elder.

"So why should he have the opportunity to have his case heard if it is not in his makeup to rectify his soul?"

"Your question brings me to the next point. We have reason to believe that his evil tendencies are incomplete. There is a glitch in his DNA, which renders him almost completely evil save for one speck of goodness, thus making him an imperfectly evil soul."

There is a stir in the audience. Souls confer with one another, question marks hovering all around them.

"Let me explain," continues the Main Elder. "This soul lived on Earth between 1869 and 1916. During this lifetime, he had the opportunity to commit adultery with a woman who loved him very much."

Somebody raised his hand. "Well, did he?"

"No. He believed in the sanctity of marriage, and once a woman is married, he felt, she is off limits to another man, including him."

"Then why does he need to go back, and what's more, why did he not come to Heaven when he died?"

"Because he did other things that were terribly immoral."

"Give us an example," said someone in the audience.

"Ironically, he preyed on married women, but only those with marital problems. He engaged in intimate relationships with them, convincing them they would 'heal' their battered self-esteems through the joy of their encounters," says the elder.

"Then why does he want to go down again?"

"He wants to change the way history remembers him by restoring his image to the world. He claims he was grossly misunderstood by humanity."

A murmur spreads from the bottom of the amphitheater to the last seat at the top.

"We are faced with an unprecedented challenge. An evil soul is requesting the opportunity to achieve goodness." Main Elder stops and looks around for reactions from the spectators. I raise my hand.

"Anastasia, do you have a question?"

"Main Elder, who is this soul?"

The Main Elder turns to seek support from the rest of the panel. Everyone is quiet.

"Main Elder?"

There is tension in the court. The elders stir in their seats. Main Elder strikes the podium with his gold hammer. It resonates throughout Heaven like thunder. I'm not allowed to ask any more questions. His decision not to answer me has been made.

Alexei raises his hand. He won't be pushed around. When he has permission to talk, he stands up and says, "We need more information, Main Elder. Perhaps we can have this soul brought up to the courts so we can learn more about it." Had he lived, he would have made a fine czar.

The elders confer with each other, some nodding, and then they announce their verdict. "It's a fair request, Alexei. We will summon the soul to come to our courts."

"Shall we be able to interrogate him?" ventured another soul.

"Yes, we will hear his case, and we'll all have a say in the decision. You will have a chance to get a feel for this spirit, and you will be able to ask him any questions. That's how we will decide whether he goes back to Earth or stays in Purgatory for eternity."

Main Elder signals the usher, who notifies the keepers at the entrance doors of the court, and the keepers in turn send word to the custodians below them, and so on until the order reaches the angel whose job is to guard the gates of Heaven. This sentinel, who has been at his job forever, hesitates. In the history of the universe, there has never been an instance where Evil was granted entrance to Heaven. But since the decision does not rest with him, he has to do his job. He touches an invisible switch, and the gates begin to open. Enveloped in a cape of fire, Grigory Rasputin comes in.

Chapter 13

"Tell us about yourself," Main Elder says.

"I was born in Pokrovskoe, son of peasants. One day I saw the Light and followed it."

"What do you mean by the Light?"

"The love of the Lord, Main Elder." Rasputin bows respectfully.

"Go on."

"I took to traveling throughout my beloved Russia learning in convents and churches, and I was given the gift of healing."

Alexei stirs in his seat, as he recalls with horror the pain in his legs during his hemophiliac attacks. He has nothing but gratitude for Rasputin.

"I traveled on foot, crossing towns and villages, and I helped the sick whenever I could."

"How did you do that?" my roommate asks.

"Through prayer."

"Let's cut to the chase," Julius Elder says. "What we want to know is why you are considered one of the most evil souls of the universe. You are aware, Mr. Rasputin, that your return to Earth depends on our votes."

"I appreciate this opportunity to explain, Julius Elder." Rasputin bows humbly. "During my travels, I got involved with many churches and learned many doctrines and philosophies that expanded my understanding of the secrets of the universe. One of these religions was the Khlysts, which are considered a pagan group, and that's why the Orthodox Church spurned me."

"So how did your involvement with that group affect your reputation?" asks Julius Elder.

"First of all, the Khlysts were a secret society, and as such, all their rituals and practices were secret. I can't share them with anybody."

"What's the main accusation against this group?" Main Elder wants to know.

"People claim that after a session of prayer, the Khlysts performed group sex as an expression of their devotion to God. The intention was not to be disrespectful but to engage all the participants in a true expression of love for each other and the Creator."

"So did you belong to the Khlysts?" Julius Elder is becoming impatient.

"No, Your Elder, I merely studied with them, just like I studied in other churches."

"So you claim you did not engage in this...practice?"

"I did as an apprentice, Your Elder. It was part of the requirements to participate in their activities, and that's why I beg the members of this court to allow me to rectify my actions."

"What else did you do that you shouldn't have done?" Main Elder takes the lead again.

"I slept with the wives of many men."

"So you caused these women to commit adultery, taking full advantage of their vulnerability."

"I am aware of that, but my intention was to help them. They were trapped in unhappy marriages, all of them, and they came to me for advice."

"And how did you exactly 'advise' them?" Julius Elder is a good inquisitor.

"I...gave them what they lacked."

"Which was?"

"He made me happy!" Lokhtina yells from the audience. She was the wife of a general, a socialite in her time. As soon as she met Rasputin, she became so devoted to him that she lost her identity and went insane.

Rasputin smiles, even though after having destroyed what remained of her marriage, he snubbed her, exacerbating her madness and her insatiable desire for him.

The usher approaches Julius Elder and whispers something in his ear. Julius Elder repeats the message to Main Elder.

"We'll take a break for lunch. We'll reconvene in the afternoon," announces Main Elder.

Before we have the chance to get up, a curtain opens to reveal a sumptuous buffet of starlight, cloud candy, and moon nectar, while silver beams flash above the entrance to the dining room with the words: "Compliments of Rasputin."

I won't be able to eat.

"Okay. You used married women, you engaged in group sex, and you defiled the name of God by engaging in magical rituals. What else did you do, Mr. Rasputin?"

"I drank excessively, and I regret it. However, I was able to summon my full sobriety when called to the palace to attend to Alexei."

"That's a remarkable ability. How did you do that?"

"I was endowed with special powers."

EXCHANGE AT THE BORDER

"Is there anything else you would like us to know about you and your case?"

"I frequented the bathhouses with several women, used prostitutes, and carried out secret schemes among members of opposing political parties."

"I see——"

"But I truly regret all my wrongdoings, Your Elder, and that's why I appeal to this respectable court to allow me to go back so I can show that I am like you: able to rectify and able to behave if given the choice."

"Good point, Rasputin. The last thing you said actually sums up the whole idea of what it is to be human: we all have a choice, and that's what separates us from the animals and other living creatures."

"That's right, Elder, and that's why I want this opportunity to choose the right path."

The faces of the audience glow in the eerie silence. He's got them.

"I have something to say!"

We all turn in the direction of the male voice. The tone sounds familiar.

"We are listening, Nicholas."

Is that Father?

"Members of this Heavenly Court, he was a perfect man of God," my father begins. "He was the only one able to help my son Alexei, so of course, he won our favor. He proved to be right in most of his assessments in politics and other personal matters." His voice quivers a little.

Julius Elder waits patiently as my father recovers his emotional composure.

"There were rumors circulating in the palace as to some very reproachable behavior," he continues. "Because Rasputin was so good to us, we dismissed the gossip without further investigation. Anybody who would dare to be against our friend Rasputin would end up demoted or sent to Siberia. But I can see now what I didn't want to see then. My wife was devoted to making our son's affliction more bearable. As you all know, Alexei was born with a terrible disease, hemophilia, for which my wife always felt completely responsible. It was up to her, then, to find a solution to his disease, and the czarina and I engaged many healers and physicians who failed to help Alexei. It wasn't until we met Rasputin that our lives changed. At first we thought it was for the better, since he was the only one able to heal our son, but then…" He becomes quiet.

"Go on," prods Julius Elder.

"This man is a fraud! He used my wife to manipulate the course of history and pursue his own agenda. Because he was good to Alexei, he had our blessings, and we consented to him being one of us. However, had we seen his true intentions, he would have never been granted the full privileges he enjoyed while in our palace."

"Be more specific, Nicholas."

"Rasputin used his magical powers to achieve his personal debased impulses, and although he could heal on occasion, he destroyed more lives than he helped."

Rasputin's eyes turn gray, deep, and mysterious. His expression is menacing like a wolf's. He stares at the angels now, one by one, with that look, and time stops. Everything freezes while his hypnotic gaze sweeps every inch of the Heavenly

Court. Then he looks at me. His magnetism is powerful, intoxicating. I remember that look.

My father turns to the audience. "Don't be fooled by him! We mustn't let Rasputin go back! He is evil and incapable of repentance. You must listen to me!" His voice rises above the dead silence of the court.

"Nicholas...you need to remember you are not the czar here. We are a democratic community, and we must give all souls the benefit of the doubt," says Julius Elder.

"How can you ignore the fate of my family? Wasn't it enough for us to be executed? You'll be making a mistake if you send him back!"

The angels frown and turn to look at him. "Rasputin deserves a chance," says someone in the second row.

"Yes! He is no different from us. We all have our share of misdeeds—" says another before he's interrupted.

"Don't you see?" says my father. "He's already influencing you without you even realizing it! Please, Main Elder! You must listen to me!"

"Your opinion is valued and will be considered, but this case will be put to a vote. Majority will rule," says Main Elder.

I look at my father and see a strength that I never saw before. He strove to please my mother whenever and however he could. I wonder what motivates him now to be so against Rasputin going back. I wish my mother were here. But she's on Earth now, living a new lifetime as...Could my father be afraid of Rasputin finding her?

The Elders turn their attention to Rasputin. "Mr. Rasputin, do you have anything else to say in your defense?"

"Czar Nicholas was a good husband, always taking care of his family, but I think I know where he's coming from. In fact, Main Elder, despite all my womanizing adventures, and God knows there were many, Czarina Alexandra was not one of them. I am aware of the strong influence I had on her character and decision-making, and you all must know it was in my power to tip the scales of her marriage in my favor. She submitted to all of the advice I gave her. She would have easily submitted to me if I had wanted her to."

"She would have never been your lover, Rasputin. Alexandra loved me with all her heart. I was the love of her life, not you."

"So you say, but my dear Czar—"

"Don't talk to me like that!"

Rasputin's gaze hardens; his smile disappears while he scouts the audience. He turns back to my father and defiantly addresses him, the late czar of Russia, as one of his own. "I should have made her my woman, and then Russia would have been at my feet." His tone is low, guttural, threatening.

A bitter smile forms on my father's face as he responds. "Don't flatter yourself, Rasputin. She knew her place then, and she knows it now. She loved you, but for your healing powers. Nothing more."

"Whatever you say, Batiushka."

That's how Rasputin referred to my father in Russia. The color drains from my father's cheeks as he realizes how powerful Rasputin still is. Nicholas's influence may not be strong enough to make the angels vote against Rasputin. He remembers that gaze, and he understands how anybody could get caught in its magnetic force. Rasputin knows he's gaining terrain, and triumphant, he takes off his peasant coat, revealing the red silk shirt that my mother embroidered for him with her own hands in Russia, 1910.

In his chambers, Main Elder paces while he scratches his long, white beard. Julius Elder knocks, although the door is open. "What can I do for you, Julius?"

"I think you need to send Rasputin back to Earth."

"It's risky. I'm not so sure we can trust him."

"We all deserve a second chance." Julius Elder waits for his words to sink in.

"I don't want to assume the responsibility for sending Rasputin back on another life mission."

"Let's make a bet then," says Julius Elder. "We send him back. If he behaves, you win and will be glorified in Heaven for having given a chance to an unlikely candidate like Rasputin. You will be promoted to the Higher Court."

"That's not a motivation for me. But what happens if he misbehaves?"

"Then you send me back to correct my misgivings from my previous lifetime. You know I won't disappoint you."

Main Elder ponders the options. While it's true that Rasputin may misbehave again, it would be nice to restore belief in goodness and prove that good can prevail over evil. On the other hand, if he has to send Julius Elder back, the improvements to his soul can tilt the scales in favor of both Heaven and Earth. After all, Julius was assassinated before he could become emperor, thwarting his chances to show his prowess as a ruler. "Very well. I vote for sending

Rasputin back. I believe he will choose the right path this time."

"Main Elder, nothing gives me more happiness than to see faith restored in the human soul. I think you're making the right choice." Julius Elder beams. He turns toward the door and hurries out before Main Elder can see the grin on his face. All Julius Elder has to do now is prepare for his own comeback, knowing that Rasputin won't live up to anybody's expectations. He will fail, and he will see to it that he fails. His chance to become emperor is finally in his grasp.

An uproar in the audience drowns out Main Elder's voice as he delivers the verdict from the votes. My father stands up to protest, but the elders motion for him to sit down.

"Because of the nature of Rasputin's soul, and out of respect for the votes against it, I am handling this matter in an unconventional way." The silence in the court resounds through layer upon layer of soundless echoes.

"Rasputin will be given another chance, but he won't inhabit a body from birth. He will occupy an existing body, forcing him to share that body with the existing soul."

"What's the benefit of this?" someone asks.

"We don't want Rasputin to have full control of the body to accomplish his goals. He will have to submit to the other soul as well. This will cause the two souls to be in conflict with one another, and each will have to struggle with the other to achieve their own goals. We are hoping that the good soul will prevail over Rasputin's."

"Whose body will he occupy?" I ask.

"Don't get ahead of yourself, Anastasia."

The gold hammer drops on the podium, and its force reso-nates throughout Heaven. The decision is final.

Chapter 14

Porro became aware that he was alive but not in the sense that he knew. He soaked up the light, watching all his troubles, his anger, and even his dreams dissolve in a sea of love and harmony. He became one with the light, and he luxuriated in this new peace. An ethereal being in white gauzy robes approached him.

"Welcome home, Porro."

"Is this America?" Porro asked, confused.

The angel laughed. "Everybody wants America. This is better than America!"

Porro looked at the angel. He was short and round, and bobbed in the air, flapping his silvery wings. The skin on his face was white and smooth like milk, and his cheeks puffed up like red balloons every time he smiled. His hair was made of angora, puffy and long, and his whole being glowed so brightly that Porro could not distinguish his silhouette against the light. The joy inside Porro was intense, unlike anything he had ever experienced before. He didn't exactly know what this was about, but he accepted it. In fact he embraced it. He felt comfortable; he felt at home.

The angel took Porro's hand, and together they flew toward the gates. As they approached, the gates opened to a breathtaking view: there were icy lakes, pristine and intensely blue; golden sand beaches; and fields brimming with birds of paradise, daffodils, African violets, and fire-engine-red geraniums. Spectacular orchids dotted the basalt cliffs that jutted among them. Their gigantic petals shimmered with velvety hues of lemon-cake yellow, vibrant hot pinks, frigid blues, and sensual reds. It was not just "seeing"; what came in through his eyes became a part of him, and it imbued him with overflowing joy and peace.

"We give newcomers a tour first, so they get acquainted with their new surroundings, but there is a lot of work to be done here, Porro. I will show you where you'll be spending most of your time the next few days, before you appear in front of the Higher Court, where you will be judged and assigned to your final domain and purpose in Heaven."

Porro was speechless before such beauty, enjoying the tour. He thought about his body, all mangled and hurt, and felt a tinge of guilt for abandoning it.

"Don't worry about your body, Porro," the angel said. "Your mission on Earth is finished. You will stay here until you are ready to go back to fulfill the next one in a different lifetime."

"I don't understand."

"You satisfied the requirements for your present lifetime. After you complete the purification process here, you will be given a new lifetime on Earth with a new purpose."

Despite the overwhelming feeling of peace and happiness that engulfed him, a twinge of discomfort nabbed him at the thought of abandoning his life on Earth. It was as if unseen forces were pulling him away from Azucena and their unborn child, as well as his mother and brother.

"I am not ready for this. I need to go back."

"That's unusual," said the angel, pensively. "Nobody wants

to go back after they've had a taste of Heaven. And remember, to be here is a privilege, not a right."

"I am not everybody. I am me, and I need to go back."

The angel took his time before responding. "Well, we certainly don't want souls that are not pleased to be here. And I can see from your file"—the angel leafed through the gauzy pages of the Book of Life—"that you are in the middle of a crossroads, no pun intended."

"I don't want my crossing over to America to cost me my life. I need to survive my journey! Please, don't get in the way. I paid my dues, tamed the desert, and reached the border. I even climbed over the fence! You must send me back and give me back my life!"

"What's the urge, Porro?"

"My mother needs me. If I live in America, I'll be able to send her money." He looked away.

"Porro, look at me."

"There is also a child on the way, my child! He will need a father, and I want to be there for him." His black eyes sparkled.

The angel listened carefully, as the images of Porro's earthly life aligned themselves on a floating blackboard to form the complete picture.

"Wait here," the angel said. He spread his silver wings and flew upward to the Heavenly Court, where Julius Elder and Main Elder pondered how on earth they would be able to accommodate Rasputin.

"Main Elder, Julius Elder," said the angel after gaining entrance to the court. "I think I found a body."

Main Elder, Julius Elder, and the angel rushed to the Welcome Hall where Porro was waiting. After the preliminary introductions, Main Elder spoke. "We have a proposal."

This sounded more complicated than he was comfortable with. "Are you sending me back?" Porro asked.

"I'm afraid it's not so simple," responded Main Elder. "Your destiny indicates that your life on Earth, this lifetime, is finished—"

"But—"

"However," Main Elder said, raising his hand, "we can accommodate special requests on occasion." He looked at Julius Elder and the angel, summoning support from them. Porro listened. "We want you to think about it carefully now. But if you insist, we will send you back, with two conditions." He stopped to give Porro a chance to absorb it all.

"What conditions?" asked Porro.

"You will have to share your body with another soul."

Porro laughed. He pictured two people trying to fit into one sweater and one pair of pants. Who would get what? His vision included images of one person doing contortions to own a leg or an arm, or fighting for the right to own the head.

"You're not serious, are you?" he said, drying his eyes from so much laughing. "What's the other condition?"

"In answer to your first question, we are serious," said Julius Elder, stepping forward. "As for the second condition, you must first agree to the first one."

"I don't believe this," Porro said, shaking his head. He was a simple man and didn't like it when he couldn't understand what was going on. What if he got roped into a situation in which he'd be at a disadvantage? Disappointed, he realized that Heaven was no different from Earth in that somebody was always trying to get one over on him one way or another. The vein began throbbing on his forehead as different scenarios paraded in his imagination. "How can I agree to one without knowing what I'm getting into? This is not fair."

"There is a soul that needs to go back, but for reasons we can't disclose, that soul—and humanity for that matter—will be better off if it occupies an existing body instead of a newborn's."

"But why does it have to be mine?"

"Because you're both going against your prescribed destiny," said Julius Elder.

"Unless, of course, you decide to stay here, and then all will be well," said the angel, trying to appease him.

"I already told you. I need to go back," Porro said, raising his voice.

"Okay then," said Main Elder.

"Wait," said Porro. "How does this work?"

"It's called transmigration of souls, when a soul descends from Heaven to occupy an existing body. It's only done in extreme cases."

"What does that mean for me?"

"It means you will have to share the objectives, mission, and desires of your twin soul."

"Oh, that's it? I can do that," said Porro. The vein disappeared.

The elders looked at each other.

"The problem is…," began the angel.

There was silence in the hall. Main Elder inhaled as he waited for the angel to open his mouth and explain. But nobody spoke. Julius Elder turned around, looking for something in which to release his anxiety.

"What is the problem?" There was tension in Porro's voice.

"This soul is…evil."

"Evil. You are sending me to live in the same body with an evil soul," Porro repeated.

"Yes," said Julius Elder.

"Why?" Porro frowned, his vein returning even more prominently than before.

"The tendency of an evil soul is, of course, to do evil. The idea is that you, being the good soul, will have to struggle with the evil soul to prevent it from doing harm. The soul we want you to share convinced the Heavenly Court that it needed a second chance, but since we don't trust it completely, we can't afford to leave it to its own devices. Therefore, if it lives alongside a good soul, it will have to struggle in order to get its way."

"And if it wins?"

"Then you will suffer the same punishment as if you had perpetrated the harm yourself."

"I don't believe this." Porro looked down on Earth. His body lay on the American side of the fence. All the possibilities available to him and his family, if he inhabited his body, paraded in front of him. He had survived the desert, made it through the border, and had almost touched his dream, and now it had all been taken away before his very eyes. If he didn't agree to those conditions, all his efforts would have been in vain, and he would never see Azucena or his child again.

"You leave me no choice," he said finally. "Let's do it."

"Are you sure now?" asked the angel. Main Elder exhaled.

"I will fight my twin soul. I will prevent it from doing harm."

"It won't be easy, Porro. This might be your biggest challenge yet."

"My middle name is challenge. What do you think? That I had it easy?" His eyes flashed.

The elders looked at Porro with approval, their faces betraying none of their concern. They knew he had no idea what he was up against.

As the gates of Heaven closed behind him, two spirits belonging to Porro and Rasputin, both in the form of holograms, pierced the atmosphere like rockets returning to Earth. Parallel to each other, Rasputin's spirit slowed down so Porro wouldn't be able to see him. He wanted Porro to enter the body first for the same reason. Darkness was his ally. It was not a coincidence that he would inhabit the chocolate skin of a Mexican immigrant.

Gradually, as they got closer to Earth, the peace and harmony they had both experienced in Heaven began to dissipate. As they entered the body, they became aware of the excruciating pain in their leg. They tried to move but the body was not responsive. The heat was like a furnace around them.

Trapped in a body confined by its own injuries, they heard dogs barking in the distance. As the sound became closer, they also discerned human voices shouting.

"Don't move!" yelled the immigration officer as he approached the body slowly. He waited for his partner to get there, one hand ready to pull the gun out of his back pocket. As the other officer got close to the body, he kneeled next to it and put his thumb and index fingers around Porro's brown wrist. He counted, waiting for the pulse to appear, and just as he was ready to give up, he gasped.

"He's alive!"

Chapter 15

"**P**ush!" The nurse wiped Gwen's forehead while the doctor waited for the crown to appear. "You're almost there, dear!"

Gwen tried to focus. She breathed in at the onset of every contraction and breathed out in five short spurts, the way she had learned in her Lamaze class. Tony wiped her sweaty hair. "You're doing great, Gwenie, great! Keep breathing."

"Shut up!"

Violet, the nurse, winked at Tony. "She's just a little uncomfortable, Dad. Don't take it personally."

"Uncomfortable? Have you ever given birth? This is murder!" Gwen lashed out. "And you," she said, slapping her husband's hand away from her hair, "leave me alone! It's all your fault!"

"Push!" the doctor summoned. "C'mon, girl, you can do it!"

She had been in labor for twelve hours and had refused the epidural, which now she regretted. All her friends had gone through it without anesthetics, and each bragged hers had been a beautiful experience. The first thing the nurse did as Gwen was being prepped in the labor and delivery room was give her the waiver, which Gwen signed without reading. Summoning the last bit of strength she had, Gwen pushed. Her abdomen was tense and rigid, the veins in her neck swollen, and her face streaked with sweat. The excruciating pressure in her lower back disappeared as it transferred toward her pelvis, and she felt her insides ripping apart. The baby's crown appeared, and Tony collapsed with a thump.

"Will somebody attend to the father, please?" The doctor laughed. A nurse walked over to Tony, took his pulse, and thrust some smelling salts under his nostrils. When Tony came to, he got up slowly, still confused.

"Is the baby okay?" he asked, walking shakily toward Gwen.

"The baby is fine," said the doctor, wiping his bloody hand and extending it to Tony. "Congratulations, Mr. Romano. You have a healthy, strapping boy!"

The nurses were busy wiping Gwen's sweat from her face and body, while another team was taking the vitals on the baby.

"Length?"

"Eighteen inches."

"Weight?"

"Seven pounds three ounces."

"Eyes?"

"Black."

"Hair?"

"Pitch black." They all laughed.

"Skin?"

"Hmm," one of the nurses pondered. "He's like...I would say...well...he reminds me of wet sand!"

"You can't put that on the chart," the doctor said, chuckling. "Let's say..." Struggling to find the right description, he noticed a dark spot on the light coffee-milk skin. His heart skipped a beat. A bruise?

"Well, Doc," said the first nurse, "is coffee with milk a better description?"

The doctor ignored her. He gently lifted the baby to examine him. The baby cried inconsolably. With horror, the doctor discovered another bruise on his back under his shoulder blade.

One of the nurses noticed the sweat on the doctor's brow. "Doc?"

But the doctor wasn't listening. His eyes were fixed on the baby, his mind racing through the barrage of information he had acquired in medical school. It wasn't that common, he remembered learning, but was not impossible. Some neonates were born with it. He reviewed in his mind with feverish speed all the symptoms. It was too soon to tell. All babies cried; he could be hungry or cold. It didn't necessarily indicate pain. But the bruise? There was no reason for it. He took off his latex gloves and whispered to the nurse, "Draw some blood and send it down to the lab immediately."

The nurse did as she was told. In the meantime, another nurse cleaned the ink off the baby's foot. After putting a diaper on and wrapping the baby in the white crocheted blanket that Tony's mother had made, the nurse walked over to Gwen. "Here you go, Mom," she said, placing the baby on her chest.

Gwen's face glistened with tears. Looking at Tony, she said, "You won."

"I may have won the bet, but you still get to name the baby."

"Aw, that's so sweet of you, Tony."

"I know it means a lot to you, Queen. So," he said, pecking the baby's cheek, "what's your name going to be, handsome?"

As the baby nursed peacefully from Gwen's breast, the teary-eyed mother whispered, "Marco. His name is Marco."

Down on the second floor, another nurse was pulling on her latex gloves. The patient's leg in Room 53C was scheduled to be amputated.

Chapter 16

"**Y**ou are one lucky little guy," the nurse said as she pushed her fingers into the gloves. "We thought we were going to lose ya," she said, trying to sound upbeat.

Porro pretended to be asleep and kept his eyes closed. He had no idea what the nurse was saying.

"My oh my, I'll be darned, I'll tell ya, one pretty lucky little guy," she went on. "Dehydrated as you were and with this infected leg, ha! The angels must be looking after ya!" She continued cleaning and disinfecting the wound. When she was finished, she patted him on the shoulder affectionately and covered him with the blanket. Poor soul, you might not have a leg by the time you wake up, she thought as she shook her head and walked out of the room.

When he heard the door of his room latch, Porro opened his eyes. *Silencio, al fin!* He looked around and inhaled. It smelled clean. It was also cool. He assessed his situation: He obviously was in a hospital, that much he knew, and he was connected to two IVs through his left arm and hand. He tried to move and saw that he could, although his leg hurt. He stretched forward and saw it was swollen and had been wrapped in white gauze and taped all around. He pulled on one end of the tape and unwrapped the dressing. The cut was open, and it showed the flesh. Even though it had recently been cleaned, green pus was still oozing from it. With his free hand, he touched it. The pain eased. Puzzled, he slid his hand over it again. This time whatever pain was left disappeared completely. He leaned back onto the pillow and dismissed it. Impossible. He drifted back into a deep sleep, on and off, aware of the constant chatter of the nurses out in the corridor.

He did not know how much time had transpired before a nurse carrying a tray awakened him. "Time for dinner!" she sang. She helped him sit up on the bed, propped up the pillows, and opened one of the dishes. A strong smell of roasted meat and tomato sauce invaded Porro's nostrils. He gagged.

"What is it, honey, don't you like it? You need to eat something. The doctor doesn't want to perform surgery on your leg until you recover your strength."

He ignored her. She would babble away anyway, oblivious to the fact that he might not understand one word of what she was saying.

"Well, I have to do the rounds to the other patients' rooms, but I'll come back, and when I do, I want to see all this gone." She smiled and waddled her big butt out of the room.

Porro waited for her to disappear into the hallway and then pushed the tray aside. He uncovered the blanket and looked for the wound, but he did not find it. He caressed both legs with his hands, prodding for the injury, but the one with the wound was completely healed. He wondered why he was feeling so good. He felt strong, alert, and in good spirits. There was another knock on the door, and another nurse entered before he could answer.

"Wait...what is this?" she said, looking at his clean leg.

He understood why she was puzzled.

"Where is the wound you had this afternoon?" Her face was as white as her Nikes.

That's when he realized that it had not been a dream. There had been a wound, which miraculously disappeared. Even the swelling was gone. The color of the skin matched the rest of his body, with no trace of redness, puffiness, or pus.

"I really don't understand," said the nurse, frantically turning the pages of his chart, hoping she had not made a mistake. "It says here, 'Trauma to the right leg, possible fracture, deep open wound, infected.' So where is it?" She bent over the leg, adjusted her glasses, and examined it one more time. Placing her hand where the wound had been, she poked. He didn't even wince. She pushed the button on the bed to call the nurses' station.

"Yes?" answered a voice.

"Ellen, I need you in room 53C right away."

Ellen waddled her big butt into the room and listened to the other nurse. Together they decided to page Dr. Fernandez. Five minutes passed before he responded.

"What is it?" he said impatiently.

"The patient in 53C is scheduled for a leg amputation, but we don't see his wound. I'm very confused," said Ellen.

"Find out exactly what happened, please. I don't have time for mistakes. Either there is a wound or there isn't. And whatever the outcome, make sure you make a note of it in the patient's file," said Dr. Fernandez.

"But—"

"I think you've overextended your shift, Ellen," said the doctor. "Put all preparations for surgery on hold for now, until I have a chance to see the patient. Go home and get some rest."

Ellen caught the scorn in his voice and knew that he did not believe her. All his opinions were based on cold facts. She acknowledged it had been a long shift for her and decided to call it a night. She tucked Porro in before leaving the room and walking out to the nurses' lounge. And I'm not writing a report either, she thought, not with my signature on it. She took her purse and cardigan out of the locker room and clocked out.

Dr. Fernandez didn't visit Porro until the next day. Before entering the room, he looked in the file, which specified a deep wound on the leg, among other things. There was no mention of the wound having disappeared. He chuckled. Ellen probably ended up seeing it after all. Since he had not been the attending physician when Porro was admitted to the hospital, he could not really attest to the truth of Ellen's claim. He knocked lightly on the door and entered the room without waiting for a response.

"*Soy el* Dr. Fernandez," he said in Spanish as he sat on the edge of the bed.

Porro looked at him sleepily, but he did not answer.

"Your fever is gone. *No tienes fiebre,*" he said, removing the thermometer from Porro's mouth. He listened to his lungs. "Good! *Muy bien!*" He pushed on Porro's abdomen. "*Duele?*"

"No."

He drew the blanket and lifted up the gown slightly, exposing Porro's legs. He verified that the leg in question was the right leg, and he touched it. Nothing. Porro didn't move. The skin was whole; there was no cut, opening, swelling, or signs of infection.

"Hmm...," he said to himself. He turned to the file once more. He read the chart, flipping the sheets with reports, numbers, and graphs. It says here that the patient had a wound in the right leg, but I don't see it, he thought. How is this possible? Could one of the nurses have mixed up the file with that of another patient? Everything is possible. He scratched his chin. Unfortunately, these things happened more often than he cared to admit, but this was no time to dwell on mistakes. He still had fifteen more patients to see this morning before heading to his office in downtown Hope.

"Porro, you seem to be fine, my friend," he said in Spanish. "I see no reason to keep you in the hospital."

"Does that mean I'm going home?" Porro asked.

The doctor shook his head sadly. "We're required to turn you over to Immigration, since they're the ones who brought you here in the first place."

Porro's eyes opened wide. He began to pant. Now it was all coming back to him. Since he was not injured anymore, he would be turned over to the authorities. His mind began to race, imagining the officers handcuffing him and deporting him back to Mexico. Once in his country, police would still be looking for him, as well as Cesar who, no doubt, would finish him off. All the effort in crossing the border and risking his life would have been in vain. Dr. Fernandez sensed Porro's fear, but there was nothing he could do about it. He had to abide by the law. He called Ellen and gave her instructions to remove all the IVs and get the patient ready for discharge.

"And make sure you call Officer Gallo," he said, looking in the file, "so they come and pick him up." He turned to Porro and extended his hand. "*Suerte,* Porro."

Porro's vein swelled. He didn't return the handshake. How could he do this to me? Porro thought. What kind of a doctor is he without compassion? Doesn't he realize what he's doing to me? Why doesn't he care? Why? I've always been a nothing; there always seems to be somebody who decides my fate. I didn't mean to break the law in coming here illegally, but I had to do it. It was that or die. And now I'll die anyway. Nothing ever changes.

The doctor shrugged and turned around, already dreading what other surprises awaited him.

Ellen came in, chirpy and refreshed after a good night's sleep, and proceeded to remove the needles and disconnect the monitors. Then she helped Porro out of bed and walked him to the bathroom.

"Agua," she said, pointing in the direction of the shower. "Pee-pee," she said, pretending to sit on the toilet.

Porro managed a smile while he tried to devise an escape.

"Gracias," he said.

Since she just stood there, he began to untie the back of his gown in front of her. He removed one arm, then the other, sliding the gown slowly over his torso. She watched him, mesmerized. He hesitated about getting completely naked and decided to cover his body from the waist down instead. As he perceived a subtle spark in a corner of her blue eye, he instinctively flexed his arms, exaggerating the muscular, well-built shape of his body and reveled in her confusion. When she didn't move, he dropped his gown, exposing his virility.

Ellen gasped. She had been a nurse for eight years and had seen her fair share of naked bodies. She regarded body parts the way a mechanic does bolts, belts, and wrenches, devoid of any sexual attraction and necessary to do their job. However, the shape of Porro's arms and his well-defined torso was enough to throw her poise out the window. Ellen became aware of the sudden heat coursing through her veins, together with the unmistakable tickle between her legs. Could it be his lack of body hair? No, she liked hairy men. Was it the silky appearance of his reddish-brown skin? What if it was a combination of both, enhanced by the way his muscles moved under his skin, sinewy and flexible?

Trying to divert her focus from his genitals, she looked into his eyes. His hypnotic gaze took her to a faraway place where she had been for a time in her life, back when she had been a mother and lover. Both types of love converged in her heart, and she was unable to separate them. She was flooded by an urge to protect this short, vulnerable man, who had just defied the laws of nature by spontaneously healing his own wound. Ellen swung toward the shower and turned on the water.

"*Caliente*," she said, trying not to show her embarrassment.

"*Yo sé!* I know!" said Porro, implying he was the hot one, not the water.

Blushing, she pulled the string on the wall and said, "Problemo."

Porro nodded.

Ellen double-checked the supply of fresh towels and soap before asking him if he needed anything else. He shook his head, a half smile on his face. The depth of his eyes flustered her, and avoiding his gaze, she said, "In the meantime I'll call Officer Gallo to pick you up." She walked past him while he stared at her, amused. He could see her embarrassment and enjoyed the power he had over her. After closing the bathroom door behind her, she disappeared into the room and then out to the nurses' station.

He had to think fast. There wasn't much time to waste. He took advantage of the strong, luxurious spray from the showerhead, lathered his body with soap, and enjoyed the freshness that had eluded him in the desert. Porro rinsed off quickly and stepped out onto the bath mat, but he did not turn off the faucet. With the water still running, he dried himself with the towel, wrapped it around his waist, and went back into the room. He opened the closet and saw that his clothes had been neatly folded on one of the shelves, even though they were filthy and smelled. A chill ran up his spine as he remembered his old life in Mexico. He opened his backpack and pulled out clean underwear, a blue long-sleeve shirt, and a pair of jeans. After shoving his tattered clothes into the backpack to avoid leaving any evidence, he put on the clean clothes and immediately felt like a new person with the fresh cotton against his scrubbed skin. He peeked through the small window on the door, waited for the corridor to be clear, sneaked out, and walked to the right. The long hallway ended, forking to the right and the left. The signs were all in English, a small detail he hadn't considered.

He looked up, trying to guess where to go, when he saw a nurse coming from the left wing. He veered to the right quickly and walked up to the elevators. At that moment, a bell rang as the double doors opened in front of him. He stepped in. There was nobody inside. Before he could push the button to go down, the doors closed and the elevator went up, the numbers lighting just below the ceiling, indicating the floors. The doors chimed as they opened on the fourth floor, and a stream of people pushed their way into the elevator. Instinctively, Porro squeezed his way out into a hall bustling with activity. People in street clothes walked from every direction as nurses went in and out of patients' rooms. A doctor trudged along, carrying a cup of coffee, a stethoscope draped around his neck. His hair looked a little disheveled, and dark circles underlined his eyes. Some patients walked alone, while others enjoyed the company of a relative or friend, pushing a pole with an IV hooked to it. Most of them were children. Therefore, nobody thought twice when a short, dark-skinned *chamaco* made his way through the floor.

He just followed the crowd as he thought, *I should get down to the lobby before they realize I'm gone, but I need to find some money first.* Porro surprised himself thinking this way, but he was determined to get it anyway. His mind racing, he peeped into the rooms as he passed by. The doors of some rooms were closed, and other rooms had visitors. Parents and grandparents spoke in hushed tones around the beds of the patients. "Get Well Soon" balloons bobbed above boxes of candy and teddy bears on the windowsills.

Suddenly he saw a room that was empty, except for a sleeping boy on the bed. He went in and closed the door quietly. The boy was hooked up to three machines that beeped rhythmically as his chest went up and down with each breath. Porro tiptoed directly to the closet, opened it, and checked inside. He found ten dollars in one of the pockets of the pants. He took the money, and just as he was getting ready to leave with it, he heard a voice in his head: If Mamá saw this, she would be very upset. You've never taken anything from anybody.

What's happening to you? Another voice jumped in unexpect-edly: *What's the big deal? You need it and he has it: take it! Those are expensive pants. The kid has money.*

Porro was confused. This was something new. Since when had he heard two opposing voices? He was proud of his up-bringing, even though he had gone through a brief period when he broke into homes. Still, at thirteen, he had never taken anything from anybody. That was the job of his peers at the time. They only used him for his speed and dexter-ity in opening locks but left him out of the spoils. His pay was to be accepted into their circle, to belong, but even that hadn't lasted. As soon as his mother found out, she sent him to the hacienda of Don Francisco Gonzalez Barista, where he'd worked ever since.

But now he needed money. His life depended on it. He turned around, facing the door, and hesitated. No, he couldn't do it. He was starting a new life, and he wanted things to work out. He had promised his mother he would be honor-able and follow the values he had learned from her. He put the money back in the boy's pants. I'll find a way to survive. God will provide, he told himself. He was surprised at the sudden acknowledgment of God, that remote and untouchable entity he had refused to believe in for so many years. *God?* said the other voice. *Now you believe in God? Don't make me laugh!* Porro was puzzled at the internal conversation taking place, but he dismissed it. It must be the drugs they gave me, he thought.

Empty-handed but with a clean conscience, he felt pre-pared to face the world.

Standing behind the door and peeking through the small glass opening, he waited until there was no staff walking by and then stepped out into the hall and followed the crowd. He blended in well; nobody seemed to pay attention to him, and for the first time in his life, this was a good thing.

When he got to the elevators, Porro pushed the button with the down arrow on the wall and waited. Nobody else was around. There would be no witnesses. The light on the indicator showed the elevator was on the second floor, where he had been for the past two days. He waited impatiently, knowing every second he remained on this floor brought him that much closer to getting caught. He began to sweat. The light on the elevator still showed it was on the second floor, and his mind began to race. What if they realized he was missing? What if they canceled service on all the elevators so they could trap him and turn him over to Immigration? As he wiped the sweat off his face with his sleeve, he suddenly heard steps behind him. Don't turn around, he told himself. His heart thumped. Closing his eyes, he braced for the worst. He'd be handcuffed and escorted to a car downstairs, there would be a trial, and he would be sent home. End of story. It had all been in vain. Once in Mexico, the police would pick him up and finish him off in a desolate field, somewhere in the country where nobody would hear his cries for help or the gunshots. Somebody tapped him on the shoulder. He jumped.

"Sorry! I didn't mean to startle you," said a black man dressed in a nurse uniform. He was all smiles.

Porro lifted his right hand, indicating that it was fine, no harm done. Although he was relieved it wasn't *La Migra*, he didn't cherish the fact that he would have to share the elevator with another person, who would be able to identify him if the situation called for it.

"Going up?" asked the friendly nurse.

What do I say? Porro thought. I must respond, or he will know I don't speak English. He started to cough loudly, holding his throat, and beating his chest with his fist. Then he looked at the black nurse to show him he couldn't talk.

Just then, another nurse came walking from the hall behind him. He was pushing a wheelchair with a young woman holding a baby. Her hair was blond and curly, the color of honey. Immediately, he was reminded of Azucena.

The nurse pushing the wheelchair kept looking at Porro. Please don't talk to me, he thought.

"How you doing this lovely morning?" the nurse said, flashing a big smile.

Trying to control his breathing, Porro forced a smile in response and closed his index finger and thumb into a circle, the sign that everything was okay. The nurse understood, and laughing, he put his thumb up.

Suddenly, the elevator bell jingled with a short metallic tone as the doors opened. Porro stepped aside to let the young mother go first and then went in himself.

As Porro hurried to leave the hospital, Gwen was getting ready to be discharged. The doctor saw no reason to keep her hospitalized, but the baby had to stay. After many tests and endless late night meetings among the best neonatologists in the area, they had all concluded the baby had leukemia. The mood was gloomy since the prognosis in the newborn was not too promising, especially when it came down to the treatment.

Gwen was in a haze. How could this happen to them? And why? Why should her little baby have to suffer like that, right from the very first day of life? Was this punishment for something she had done wrong? And if it was, why should it fall on her baby? She insisted on staying there, but the doctors were adamant.

"No, you need to go home. We'll take care of the baby. He needs to undergo frequent testing before we determine the best way to proceed. He's too young to receive treatment, and while untreated, he needs to be under observation."

She and Tony left the hospital with a mixture of numbness and anger. Life was unfair.

In the meantime, an angry Officer Gallo paced the second floor, hoping to find a clue to the whereabouts of the little *chamaco* who had the nerve to slip through his expert hands.

"How the fuck could you let this happen?" he cursed at the nurse in charge.

"What difference does it make anyway? One more, one less, the truth is you guys suck at your job," Ellen retorted with a smirk, "and that ain't my fault."

Officer Gallo lifted his index finger. "I will find him. And when I do…"

Ellen waddled her big butt out of the nurses' station. *And when I do, my ass. Good for him*, she thought. *I liked that boy anyway.*

Chapter 17

"I still don't believe Porro could have tried to steal from me. It's just not him." Don Francisco sat down on the leather couch in the hospital waiting room. Carlos was in the recovery room after his shoulder surgery. "He was too good to have done something like that. Are you sure it was him?"

"I'm sure, Papá," said Cesar, shifting in his seat. "It's been thirteen days since he disappeared. Too much coincidence." His father kept pondering and revisiting the situation, making it harder for Cesar to keep the story straight.

"I will meet with the chief of police and ask him to assign a special force to investigate the case. I appreciate the confidence they have in your report, but they shouldn't rely on that alone."

"Do you doubt my word? Is that it, Papá? Why don't you just say it? I have always been treated differently in this household, no matter what I do. It has to do with me, not with Porro, isn't that right?" Cesar's eyes flared, his anger mounting by the minute.

"You can take it personally, Cesar, but we must be fair. If they are going after the wrong person and they catch him, it could ruin his life, and for no reason. Think about it."

Cesar was quiet. He couldn't argue with that. His father's words resonated with him. He tried to push away an emerging guilt about putting Porro behind bars, knowing that Porro's only sin was being a laborer in love with his employer's daughter.

"Well, you know how they are: sooner or later they show their true colors, Father," Cesar continued in an attempt to convince himself.

Don Francisco didn't respond. He knew a good person when he saw one. He would make inquiries until he found out the truth.

When they got home that night from the hospital, Azucena was in her room. Don Francisco and Cesar went directly to the main dining room, where dinner was waiting for them. As they took their seats at the table, Don Francisco placed a napkin neatly on his lap.

"Azucena hasn't been down for dinner lately," he said casually.

"I wanted to talk to you about that, Father. In fact..." Cesar paused while he signaled to the butler to pour wine in his glass. Cesar's hand trembled slightly while he took a sip.

"I think she should go to Ciudad Encantada," Cesar said abruptly.

"Why?"

"Perhaps the change of air will suit her."

"Why does she need the change?"

"I think she's shaken up about what happened to Carlos."

"Carlos is not dead, even though it was a close call," conceded Don Francisco.

"It's been stressful for her, and she could probably use some time away."

"But where is she going to stay?" asked Don Francisco.

"She can stay with Aunt Sofía. I'm sure she wouldn't mind the company."

Don Francisco shook his head. "That's out of the question. Your mother's sister left the family a long time ago."

"Well, maybe it's time you two made up," said Cesar, wiping his mouth with a napkin.

Don Francisco scrutinized Cesar as he cut a piece of meat and delicately placed the knife on his plate. "What's your agenda, son?"

"No, no agenda, Papá. Sooner or later you're gonna have to talk to Sofía again. You can't hold grudges forever."

"Ha! Since when do you like peace in the family, Cesar?" Don Francisco's glare rested on his son's eyes.

Avoiding his father's stare, Cesar stuffed his mouth with carrots and potatoes, and Don Francisco took this opportunity to assess the overall situation. He had noticed Azucena appeared plumper than usual, and her rosy cheeks had turned a pale yellow. She spent most of her time in her room, and a desolate expression clouded her eyes. Suddenly, Don Francisco called Manuel, the butler.

"Get Señorita Azucena downstairs, please. Tell her I need to talk to her."

"Yes, sir."

A few minutes later, he returned with Azucena who was holding her stomach with one hand.

"Did you want to see me, Papá?"

"Darling! Come here!" He kissed her on the forehead. "Sit next to me."

The smell of the onions and garlic in tomato sauce worked their way into Azucena's delicate system. She gagged.

"What's the matter?" asked Don Francisco.

Azucena looked at Cesar. He looked down.

"Azucena?"

She burst into tears. She didn't know how much longer she'd be able to keep it a secret. Cesar had suggested she tell Tía Sofía, but Azucena felt she would need to talk to her in person. She couldn't just pack up and leave without telling her father first. Also Azucena didn't want to be far from home and Carlos, so she could visit him at the hospital every day.

Don Francisco looked at the two of them. While Azucena had her father's deep green eyes, Cesar displayed his mother's light brown hair. His skin was darker than the rest of the family, and he wasn't tall like Carlos. Don Francisco loved him just the same. He had been at his birth twenty-eight years ago and had vowed to love him as if he were his own. After all, if it hadn't been for Cesar, he wouldn't have…but that belonged in the past. He needed to concentrate on today and the matter at hand. "Something tells me this is more involved than you make it sound, Cesar. Tell me right now what's going on."

"There's nothing to tell, Papá. We heard a noise that night, and when I saw the shadow running in the hacienda, I went outside with my rifle. I followed it all the way to the woods, and as I aimed to shoot, Carlos got in the way. The man escaped. I didn't mean to shoot Carlos, of course. You know that, don't you?"

"I didn't ask you about that night, son."

It was true. The events of that fateful night haunted Cesar incessantly, and all he could think about was getting caught in the lie.

Don Francisco got up from the table and paced the dining

room thoughtfully. Too many holes in the story. He went over the facts one more time, putting scenarios together with the information he had.

"You know what I think?" he said suddenly.

Cesar held his breath. Azucena looked up.

"The police came that night, allegedly looking for the robber, after which Porro never showed up again; my daughter loses her appetite yet gains weight; and you, Cesar," he said, pointing a finger at him, "you act as if all is well under the Mexican sun." Don Francisco waited for an answer. When none came, he walked to the telephone on the side bar by the window. "I will put an end to this mystery immediately," he said, picking up the phone and dialing.

"Doctor Gómez? Francisco González Barista here." There was a pause. "Yes, thank you. Everything is fine, except I want you to see my daughter tomorrow and do a complete physical. I want the results sent to me directly."

Azucena gasped and looked at Cesar.

"What?" Don Francisco yelled on the phone. "What do you mean you saw her? When?" There was a pause again. "Impossible!" His moustache quivered as the words hurtled out of his mouth. The hand holding the receiver began to shake, and little beads of sweat formed above his thick eyebrows. He took a handkerchief from his pocket and wiped his face. His breath became more laborious, and then he pressed on his heart. "I need to get off," he said in a whisper. "No, I believe you."

Don Francisco hung up the phone. "I should have known," he muttered.

"I wanted to tell you, Daddy, but I was so afraid!" Azucena was crying in her father's arms.

"Didn't I always tell you that you could come to me for anything? How could you think I wouldn't stand by you?"

"I don't know. We thought you'd be mad."

"Well, I'm not particularly happy about it, but…" Don Francisco stood up from the chair and started pacing the room, his hands clasped behind him.

"Cesar was worried that this would affect your health, but we didn't mean to lie to you, Papá," she said between sobs. "I guess it was bound to come out sooner or later."

"Who's the father, Azucena?"

She did not respond.

"I need to know who the father is," Don Francisco repeated.

"I can't tell you," she said, wiping her tears.

"I hope he realizes that he will have to marry you, Azucena. I want to meet him."

A shadow veiled Azucena's green eyes as she remembered that she hadn't heard from Porro since that eventful night. She knew he hadn't been caught because the police reported to Cesar they were still looking for him. She understood why he would stay away from her, but would her father insist on marriage if he knew Porro was the one?

"What if you don't approve of him?" Azucena asked.

"Does he love you?" he asked.

"Yes."

"Then I'll approve."

"You mean it, Daddy?" she said with a glimmer of hope in her voice.

"Of course! The child needs a father, and it will legitimize your love for each other. I would have preferred that you had waited until you got married, but what's done is done. No sense in crying over it."

"Father, I think you need to consider the situation more carefully. It's not as simple as it sounds," said Cesar.

"Don't tell me what to do, son. There's nothing to think about! Azucena, you will invite this young man tomorrow for dinner. I want to meet my future son-in-law."

"Now what do we do?" asked Azucena, annoyed. She waited until Don Francisco retired to his room.

"I don't know. The police say Porro has vanished. Nobody can find him. Tell me the truth: are you sure you haven't been in touch with him?" Cesar asked.

"No, I swear. Ever since that night I haven't heard from him once. But then again, can you blame him? After the way you chased after him? Who knows where he's hiding now and if he'll ever want to see me again!"

"If he loves you, he'll come back."

"You threatened him, remember?"

"If he's a man, he should do the honorable thing and…" Cesar paused at the epiphany. That's what Porro had wanted to do in the first place. He had acted like a gentleman, and in return Cesar had chased him away at gunpoint. He was always so angry about everything. He had always felt inadequate in the family, as if he didn't belong. Despite the fact that he had been surrounded by love, it wasn't enough. He even looked different. While Carlos had white skin and Azucena those lovely green eyes, he often wondered where his short stature and dark skin came from. Neither of his parents had those features, and he had always been the target of scorn and laughter in school. The only way to deal with it was to strike back.

"Azucena, I'm so sorry I got carried away," he said, still in shock.

"You always do. You're so angry all the time. But this time, you really screwed up," she replied.

"I am truly sorry," he said, almost in a whisper. He couldn't even look at her. What kind of person was he, really? And why had they all loved him in spite of it?

Azucena took a deep breath. "What's done is done," she said, putting her hand on his.

Cesar was touched. How could she forgive him for what he had done? And how could he repair the damage? "I'll tell you what," he said.

"What?"

"I'll make it up to you. I will go to Porro's house personally, and I'll apologize to him. After I drop the charges with the police, I'll convince him to come to the house and talk to Papá."

Azucena studied him. "You really mean it, don't you?"

"It's the least I can do."

Chapter 18

Although he was aware that Immigration might be looking for him, this time he didn't run. He had survived the crossing and miraculously healed, and to him this meant he must have special permission from Heaven to walk the streets of Hope at his leisure, and this made him feel invincible.

A cool breeze descended from the cloudless sky. He headed east, squinting to shield his eyes from the morning glare. Clothes boutiques, a bookstore, an arts and crafts supply store, and a hair and nail salon populated the shopping center behind the parking lot. Porro inhaled, and the smell of freshly baked pastries filled his lungs, mixed with the pungent smell of strong, black coffee. He realized he hadn't eaten in a few days.

The Bittersweet Café was a little shop tucked in a corner of the shopping center. The curly font in the window was painted pink and brown in stark contrast to the interior decor. His stomach rumbled, but he had no money. He stood by the window looking inside with longing. Three dark mahogany booths were arranged against the burnt-orange wall on the left. The rustic, sturdy shape of the tables was in line with the simplicity of the rest of the furniture. A bamboo candleholder on each table held a single fresh sunflower. The benches were covered with red and brown fabric with circles and squares asymmetrically arranged against a backdrop of blue triangles. Three equally rugged square tables stood in the center of the café, perpendicular to the booths. Four heavy chairs, covered with cushions in the same design as the benches, surrounded each table. A loveseat with a small table on each side and a coffee table in front of it framed the yellow mustard wall on the right, across from the booths, creating a whimsical and cozy ambience that attracted even those who were too full to eat. It was the kind of place where people gathered for comfort, the soul kind. Porro went in.

"I'll be right there!" a friendly female voice with a strong Texas twang called out from the kitchen. Porro waited, realizing that he might not be able to communicate with her.

The young woman, who appeared to be in her twenties, came in wiping her hands on her apron. Her long neck held her diamond-studded face, highlighted by a strand of strawberry-colored hair against her shiny black bob. She walked like a heron, poised and cautious, lifting her skinny, jean-covered legs as if she were wading in a gator-infested mangrove. She was sexy despite her flat chest, but what stirred Porro's excitement was his perception of her loneliness.

"*Yo...quiero,*" he began.

The young woman looked at him amused.

"*Necesito trabajar,*" Porro said, suddenly identifying an urge to reach out to this pitiful creature.

She recognized one of the words from her Spanish class in high school but didn't know how to respond in Spanish. Instead, she shook her head. Porro pretended to wash imaginary dishes in the air. This time the message was unmistakable, but she was alone in the bakery, and he was a complete stranger. She played dumb. Thinking that she wasn't getting the message, he got to the point.

"*Tengo hambre*," he said, making circles in his belly with his hand.

This time she understood—he was hungry—and she let down her guard. She had seen hunger when people came to the church on Sundays for their weekly bowl of soup. She pointed her index finger for him to stay where he was and disappeared into the kitchen. A few minutes later, she came back carrying a big loaf of French bread slathered in butter. She put the plate on the table and signaled for him to sit down. Then she disappeared again, and when she came back, she was carrying a mug of black coffee, so strong that the smell alone could wake up a sloth and make him dance.

"Eat," she prodded.

Porro couldn't help but dig into the bread, lapping up the warm and silky butter that dripped from the corner of his mouth. The girl handed him a paper napkin and smiled. She watched him chew the fresh baguette, making a crunching noise with every bite. He smelled of disinfectant and was neatly dressed. His black hair was combed back, sleek and shiny and all one length, as if he hadn't cut it in a few weeks. When he swallowed, the veins in his neck swelled, suggesting a virility that frightened her and attracted her at the same time. She wondered what his story was. He wasn't really handsome but had this magnetism that she found irresistible: the dark skin, white teeth, and those eyes, so deep she felt as if she were falling into a mysterious black hole. Despite the fact that Hope, Texas, swarmed with people like him, he was unique, an exotic species maddeningly appealing.

"What's your name?" she asked with a smile.

Porro didn't understand.

"Name," she repeated. When he didn't react, she patted her chest. "Trixie," she said.

"Oooh!" he said. "Porro." He also touched his chest.

"No English?" she asked, already knowing the answer.

"No, Español *solamente*," he said, indicating he only spoke Spanish.

"*Yo un poquito*," she said, making a gesture with her hands that she only spoke a little Spanish.

He smiled, amused at the way the two diamond studs in the middle of her milky cheeks disappeared in the hollow of her dimples when she smiled. Her eyebrows were excessively thin above a pair of Siamese cat eyes. Porro compared her to Azucena, who had the stout demeanor of a Spanish queen. But he was impressed that she knew a little Spanish and wished he had learned English when he had the chance in elementary school.

Porro finished eating. "Gracias," he said. He gulped the coffee and wiped his mouth with the napkin. He felt much better, even though he had room for a lot more. Unable to communicate with her, he looked out the window. He realized he didn't want to go yet. He enjoyed being around her and felt more comfortable in the warmth of the bakery than he had anywhere else in this new country. It would be great if he could work there. Again, he tried to make her understand that he'd be willing to wash dishes in exchange for a few dollars, but when she said no, Porro stood up. There was no reason for him to stay.

He didn't want to leave without paying. He took out the silver locket from Marco's backpack. Opening it, he removed the photograph and tucked it in his pocket.

"*Para ti,*" he said, giving Trixie the empty locket.

Without taking it, she pointed at the picture. "Show me that," she said.

When he didn't understand, she tried to get her hands in his pocket, but he balked. "Show me!" she repeated.

Reluctantly, Porro took out the photograph and showed it to her.

"Your girlfriend?" she asked, hugging herself and mimicking kisses.

Porro began to laugh. *I wish,* he thought. Then he shook his head, putting the photograph back in his pocket. He took Trixie's hand, opened it, and placed the locket in it.

"Oh no, it's not necessary," she said, blushing.

"*Sí!*" he insisted.

She looked at the locket. It was pure silver, probably very valuable. She decided to keep it, but only because it was from him. She hung it around her neck. "Thank you."

He nodded. "*Muchas gracias por la comida,*" he said, thanking her for the food. He walked toward the door.

"Wait!" she exclaimed.

"Hmm?"

"Come with me," she said, motioning him to follow her into the back area where the kitchen was.

Two cakes rested on a long stainless steel table. One was decorated with chocolate cream swirls, topped with strawberries, and the other looked like a wedding cake. It had several tiers, each smaller than the one below, covered in wavy layers of white and silky cream. The soul-warming smell of French bread wafted from the oven to his right.

She brought him to the sink, where a few plates and

silverware soaked in sudsy water. As in a game of charades, they held a conversation with hands, gestures, and giggles. Trixie took an apron from a hook on the wall and put it around his neck, tying the strings around his waist. He was solid and muscular. The strength of his arms made her heart race and hands tremble. Hoping he hadn't noticed, she pulled away quickly and was relieved when she saw he was already rolling up his sleeves, as if the only thing on his mind was the task at hand. Before she had a chance to explain with gestures, he had begun to wash the dishes.

The bells jingled as the door of the bakery opened. Two men dressed in solid green military uniforms walked in.

"Immigration," said one of them, flashing his badge in front of her.

"Yes?" Trixie answered, smoothing her hair with her hand.

"We're looking for a man about this tall," Officer Gallo said, putting his hand below his chest. "Have you seen him?"

"What does he look like?" she asked, solicitous and still playing with her hair.

Officer Gallo and his partner fumbled in embarrassment. "I'm afraid we don't have a picture of him," he admitted, "but he must be around here somewhere. He couldn't be too far."

"Can you describe him?"

Officer Gallo eyed her. "Why, have you seen him?"

"How would I know? A lot of people come in and out. If you describe him to me, I may be able to help you."

"He's short, dark skin, black hair of course," he said, rolling his eyes at the ridiculousness of it all. "All right, look," he continued, making an effort to cover up his embarrassment, "he left the hospital about an hour ago. You might have seen somebody that fits the—"

"Description?" she mocked. "Half the population of Hope fits that profile to a T."

Just then Porro finished doing the dishes and came out of the kitchen looking for more things to do. Officer Gallo spotted him first.

"That's him!" he said, running toward the back. Trixie got in front of him yelling, "Wait!" but Officer Gallo was already dodging tables and chairs. In the confusion, Trixie pretended to fall, taking down more chairs with her.

"Ouch!" she yelled, holding her arm. Officer Gallo hesitated, but then he turned around to help her, bumping into his partner, David Striker, who was already bending down and helping Trixie to her feet. Like the Three Stooges they fell, one on top of the other, legs tangled with arms, chairs, and everything in between. Trixie moaned, trying to climb out from the knot they had become, while Officers Gallo and Striker fought to detangle from each other. Once up, they dusted off and ran to the rear of the bakery, but the door going out into the back lane from the kitchen was locked from the inside. Jumping over the upended chairs, they ran to the front door and exited into the street. They looked in both directions but didn't see anything. Officer Striker came back in, followed by Gallo, and headed toward the men's room. He opened the door. "He escaped through the window!"

Trixie repressed a laugh. "I guess you lost him again," she said. "You might as well stay here and have something to eat. It's on the house."

Officer Gallo hesitated. It did smell good, and although he'd had a big breakfast that morning, the appeal of the place was irresistible.

"What was that man doing here?" he asked, fighting the temptation to stay.

"He came to eat."

"So why was he in the back?" Officer Striker asked.

"The restrooms are in the back, sir. He ate. Then he went to the bathroom."

"He's illegal, ma'am," said Officer Striker.

"Am I supposed to ask my customers whether they are legal or not?" Her purple eyes flickered.

Ignoring her, he continued, "How did he pay?"

"He didn't. You chased him out before he could. Maybe you should pay me for his meal."

Officer Gallo overlooked her sarcasm. "In that case, we'll take you up on your first offer, right, David?" He looked at his partner, who was picking the chairs up from the floor and putting them back neatly around the tables. Then they sat across from each other in a booth.

"What do you recommend?" asked Officer Striker.

"Death by chocolate," Trixie said matter-of-factly.

"I don't like the sound of it," he said, shifting in his seat.

"Mud pie drizzled with warm raspberry sauce then?" she went on.

"I think I'll just have coffee," said Officer Striker, dryly.

"Napoleons are fresh today," she said, looking at Officer Gallo.

"I prefer cannoli," he replied.

"I have elephant ears."

The officers looked at each other, wondering whether she was making fun of them and getting away with it.

"Just bring me an espresso," Officer Gallo said.

"Coming right up!" said Trixie with a smile.

"Fucking illegals," mumbled Officer Gallo, once she was out of sight. "Wait till I catch him, and when I do, I'll kick his ass right back to where he came from."

A few minutes later, Trixie appeared with the coffees, which she arranged neatly on the table in front of them.

"So," she said, her hands on her waist, "why are you so interested in this guy anyway?"

"He crossed the border illegally. Perhaps you can tell us something unusual you noticed about him that can help us find him." Officer Gallo tried to sound nice since force didn't seem to work with her.

"He's probably dangerous," offered Officer Striker, changing tactics again. "Here is my card. If you see him around, give me a call."

Trixie was happy Porro had been able to escape but wondered where he could have gone, and if she would ever see him again. One thing she regretted was not having been more direct with him. She conjured up a mental vision of his sturdy arms, sinewy and strong, as he washed the dishes. She took the card with both hands, reading the information on it. With another flash of her purple eyes, she said, "I will, Officer...David, is it?"

"Yes."

"Striker?" She narrowed her eyes in disbelief.

"Yes, what's the problem?"

"I've never met anybody in law enforcement who was Jewish."

"Who told you I am Jewish?"

"Oh, c'mon, anybody can tell…"

The words of his mother resonated with Officer Striker: "You can change your name, you can change your looks, and you can change your lifestyle, but you can never ever change who you really are. Ever." He had been born a Striker, and he had no reason to want to change it. He considered himself as American as the Statue of Liberty. But the history of his grandparents seemed to follow him wherever he went and whatever he did—an invisible seal of authenticity to his true identity. Like the imaginary ghosts that lived in his closet when he was little, the story of his grandparents' journey toward freedom popped up at the most inconvenient times to remind him that his family had a secret. Would he ever be able to escape the karma that followed him through three generations? When his grandfather Jacob Strikowsky landed in America, he had no idea that one day his own grandson would have to confront, face-to-face, the savior of his ancestors in the skin of an illegal Mexican. Like Porro, his grandfather had been an immigrant. But unlike Porro, he was trying to escape the incipient persecution of Jews in Europe. Like Porro, his grandfather had kept Rasputin close to his heart, but for very different reasons. When he landed on Ellis Island, Jacob Strikowsky became Jacob Striker, so nobody could trace him back to the time when his parents had to pay excessive sums of money to Mr. Rasputin to obtain exit visas from the czar and the czarina of Russia.

Chapter 19

They drove in silence. Little Marco was in the care of the doctors, who promised they would do everything in their power to cure him. Bebe had stayed at Gwen and Tony's house watching Daniel and Melody. Tony turned at the corner, past the Bittersweet Café, and continued on straight toward the highway.

"Watch out!" Gwen screamed.

Tony slammed on the brakes. "What's the matter with that guy?" He rolled down the window of his SUV and yelled, "Watch it!"

Porro continued to run, zigzagging through the traffic, looking over his shoulder every so often.

"I don't see anybody chasing him," said Tony.

"He seems scared. Follow him," said Gwen.

"We should get home soon. The kids are waiting."

"I hate the idea of going home without the baby. I can't stand it. Slow down," she whispered, watching Porro.

Tony drove the SUV up the street, following Porro's lead the whole time, but he had begun to slow down. Gwen kept her eyes on him. Ever since she had seen the news that night, she hadn't been able to control her thoughts. She kept thinking about her brother, Marco, and wondered if he had been in the group that was sent back. And if he was, what if he had managed to escape? Could this be him?

"Stop the car," she said.

"Are you out of your mind?"

"What if he's my brother?"

"How could it be?"

"You never know."

"You don't even know if your brother was among those crossing."

"I know. Don't ask me to explain because I can't."

"You're not being yourself," said Tony, shaking his head. "And here I am, like an idiot, following a perfect stranger because my wife thinks he's her long-lost brother."

"You're not an idiot. You just want to please your wife," she said in a conciliatory tone.

Tony closely followed Porro, who was now walking. They were a few blocks away from the main avenue, so there were no cars around and only a couple of people walking. Without warning, Porro started running again, but this time he tripped and fell. A small piece of paper slipped from his pocket. Without noticing, he got up again and continued to run.

"Now you have to stop," said Gwen firmly. "He dropped something!"

Tony pulled up to the curb and parallel parked between two other cars. He looked at Gwen. "What are you going to do now, get out of the car and give it to him?"

"Yes," said Gwen.

"I don't believe this." Tony looked out his window.

Ignoring him, she opened the door of the SUV. A gust of cold air rushed in. She got out and ran toward Porro. Slowly, she bent down and picked up what had fallen from his pocket. It was a photograph of her when she was twelve.

"Marco!" she called. "Please wait!"

Porro stopped in his tracks. Did she say Marco? He watched her approach, slowly and cautiously. He squinted to focus. It's Marena! What do I do now? What should I say? Wow, she's more beautiful than her picture!

That's right, we need to connect with her, Porro. C'mon! Go talk to her!

As she got closer, Gwen noticed he was young, probably in his twenties, and short but well built. He didn't look like her brother, although she hadn't seen Marco since he was five. Still she felt irresistibly drawn to him.

Porro held his eyes on Gwen as well.

"This…," she said out of breath, "this picture…where did you get it?"

"Marena," he finally said.

"My name is Gwen," she said in Spanish. "Who…who are you?" She was holding back her tears. Her lips quivered.

He stood there, glued to the pavement. His head spun in a whirlwind of thoughts, doubts, and questions. Why was she denying who she was? He decided to take a chance.

"*Yo soy Porro, amigo de Marco*," he said, telling her that he was Marco's friend.

For a brief moment, Gwen stopped breathing. "Where's my brother?"

Porro could only shake his head. He had never envisioned this would happen, and he wasn't prepared to give any answers. "We crossed together."

"Where is my brother?" she repeated, her voice rising.

Porro kept silent. How could he possibly tell her?

Gwen felt as if she was going to lose her balance.

"Your brother didn't make it. *Lo siento*," he finally said.

So that's what it all had come down to. All those years of wondering and not knowing had finally come to an end. The desert had claimed her mother and father, and twenty years later, her only brother. "Did he die?"

"Yes."

"How?"

He was about to answer, but she interrupted him again. "You killed him!" she said in Spanish; her eyes widened in horror.

"No! I didn't!"

"And then you took his belongings and tried to take his place as my brother!" she went on.

"I swear, Marena, it's not like you think at all!"

Gwen lunged toward him and began hitting his chest with her closed fists. "You did! You did!"

"Marena, stop!" Porro held her hands. "It wasn't me who killed your brother."

"Then who did?" she whispered.

"Coyote."

Gwen's legs couldn't hold her any longer. Coyote, how convenient. How could she know if he was telling the truth? Covering her face, she sat on the pavement and wept.

Tony had been observing the scene from the car, but when he saw his wife hitting the ground, he rushed to her side.

"Gwen! What's wrong?" he asked, reaching down to lift her up.

"He killed my brother," was all Gwen could say.

Porro sensed what she was saying. He approached her and looked her in the eyes.

"I did not," Porro said in Spanish, holding her gaze.

And then it was as if she were suspended above the big beyond, a peaceful valley of love and recognition, a place where she felt intimately at home. She stopped crying and lifted her face, seeing her own reflection in the obsidian mirror of his dark eyes. She was mesmerized by the depth and mystery of it. She suddenly had the sense that she had met him before. The way he looked at her was vaguely familiar, as if it had happened a long time ago.

"You didn't?" She wanted to believe him so badly.

"No, I swear," said Porro, shaking his head.

"I don't know why, but I believe you," she said, an immense peace passing through her entire being.

Porro exhaled, relieved. I should give her the letters and Marco's belongings now. That will make her feel better, he thought.

Don't do it, Porro.

Why?

She is the reason for my coming back, do you not realize? This is my chance to reconnect with her!

Who?

My Czarina Alexandra...

What the hell are you talking about?

Sorry, I forgot you are not well versed in Russian history, Porro.

Russian history? Who are you? Porro asked, grabbing his head in his hands and trying to ignore both voices that had been hammering at him since the crossing. You always want to do bad things! I don't know who you are, but I'm not going to let you harm Marena. She is my friend's sister.

You can try to stop me, Porro, but I am powerful, more than you know. She and I go back a long way.

The time had come for Gwen to make peace with it all. The fact was she had lost her brother when she and her parents came to the United States. He had become a memory, a blurred image tossed like a toy by the fury of time. Now she could finally have some closure and put it all behind her.

"I'm just overwhelmed, that's all. Why don't you come to our house?" Gwen asked.

His eyes lit up. Actually, it wasn't a bad idea. He had nowhere to go.

"Gwen, dear, we don't know him," protested Tony.

"Thank you anyway," Porro said, sensing his disapproval.

"Perhaps another time then. You can tell me all about my brother. I'll give you my address and phone number," she said, fumbling inside her purse in search of a pen and paper.

"Okay. I'll call you sometime," Porro said, although he didn't really know why he had said that. Fate had delivered Marena effortlessly right in his path. Why? What was her role in his life? Or was it the other way around? Was she the reason he had met Marco in the first place? What was the meaning of all those snippets of conversations he had with that strange voice inside him? Somehow he felt he should keep in touch with her. She was kind and beautiful, and she could be helpful to him in a foreign country. But when his "other" voice spoke, it was as if someone else was living inside of him, making him powerfully attracted to her. It wasn't a sexual attraction, but he felt a strong need to be connected with her. Perhaps it was the lure of the "forbidden fruit"? Not only was she married but she was also older than him.

Suddenly, he resolved to end the connection right then and there. There was no reason to see her again.

"Before I go, these are the letters Marco carried with him," he said, handing her the bundle, neatly tied with a red crocheted chain.

"These must be the letters my adoptive mother sent to my aunt years ago," she said, shuffling them like a deck of cards. She looked at Porro. "May I keep them?"

"Of course." Now it was officially over. There was no other reason to stay connected.

"We must meet again," she said, her eyes oozing honey.

See? What did I tell you? She wants to see me again. She is already caving in to my charm.

"I think it would be a mistake," Porro said.

"Why? You were meant to be in my life. Perhaps you're a gift from my brother."

He struggled with his voice. "I don't think so. I must go now."

She looked at him one more time. "It's funny...haven't we met before?"

This is good, Porro. This is very good.

The cold air was what Gwen needed to slap her back to reality. Was it possible that she had coasted along all her life without direction? If she had, then she finally had landed on an island of understanding and revelation, where all her answers lay scattered about like coconuts on a tropical beach. Even though her brother's death had come as a shock to her, the fact that it wasn't a mystery anymore had brought closure to years of wondering. Now she could put all that behind her and go on with her life, living and loving each moment fully without being half-anchored in the past and the land of her birth.

After they said good-bye, Porro disappeared quickly around the corner, leaving her dumbfounded. She regretted that he had left without giving her a means to get in touch with him. Feeling an obsessive need to see him again, she rationalized it was to know about Marco's last days of his life, but she secretly knew she had fallen prey to his fierce magnetism.

Gwen laced her arm into Tony's, and together they walked to the SUV, a few feet down the street. Even though she wasn't in a hurry to leave, she sprinted with renewed energy.

"I can't go home," she said, smiling.

"What do you mean?" asked Tony.

"Let's go somewhere." She gazed at the blue sky and took in a deep breath, closing her eyes.

"I don't get it," Tony said. "You just found out your brother is dead, and you act as if you just met the king of Spain. What's going on, Gwen?"

She opened the passenger door and got in. "I don't know. I feel as if my life came full circle somehow, almost as if my brother's absence has somehow been filled by…" She couldn't finish her thought. Fear took hold of her. How could she even entertain the idea that Porro could ever replace Marco? It was ludicrous. "It's hard to explain."

"You're being irrational."

"Are you going to blame my hormones again?"

"You said it."

"Take me out for coffee," Gwen said.

"That's the last thing you need. We're going home. The kids are waiting."

"I saw a bakery on the way from the hospital."

"Well, if you insist, I can drop you off there."

"And you?"

"If we're not going home, I might as well go to the office and work on that estimate."

"But I thought you were taking the day off! You won't go with me for a cup of coffee?"

"I'm tired. I have a lot of work to do, and I can't waste time."

"So going on a date with me is a waste?"

"I didn't mean it that way," said Tony, shaking his head.

"Sure you did. Drop me off here."

"But we're not at the bakery yet."

"I'll walk."

Tony stopped the car. It was no use arguing with her. He watched her get out.

"I'll pick you up from the bakery in an hour, then?" he said, rolling down the passenger window.

She nodded. As she turned to walk in the opposite direction, she acknowledged that he had been under a lot of stress lately, and she wasn't making it any easier on him. It would be best if she walked off her anger.

Gwen welcomed the open air and the chance to release her anxiety. There was no trace of Porro. She followed the scent of freshly baked pastries, punctuated by the sobering bitterness of strong, dark coffee. The bells on the door jingled as she entered the Bittersweet Café. The cold in her ears melted like ice under hot water. She noticed two officers sitting in one of the booths. Officer Gallo nodded with a smirk of approval as she sat down in the booth behind them. Trixie appeared shortly after.

"What can I get for you?" she asked, tapping the pen on her pinky. She didn't even look at Gwen.

"Double espresso, please, and chocolate marble cheesecake with raspberry sauce." After nine months of watery decaf, she was ready for the real thing.

Trixie's diamond studs twinkled in her cheeks as she smiled on her way to the kitchen. When she came back with Gwen's order, the officers got up from their table.

"Thanks for the coffee, miss," said Officer Gallo, throwing a five-dollar bill on the table.

"No problem!" said Trixie.

"We're counting on you," said Officer Striker with a wink. "If you see him again, you must call us immediately."

Trixie watched them get in their vehicle and drive away. Just thinking that she might see Porro again was enough to throw her into a tornado of emotions. But what was the likelihood of ever seeing him again? He wouldn't dare come back to the bakery, and the chances of him being a part of her life were as inconceivable as Jimmy Stewart stepping out of the screen and shaking her shoulders, saying, "It's a wonderful life!" But if he did come back, would she hand him to the authorities? Of course not. She'd protect him and make sure he was safely hidden, even though it meant she would be breaking the law once again. She sighed.

"Who are they looking for?" Gwen took her by surprise.

Trixie looked at Gwen for the first time. Her heart jumped.

"It must be somebody special, by the way you blushed." Gwen took a sip of her espresso.

Trixie stood transfixed. After a long pause, she managed to stammer, "No, it's not that. It's just that you...you look familiar."

"Have we met?" asked Gwen.

"No, not really," Trixie said, hurrying back to the kitchen. Once there, she turned on the faucet and splashed cold water on her face. Her hands were trembling. She leaned forward on the sink, connecting the dots. There was a strong resemblance between the woman sitting at the table and the teenager's photo. Could she be Porro's wife? Unlikely. She was considerably older than Porro. Was she his sister then? Except for their black hair, they didn't look anything alike. So who was she, and why was she in the bakery the same day Porro appeared in her life? Porro had made sure he removed the photograph from the locket before he gave the necklace to her. Now she had to know who this woman was. She might lead her back to Porro. Trixie dried her face and hands, and went back to the front.

"How is everything?" said Trixie, trying to sound casual.

"Great! I like this place."

"Can I get you something else?"

Gwen was about to answer when she noticed the silver locket on Trixie's neck. It looked exactly like the one her father had given to her mother when Marco was born. The locket was triangular and had a ruby stud at the vertex. How many heirlooms like that were there?

"Where did you get that?" she asked, putting down her spoon.

"What?"

"The locket." Gwen's eyes were fixed on it.

"Someone gave it to me." Trixie closed her hand around it instinctively.

"Who?"

Trixie ignored her.

"May I?" Gwen stretched her hand.

"No." Trixie turned her back to Gwen.

"That's my brother's locket!" Gwen said, getting up.

Trixie stepped back so fast that she almost lost her balance. "Porro is your brother?"

Gwen covered her mouth to suppress a scream. "Is that what he told you?"

"No, he just gave me the locket in payment for food."

"But the locket is not his. It's my brother's."

"Wait, I'm confused...," said Trixie, scratching her head.

"Look on the back of it; you'll see my brother's initials," Gwen said. She walked around Trixie and stood in front of her, so she could verify that the locket had belonged to Marco.

Trixie turned the locket over in her hands. "M. S.," she said.

"Marco Sanchez, see?" nodded Gwen.

"So who's Porro?"

"He crossed the border with my brother."

"How do you know?" Trixie asked.

"My husband and I almost ran him over in the street and—"

"Oh my God! Is he okay?" Trixie interrupted.

"Yes. He kept running, and we followed him until something fell out of one of his backpacks. It turned out to be my photograph."

"So you just saw him? Where was he headed?"

"I don't know. But I need to see him again."

Well, isn't that interesting, Trixie thought. Why would you want to see Porro again, bitch? You're married, she said to herself. She went behind the counter and punched a few numbers into the cash register. "Twelve seventy-five," she snapped.

"You're keeping something from me, aren't you?"

"I don't know what you're talking about."

"First of all, you need to give me that locket."

"That locket is mine now."

At that moment, Tony walked in. "Ready, dear?"

"No, I'm not leaving until she gives me the locket."

"What locket?" he asked.

"Tony, Porro gave her my brother's locket, and she doesn't want to give it back to me." Gwen's voice quivered.

Tony looked at Trixie, but he didn't see anything. "Gwen, please…"

She saw with horror that Trixie didn't have the locket anymore. "But she just had it! I swear!"

Tony smiled faintly and shook his head. "I'm sorry, miss. My wife just had a baby who's very sick and had to stay in the hospital. I also think her hormones are still playing tricks on her. You'll have to excuse us," he said, leading Gwen out the door.

"But…" Trixie realized they were walking out without paying.

Gwen freed herself from Tony and walked back in. "You want your money, don't you?"

Trixie nodded.

"Well, I want my locket," said Gwen, her hand stretched.

Trixie shook her head no. Her diamond studs flashed defiantly.

"Okay, then, if that's how you want to play this, here's your money. Now you listen to me, bitch, and listen well. There's a possibility that Porro might have killed my brother."

"Oh, please…" Trixie said, rolling her eyes.

"And if you protect him, you will be held accountable."

Blood flooded Trixie's cheeks under her white skin.

"So," Gwen continued, waiting for her words to sink in, "when you see him again, you call me." She handed Trixie a piece of paper with her phone number on it.

Trixie felt a surge of protection growing within her. The feeling took over her mind, her logic, her ability to reason. She admitted to herself that she had to see Porro again. It was an urge, an obsession—completely unexplainable. The only other time she had felt like this was when Jared, her boyfriend of two years, suddenly left her to marry somebody else. She was never able to understand why, and because she never had closure, he became an obsession for her. That is, until she met Porro. Now that he had walked into her life, she was not going to let him go so easily. The fact was she could care less about the locket, except that it reminded her of him.

"Did you see the two officers who just left?" Trixie asked Gwen.

Gwen nodded.

"They're from Immigration, and they're looking for him. I have their business card because I'm supposed to call them if I know of Porro's whereabouts. They told me that if I don't report him, I'll be breaking the law." Trixie waited for Gwen's reaction.

Foreboding thoughts swarmed in Gwen's mind. She had already lost Marco when she left Mexico, and now fate had brought her face-to-face with the last person who had seen her brother alive. She had to see Porro again, but she couldn't quite explain why.

Trixie continued. "Now, I can tell them where he was seen last, and they'll scope the area again. If they catch him, they'll put him on an airplane, and we"—she pointed at herself and then at Gwen—"will never see him again. Ever." When no reaction came from Gwen, she went on. "Very well, I guess I'll have to do my duty as a citizen." She pulled Officer Striker's card from her pocket, walked over to the phone in the corner of the counter, and picked up the receiver.

The trick didn't work. Gwen was not the type to be bullied by someone like Trixie. She knew Trixie was bluffing because if she were to call Immigration, she would never have the chance to see Porro again. And since the officers had just left the bakery, it would be a while before they got her message.

Gwen perceived Trixie's need for Porro. She sensed the lack of love in her life, her loneliness, and her clinginess. If the locket provided some kind of emotional anchor for her, she was okay with that. Gwen's memories were intact, and she didn't need a locket to remind her of her roots. Suddenly, having the locket wasn't important anymore. Relieved, she signaled to Tony with her finger. "You owe me a date," she said.

He held her hand and walked over to the booth. Sitting across from her, he took her hands in his. "I shouldn't have gone to the office."

When Trixie saw Gwen and Tony looking into each other's eyes, she hung up the phone. They looked like two lovebirds. She didn't feel threatened anymore. Perhaps, if she befriended Gwen, she might see Porro again. She tightened her apron behind her back and walked to the table. "Here, take it," she said, removing the locket from her apron pocket where she had hidden it.

"You keep it," Gwen said and held out her hand. "My name is Gwen, and this is my husband, Tony."

"And I'm Trixie." The two studs in her cheeks smiled along with her.

Chapter 20

Cesar woke up early the next morning. He went downstairs and had a quick breakfast. Now that he had assumed responsibility for what he had done, he would repair the damage inflicted across the board on his family. For the first time in his life, he pushed his selfishness aside and considered the consequences of his behavior. He had no idea how things would turn out. What if Porro started a fight with him? What if the whole thing turned violent? This could end up being more detrimental to Azucena, but he needed to take a chance and act like a man.

The chauffeur drove him from the posh neighborhood in Las Colinas into the humble section of Quetzal, where Porro's mother lived. They arrived at eight-thirty in the morning. He got out of the car and told the chauffeur to wait for him outside.

It was a modest house with small square windows, from which the smell of stew emanated, even this early in the morning. The sun's glare reflected on the white little house, making it hard to look at. The shutters were painted bright yellow, and bougainvilleas in fiery orange and hot pink added a splash of color to the wall. A black iron fence carved in elegant Spanish designs surrounded the house, separating it from the neighbor's. It was reminiscent of the architectural style that prevailed during the colonial period. A few stepping-stones led up to the front porch dotted with terra-cotta pots, which overflowed with geraniums and orange pepper bells. Cesar buttoned his jacket and walked to the door. He rang the bell.

After a few moments, a short woman in her mid sixties leaned out of one of the windows and asked, "May I help you?"

"I am looking for Porro Camorra," Cesar said.

The woman's eyes flickered at the mention of his name. "He's not here."

"May I come in?"

"Who are you?"

"I am Cesar Gonzalez Barista."

The woman gasped. She disappeared from the window, and a few moments later, she unlocked the door. Stepping aside, she said, "Please come in, Mr. Barista."

"Thank you," said Cesar.

"Make yourself comfortable, please," she said, indicating the green sofa under the window. "Can I get you something to drink?"

"Sure, coffee would be perfect. Thank you." He wondered how she would have reacted if he had asked for whiskey, which was what he really needed.

Celestina went into the kitchen and came back a few minutes later with a tray. She placed it on the coffee table, picked up the cup of coffee, and handed it to Cesar. "Please," she said, pointing to a bowl filled with tamarinds.

Cesar took the cup. It looked like tea. He took a sip and winced at the lack of flavor. Celestina sat on the chair across from him, her hands on her lap and her fingers fidgeting.

"What can I do for you, Mr. Barista?"

"I need to talk to your son," Cesar said, assuming the

woman was Porro's mother. Her eyes were the same shape, slightly slanted toward her eyebrows.

"I told you. My son is not here."

"When will he be home?"

There was a long silence. Finally, Celestina said, "I don't know where my son is. I was hoping you would know what happened to him."

Cesar was quiet, and he looked at the floor. *So she doesn't know,* he thought.

"Something happened to my Porro that forced him to leave his job so suddenly. What happened, Mr. Barista?" she asked.

"Señora," Cesar said, "I—"

"What did he do?" she whispered.

"It really wasn't his fault..." he began. Cesar stared down at the coffee in his hands. How could he explain to Celestina what he had done? And if he told her the truth, would she be willing to disclose where Porro was? Was he prepared to deal with her reaction?

"Señora," he began in a low voice, "I made a mistake, and I'm here to correct it."

"What did you do to my son?" she asked, measuring each word.

"I threatened him."

"Why? What could Porro have done to deserve that?"

"There's something you must know before you jump to conclusions, Señora."

"This better be good," she said.

"Porro is in love with my sister, Azucena. They've been lovers for a few months now—"

"Your sister? I didn't know that," interrupted Celestina.

"Yes, and she...became pregnant."

Celestina gasped. "Oh my God!"

"You must know, Señora Camorra, that Porro did the honorable thing. As soon as Azucena told him she was pregnant, he wanted to see my father to ask him for my sister's hand." He waited for Celestina to take it all in. "But..."

Celestina was crying now.

"Are you okay, Señora?"

Tears poured down her wrinkled cheeks like sap from an injured tree. "So Porro is going to be a father," she repeated, sobbing.

Cesar nodded. "When my sister told me about it, I assumed he had taken advantage of her. For the sake of her honor, I went after him with my rifle through the hacienda, but he managed to escape. In the process I accidentally shot my brother, who was with me, and when the police came, I was too scared to tell the truth. I didn't know if my brother would live or die, so I told the police Porro shot him."

"That explains why he left so suddenly," she said, covering her face with her hands. "My poor son."

"I'm so sorry, Señora."

Celestina looked up. She dried her face with the apron. She clenched her jaws, forming a square around her otherwise round face. "Well, then, I hope you're happy, Mr. Barista. You managed to destroy two families, ours and yours! The real reason you chased him is because you don't think he's good enough for your sister, and on top of it you accused him falsely!"

"Like I said, Señora, I came here to make it right," said Cesar, looking down.

She stood. "Get out of my house."

"But——"

"Now!" She pointed to the door.

Cesar got up from the sofa. "I'm afraid you don't realize the extent of the damage, Señora Camorra. I need to take Porro with me, today."

"Why?"

"Because if I don't, my father will hunt him down until he has him killed."

Celestina excused herself. She walked to the back of the house through a narrow hallway. She needed time to think. Between not knowing if Porro had made it over the border and his employer and the police looking for him, she was torn. Should she believe him? What if it was a trap? He sounded sincere, and he did look distressed. Then again, you never knew with people. Everybody had his or her own agenda. What if she told him Porro had left? If Cesar was telling the truth, he needed to find him, but if it wasn't true, Porro was safe in America. That is, if he made it.

It had always fallen on her to make the big decisions for her family. In the absence of a steady man in her life, she had to be mother, father, friend, confidante, caretaker, and shield from the outside world. Let him wait, she thought. She went to her bedroom and sat on the bed. Unable to concentrate in the solitude of her room, she returned to the kitchen. The comforting mix of warmth and aromas was where she had always been able to find her answers as she washed, chopped, and mixed. A few dirty dishes lay in the sink from the morning.

She ignored them. She needed to gather all her energy and make the right decision. A mistake could cost Porro his life, and she would not be able to live with that. She lifted the lid of the pot in which her stew simmered and inhaled. The savory smell of peppers and tomatoes spoke to her. You don't have to be sweet. You don't have to comply. Your son's life depends on it, she told herself. Resolute, she walked back to the living room.

Her hands on her hips, she asked him, "And what if you're not telling me the truth?"

"This is about my sister's honor, Señora. My father wants Azucena to be married, and when he finds out that Porro is the father, he will be very pleased. He always had a high regard for Porro."

"And if Porro doesn't show up?"

"In that case, my father will assume that Porro is avoiding his responsibility, causing embarrassment to the family. I promise you that he'll use his influence to have him killed if he refuses to marry Azucena."

"So what will happen to your sister in the meantime?" asked Celestina.

"She'll go to Ciudad Encantada for the duration of her pregnancy. My aunt Sofía will care for her until she gives birth."

"Why Ciudad Encantada?"

"To spare her the bad tongues."

"And what will happen after she gives birth?"

"She will have to give up the baby for adoption, and my father will send her to a convent."

Celestina was quiet. No matter how much they looked,

they would never be able to find him in Mexico, which meant Porro was safe—at least, safe from them. But was he really safe? She hadn't heard from him since he left thirteen days ago. What if he was dead? But it also meant that she would have a grandchild she'd never know. Somebody else would hold it, feed it, laugh, and play with it. She'd never have the chance to caress its soft skin or sing lullabies while rocking it to sleep. And somebody else would watch it grow into adulthood. Somebody else would walk away, reaping the harvest of love and happiness that belonged to Porro and Azucena, and to her, the legitimate grandmother. It was heartbreaking. But what could she do now?

"I have rights to that child. I can adopt him if your father is so afraid of what people think," she said.

"I'm afraid my father won't approve of it, Señora Camorra."

"It's not up to your father, Mr. Barista. The Spanish Inquisition is over. I have rights too."

"My father is a powerful man, Señora. He's used to getting his way."

"And what is his way?"

Ignoring the question, Cesar said, "Make sure Porro comes to my house tonight and speaks with my father." He got up and buttoned his jacket.

Celestina was trapped. "I'm afraid I won't be able to do that."

"And why is that?" he asked in a condescending way.

"Because Porro went to America."

Chapter 21

From the outside, it looked like a storybook church: an A-frame structure, with double doors centered atop five steps, a round clock above them, and a steeple with a cross on the roof. Simple lines and a whitewashed front concealed the elegance of the sanctuary inside. The walls were covered with mahogany panels, evenly set between square sections of carved wood. The shiny luster of the reddish-brown veneer reflected a warm atmosphere when the sun filtered through the stained glass windows. The combination lent a copper ambiance to the room. The flat wood benches were upholstered with red velvet, comfortable in their clean simplicity. There were twenty rows on each side, each with a Bible and the announcements for the upcoming week, neatly arranged in a book holder on the back of the preceding seat. The podium, from which the sermon had been delivered each Sunday since 1918, was tucked humbly to the left of the altar, surrounded by a railing of dark wood columns, as if to keep bad spirits away. It was considered a young community, and despite having grown from three founding families to a congregation of one hundred, the church had managed to keep its quaint, inviting atmosphere for everyone who entered through its doors.

As Porro pushed the door open, the first thing that struck him was the scent of sandalwood emanating from the pages of the Bibles. Like ghosts dancing in the guttural silence of the church, the confessions that Father O'Leary had endured and absolved over the years had been permanently sealed in the safety of the sanctuary.

Leaving his two backpacks on the floor, Porro tiptoed to the front of the church. The marble tile squeaked under the rubber soles of his sneakers.

Childhood memories flooded his conscience. The last time he had been in a church, he was eight years old. Every Sunday, his mother woke him up early and dressed him in a clean, ironed and starched white shirt tucked into a pair of navy pants. She polished his black shoes the night before and combed his black hair to one side. One day, too bored with the service, he wandered off to the courtyard. He joined some of the other children who, like him, were bored and had gone outside to play ball instead. As he approached the group, he stood by the side waiting to be acknowledged. They don't seem to notice me, he remembered thinking. They were all white kids from middle-class Spanish families, and even though their parents listened to the sermon every Sunday, it didn't seem to make a difference in the way they treated the descendants of the native Indians. When he finally gathered the courage to ask if he could play, Jacinto, the son of the school principal, said, "No, we don't play with darkies." It was enough to send Porro running to his mother, hurt, humiliated, and feeling lonely and excluded. When he entered the sanctuary, the priest was delivering his sermon, and he held a pair of accusing eyes on him as he made his way to his mother. When the service was over, people turned to one another to greet and mingle, but no one looked at Celestina or him. He tugged at his mother's skirt, urging her to leave. She kept a smile on her face as her eyes swept the room, trying to establish eye contact with somebody, but again nobody responded. After that, Porro learned to lie to his mother. He began pretending to be sick or busy doing homework; he made up one excuse after another until he ran out of them. And when he did, he threw the biggest tantrum his mother had ever endured.

Now in America, Porro wondered if it would be the same here. When he walked from the hospital to downtown, he had noticed the diversity of faces, sizes, shapes, skins, and eyes. There was a dizzying variety of cultures—Chinese mingled with African Americans, Irish with Spanish, Germans with Native Americans. Nobody was looked upon with disdain, and everyone wore the colors of their culture like a flag of pride, proclaiming their uniqueness. It was as if they were blind to their differences.

Porro heard steps coming from the right side of the altar, where a door led into the priest's study. The echo resonated in the church and wafted to the high ceilings like smoke from a sacrifice. A dark silhouette emerged from the room behind the door. The priest walked to the altar and saw Porro standing there. Since he wasn't sitting and didn't seem to be praying, the priest approached him. Porro hated to have to ask for help from an institution he had learned to resent.

"May I help you?" said the priest. His voice was kind and soft.

Porro just looked at him, unable to understand. The priest smiled. His accent was markedly American as he repeated the question in Spanish. Porro was pleased.

"You speak Spanish!"

"If you don't speak it in these parts of town, you're lost. It would be a mistake and a disservice to our guests from neighboring countries not to be able to communicate with them." His *r*'s rolled softly like waves lapping against the shore, and his vowels prolonged the syllables like a dance in slow motion.

"I am lost," Porro said finally. "I need a place to stay."

"What's your name, son?"

"Porro Camorra."

"Porro." The priest rubbed his goatee as he said this, then walked around Porro and eyed him from the side. "I take it you just got here, meaning the United States."

"Yes, Father."

"And I assume you're running from Immigration," he said, avoiding Porro's eyes to spare him the embarrassment.

Porro didn't respond.

"Don't worry. We won't turn you in to the authorities. We don't turn anybody away, but you need to know that we have to abide by the law."

"I know."

"Do you have any friends or relatives?"

"No, sir, I am on my own," responded Porro.

The priest sighed. With his hand on his chin, he turned toward the altar, searching for answers. Then he said, "You may stay here for a week. There is a guest room in the east wing with a cot and blankets. You can also help yourself to the food in the kitchen. Every Sunday we have a community soup kitchen for all who need it. But I'm afraid that after a week you'll have to find another place to stay."

"A week is better than nothing, Father, and I appreciate any help," said Porro. This wasn't even his country and he already felt welcome.

"You must find work," he said, lifting his palm between him and Porro, "even though I'm not suggesting in any way that you break the law."

"I prefer to break the law of the land, rather than the law of the Lord."

"I'm not sure I understand you, son."

"If I work, I'll get paid for my services. The alternative is to steal, right? In that case, I'd be sinning."

Father O'Leary studied him. Porro wasn't the typical immigrant who roamed the streets of Hope. Something he couldn't pinpoint set him apart from the rest. He possessed a certain confidence that could only come from knowing he had a special permission to be there, legal or not.

"I can't argue with your reasoning, Porro. I certainly commend you for not wanting to steal."

"Thank you, Father." Porro sensed that he had caught the priest's curiosity. He also noticed the priest looked at him with a reverence that nobody else, except for Trixie, had ever displayed toward him until now. Where had this newfound respect come from? Were Americans that open-minded? What was so admirable about wanting to work? Didn't people in America work?

"The members of this congregation are pious people," the priest went on, "You might want to make some connections on Sunday, after services."

Porro nodded. He had learned to take life one day at a time. Circumstances could, and would, change at any moment, so there was no sense in worrying about it. For now, he had food and a place to sleep, safe from the clutches of Immigration. In the silence of the church, his stomach growled.

"You're hungry, son. Let's go to the kitchen and eat something. Then I'll show you around," said Father O'Leary.

That night he dreamed of his mother. She was wearing a red gown and holding a candle in her hands. As she walked toward him, the candle flickered, making her face look like an angel on fire. Celestina was saying something to him as she came closer, but he couldn't make it out. Walking toward the window in their little house and looking out, she asked the stars and the moon if they were taking care of her Porro. The moon laughed and the stars aligned in response, forming a word that started with the letter *r*. Celestina tried to read it, but it dissolved in a rain of red drops, like blood falling from the sky, and she was startled. Scared, she sat down on the green sofa and started to cry. Then Azucena appeared, more beautiful than he remembered, and caressed Celestina. In the background, a swelling sea sputtered red foam as the waves broke against the rocks. The image of Cesar swimming against the current, trying not to drown, appeared like a hologram that enveloped the whole scene. "Porro! Where are you?" Cesar cried. "Answer me!"

Porro woke up in a sweat. Sitting up, he had no doubt that either Cesar or the police were looking for him, and somehow his mother was involved. He had wanted to keep her out of this. By now they had probably caught up with her, putting pressure on her to disclose his whereabouts. The night before, Porro thought about writing to his mother to let her know he was safe, that he had made it through the border, but now he knew it would be risky. His mother would have to wait, and his heart ached for her.

He got up quickly and took a shower, washing off the fear the dream had left on him. He put on clean clothes, made the bed, brushed his teeth, and went to the kitchen. He made some coffee and toast with grape jelly and ate in solitude.

Once in the sanctuary, he entered the second row and kneeled down. A statue of the Virgin Mary looked down on him with merciful eyes as he uttered a prayer. He wasn't even thinking consciously about it. The words just poured out.

"*Padrenuestro que estás en los Cielos*, our Father in heaven, I know I haven't been good about fulfilling my obligations as a Catholic. I beseech you to forgive my shortcomings and listen to my pleas on behalf of my mother. Please protect her from harm. Give her strength to endure any harassment coming her way. As for Azucena, give her wisdom to make the right decision with respect to our child. Heal Carlos, and…Cesar as well. Amen."

When he crossed himself, a current of electricity crawled under his skin, and all of a sudden, he felt so close to heaven that it seemed as if he was floating. He couldn't understand the change taking place in him, the fervor with which a desire for good things kept pouring out of his heart on behalf of those he loved and even those who wanted to harm him.

He felt so elated that all his doubts and worries dissipated like fairy dust in the wind. He felt a kinship with the church and all that it represented.

Chapter 22

The preparations for the soup kitchen had been under way since six o'clock Sunday morning. The kitchen came alive with the chatter and laughter of the volunteers who poured in carrying celery, onions, garlic, and carrots. The beef was already in the refrigerator, ready to be chopped. By the time morning mass was over, the soup would be ready for any and all who wanted it.

Father O'Leary introduced Porro to the group of volunteers. Women sliced, diced, and shredded, the chop-chop of their knives punctuating the hectic rhythm of the morning. The men carelessly plopped vegetables into pots, splattering the boiling broth all over the stove and counter. Porro offered to wash the utensils as they were being used since he didn't know what else to do.

"Good morning." Trixie came in, dragging her feet. "Sorry I'm late." She yawned.

"Hey, Trixie!" said Cecelia, one of the volunteers. "Can you stir this pot while I get the parsley from the fridge?"

Trixie did as she was told and then, out of the corner of her eye, she saw Porro by the sink, washing the dishes. The blood drained from her porcelain white face, and she started breathing fast.

"You okay?" asked a man with red freckles.

"Yes, a little dizzy," she said, steadying herself on the counter.

Porro turned around. Trixie was staring at him, unable to move. Heat rose from her belly, firing up her face and making her look like a beet. He turned off the water, dried his hands on a towel, and swaggered toward her, his eyes fixed on her the whole time. When he was close to her, with his gaze steady and his eyes piercing hers, he noticed a faint odor seeping through the sweat that glistened on her chest. He relished the power he had over her.

The man with the red freckles turned to Porro. "Let me introduce you to Trixie," he said, unaware of the spell they both were under. "She does community hours once a week." He winked.

Porro gave him a blank stare, as if shooing away a pesky bug. The man turned around before he could see Trixie stick her tongue out at him.

"Trixie, we have the cooking under control," said another volunteer, tying her apron around her. "Why don't you show Porro where the dishes are? The two of you can go out and set the table in the courtyard. Don't wait until the last minute. The service will be over soon."

Trixie walked to the chest, followed by Porro. She opened one of the cabinets and removed a stack of paper bowls. She put them in Porro's hands and took another stack for herself. She led the way to the patio, with Porro following closely behind. As she set the bowls in towers on a corner of the table, he imitated her movements, staring at her the whole time and mindful that she knew it.

When the service ended, the homeless and the poor flocked in. They formed a line, each grabbed a bowl and a spoon, and then they walked down the long table to receive their share. Porro and Trixie were serving.

"So," said Trixie, "where did you go after those jerks chased you away?" Her voice was chirpy.

Porro didn't understand. He was beginning to realize the need to learn English. He shifted on his feet, knowing she must have forgotten he didn't speak the language and was probably waiting for him to respond.

"Emmm…," he began, trying to find a way to communicate.

"Oh, I keep forgetting you don't speak English!" she said, laughing.

Father O'Leary appeared from the main sanctuary, bowing and greeting the congregants as he walked toward the table. "How's it going?" he asked Trixie.

She put down her ladle and walked around the table. "Father, I need to talk to you."

"What's it about, child?"

"I prefer to talk in private," she said. Turning toward Porro, she raised her index finger and said, "Give me a few minutes. I'll be right back."

Porro nodded.

Trixie and the priest walked over to a corner of the courtyard. They sat under the magnolia tree, which was in full bloom, infusing the air with an intoxicating fragrance.

"How long is he staying here?" she asked.

"I'll give him a week, but then he'll have to figure out what to do. I can't compromise the congregation."

"Father, I want your blessing," she said.

"You? You want my blessing?" Father O'Leary laughed. "For what?"

"I'm gonna ask Porro to come live with me."

The priest winced. "First of all, you don't know him. It's very commendable you want to help, but you're asking me to bless a situation that could be dangerous for you."

"I feel as if I've known him all my life," she lied. "And besides—"

"The answer is no, Trixie, I won't do it. He came here knowing the odds. He probably has an idea of where he'll be staying. He must have friends somewhere, and it's just a matter of time before he finds them. Please don't get involved in his life."

The Father's words echoed in her head. She had heard her group therapist say something similar, not exactly, but close. It had to do with her clinging to people, a pattern she had held on to all her life and that had pushed her to find comfort in pills, which eventually landed her in rehab. Wanting to live with Porro was exactly what her therapist would advise her against, but she was addicted to whatever made her feel good, loved, and secure. This time, the drug was Porro. She shook her head.

"Well, then, if you don't bless us, it's okay. The one time I want to help and I get objections. I will offer my home to him, and he can count on me for anything, with your blessing or without it."

Stomping back to the serving table, now empty of bowls, she noticed a group of men, mostly in their fifties, who lingered idly after lunch. Porro sat alone, playing with a paper napkin. Trixie approached him.

"I can see you're finished," she said, taking his plate away.

"Yes," he said, wiping his mouth.

"Okay, then, let's go." She tilted her head and made a gesture with her hand. "We're going *mi casa*." She didn't smile while she said it.

"*Tu casa?*" Porro stood up, hesitating.

"Sí." She held her hands out to him.

Just then, the priest returned and approached them. "Well, well, well," he said to Porro in Spanish, "it looks like you've found a place to stay."

"Yep," he replied in his native tongue. His mouth twisted into a half smile.

The priest eyed him gravely. "I don't know who you are, Porro, but I'd better not find out anything happened to Trixie. You hear me?"

"What do you mean?" Porro became serious.

"All I know about you is that you just crossed the border illegally. For all practical matters, you could be a fugitive, and only God knows why," said the priest boldly. "The other thing is that you'll be living in sin."

"Sin?" Porro's vein swelled up under his skin. "Sheltered between the walls and stained glass of your church, what do you know about sin? People come here each week, wearing their fancy clothes and Sunday behavior. You haven't seen sin and wouldn't know when to recognize it. Don't talk to me about sin." He punched the air in defiance.

Father O'Leary nodded. His hunch had been confirmed. Not only did he know nothing about Porro, but he also had just witnessed an outburst he didn't like. He was glad to get rid of him, but he'd have to keep an eye on Trixie, even though she was a hopeless addict.

Chapter 23

"**I** need the phone number of the Consulate of the United States, please," said Don Francisco to the operator. He waited a few moments for a response. "Thank you." He hung up the phone and dialed another number. "What time do you close today? Five? Do I need an appointment with the consul general?" Pause. "It's for a visa. Sure, I can provide you with all those documents. Yes, my passport is valid. How long will it take to issue the visa? No, I need it sooner. Yes, it's urgent. I'll be there tomorrow first thing, then." Don Francisco put down the receiver. "Start assembling these documents," he said to Cesar, handing him a handwritten list.

"But, Papá, once we are in the States, how are we going to find him?" Cesar had come to terms with the fact that in order to help Azucena, he would need their father's help. Contrary to Cesar's assumption, Don Francisco took the news calmly and didn't dwell on technicalities. Being the practical man he was, he devised a plan to bring Porro immediately back to Mexico.

"We need to get in touch with the Coyote who crossed him. He can tell us whether he crossed through Texas or Arizona. Then we'll trace his whereabouts based on that. Porro can't be too far from the border."

"There are a million Coyotes, Father. We'll never find the one he used," answered Cesar. "Unless..."

"Yes?"

"Unless we find the person who financed the crossing. He might have recommended a Coyote too."

"Good thinking. Porro's mother must know. In the meantime, get all the necessary papers ready for the visa. Time is of the essence," said Don Francisco. A glimmer of hope shone in his eyes. Soon his daughter would be reunited with the man she loved, and he would throw the biggest fiesta Mexico had ever seen.

In her room, surrounded by red and gold pillows of embroidered silk and brocade, Azucena flipped through bridal magazines, savoring the moment she would be Porro's wife. Despite the fact that he had fled in such a hurry and gone to the United States, she wasn't worried. Now she had her father's blessing, and that made all the difference in the world. She had full confidence that her father would put all his connections and resources to good use. Azucena also knew Porro was a survivor, and she felt that, because he was so good, God would protect him from harm. Good things happened to good people, she rationalized, and she was sure he had crossed successfully. The challenge now was to find him. But for that, there was Papá, who through his unconditional support would do everything in his power to reunite her with her beloved. From the comfort of her room, she remained oblivious to the flurry of activity downstairs, where painters had already begun coating the walls in the living room and dining room with fresh layers of burnt orange. At the same time, the housekeeping staff was busy taking down curtains to wash. The just-polished mahogany furniture glimmered in the afternoon sun.

Don Francisco had also hired an extra crew to help in the kitchen. The china was brought up from the basement to be washed with the crystal goblets, tumblers, and silverware.

She caressed her belly. What would it be, a boy or a girl? And what if she had twins? What would Porro prefer to have? What would they name the baby?

Back in Hope, Texas, Porro was stepping into a very different realm. As he entered Trixie's apartment, the chaos slapped him in the face. He noticed how small the room was, how stuffy and untidy. A black lacquer bookshelf held everything but books. Old coupons, newspapers, and magazines cluttered the top shelf; videos overflowed from the bottom shelf, and a cassette collection lay scattered on the middle shelf. Halfway into the room, a dried-up peace lily leaned toward the window, begging for water. Dust covered everything. A dirty crocheted blanket draped the back of a black suede futon. Blue and red pillows were strewn all over the floor, and dirty cups and plates caked with dried food littered the coffee table in front of the TV.

Trixie took Porro's backpacks to the bedroom. "This is where we're going to sleep," she said, showing him the room. A single picture of a young woman in black leggings and hot pink boots hung from the wall adjacent to the bed. Her short blond hair, à la Marilyn Monroe, was surrounded by a cloud of smoke from the cigarette she held in one of her black-gloved hands. Purple- and white-striped sheets were rumpled together with a lavender comforter, the pillows thrown carelessly at the foot of the bed.

As Trixie walked in, she almost tripped over a couple of empty containers of Chinese food. The room reeked of beer and dirty underwear.

"How do you like it?" she asked cheerfully.

Porro recalled the smell of fresh linens drying in the Mexican sun. He heard his mother's words as she justified her daily activity as a homemaker. "*Así se duerme mejor*," she said time and again, alleging that a person slept better on a clean bed that had been made since the morning, the sheets stretched taut. His sheets had always been white since the ones with designs cost more. A splash of color came from the red flannel blanket, solid and flat, although when you cuddled in it, you inhaled sun and fresh grass.

His nose twitched as he looked around the room. He had to admit it was an upgrade from the desert. Turning away from the room, he looked around for a second bedroom, but he only saw one more door, which Trixie opened in anticipation.

"*Baño*," she said, pointing at the toilet.

Porro understood what only one bedroom and one bathroom implied. He walked back to the bedroom and went inside. Sitting on the crumpled sheets, he started bouncing playfully like a kid. Trixie joined him.

"First thing we're doing is enrolling you in English classes at the local high school," she said, opening one of the backpacks. She took out the few clothes he had with him and made room in the closet for them. It only took ten minutes for him to get settled.

"Let's go for a walk," she said, grabbing his hand.

It was a beautiful, breezy afternoon and the leaves in the

trees danced under the sun. They walked in silence until they reached Laredo Street.

"Ah!" Porro said, recognizing the street. After three more blocks, they were in front of the bakery.

"You live with me," said Trixie, pointing at him and then at herself, "and wash dishes." She made circles in the air pretending to be washing.

Porro's teeth flashed in a smile of relief. He had a house, food, and a job! What more could he ask for?

"Yes!" he said in English.

"Wash to eat," answered Trixie, making a gesture as if she was eating something. "No money," she added, rubbing her thumb against her index and middle finger.

"No *dinero*?" Porro was surprised.

"Nope, you wash so you can sleep and eat," she said, her hands on her waist.

So this was what it had come down to. He'd have a place to stay, but he had to pay for it with his work. He'd have no money to be independent. To make things worse, he would have to share her bed, unless he managed to sneak out onto the couch. He didn't know what Trixie expected from him exactly, but he knew she was hopelessly attracted to him and had manipulated the situation so he'd be completely dependent on her. He realized he was in no position to be picky, and this arrangement would have to do until he found an alternative.

They went inside the bakery.

"Hi, Grandma!" said Trixie.

"Darling! What a nice surprise! What are you doing here on your day off?" asked Grandma Letty.

"Oh, I was just in the area. This is my boyfriend," she said, looking at Porro.

Grandma Letty stared at the chocolate skin of the young man accompanying her granddaughter, whose purple eyes flickered against her ivory face. They couldn't have been a more mismatched pair.

Chapter 24

Manuel Tejadas's house was in the little village of Valle de las Serpientes. Cesar drove three hours straight from the city. Celestina had been diligent in guiding him to Porro's friend Alvaro, who immediately disclosed who the Coyote was and where he lived.

It was 8 o'clock on Sunday night. Cesar felt like a hound tracking his prey. He could even smell victory. The Coyote would tell him everything he needed to know; he was sure of it. But just in case, if he had to be nudged, Cesar was prepared for that as well.

As he reached the neighborhood, he stopped the car in front of a *taqueria*. All he had eaten that day was breakfast, and the excitement kept his appetite at bay. He didn't want to waste one minute more than was necessary. There would be plenty of time to celebrate later. Turning on the inside light of his car, he took a map from the glove compartment. He followed with his index finger the names of the streets, looking for *Calle* Oviedo. He was close. He counted how many blocks he had to drive before he needed to turn left, until he reached the number 1916.

Coyote's house was a small, square terra-cotta building with a flat roof. The single window in the front was partially covered by a flowery curtain. Cesar couldn't decide if it looked friendly and inviting, or outright sinister. He got out of the car, buttoned his jacket, and rang the bell.

A small woman in her forties opened the door. She was plump, and her black hair, streaked with silver strands, was pinned back in a bun. She wore faded clothes, and melancholy showed in her eyes.

"Yes?" she said.

"I'm looking for Manuel Tejadas," said Cesar.

"Is he expecting you?" she asked.

"No, not really."

The woman's expression changed from sad to wary, and a tinge of fear appeared on her worn face.

"Don't worry," Cesar reassured her, "I didn't come on official business."

"Who are you?" Her eyes became two black slits.

"A friend of mine crossed with your husband this last trip, and I need to find him. His mother is sick," he lied.

The woman's features softened. "Wait here," she said, closing the door behind her.

A few moments later, an unkempt and unshaven man came to the door, buckling his belt. His white undershirt was stained with salsa, and black hair protruded from under his arms. He smelled of sweat.

"What do you want?" he asked, keeping Cesar outside.

"I'm looking for Porro Camorra. You crossed him about three weeks ago."

"Sorry, can't help you," said Manuel Tejadas, closing the door.

"Oh no, you don't," said Cesar, intercepting the door with his foot. "He was in your last group—I know that for a fact—and I need to find him."

"I cross a lot of people. I don't remember all their names."

"Listen, I need to find this kid. His mother needs him."

Coyote sized up Cesar. He was well built but short and considerably younger than him. Although he wasn't fully white, he carried himself like an aristocrat and probably had connections in high places. He could use someone like that.

"What did you say his name was?"

"Porro. Porro Camorra."

The expression on Coyote's face changed. An imperceptible smirk appeared at the thought of that little punk who had dared to challenge him in the desert. "What does he look like?"

"He's short, shiny black hair, dark skin, fast on his feet," Cesar said, remembering how Porro had outrun him on his own hacienda.

Coyote started to laugh. "You are describing eighty percent of the people that cross," he said, scratching his belly. "I'm sorry. I can't help you." He started to close the door.

"Wait!" Cesar said, pulling out a wad of money from his pocket.

At the sight of the money, Coyote stopped. "I think I remember vaguely now. Why don't you come in? Zulema," he called, "bring us two beers."

The two men sat at the dinner table while Zulema hurried to the kitchen. When she came back, Cesar was counting the money. He slammed $200 down and pushed it across the table toward Coyote.

"Now, where is Porro Camorra?" he asked.

Without counting it, Coyote put the money in his pocket and said, "I don't know."

"Bastard!"

"Easy now," said Coyote, unperturbed.

"You told me you remembered him!"

"That doesn't mean I know where he is," said Coyote.

"Why wouldn't you know? I gave you all I had," said Cesar, trying to keep his cool.

"It's not a matter of that," said Coyote. "It's just that I'm telling you what I know, and the truth is I don't know where he is."

"I don't expect you to know where he went once he was in the United States, Señor Tejadas." Cesar spoke slowly, measuring each and every word, and emphasizing Coyote's name as a sign of respect, but what he really wanted to do was punch him in the face. "If you just tell me at which point he crossed and if he actually made it all right, I'll take it from there."

"I'm telling you the truth." Coyote spit out the toothpick he had been chewing on and took a swig of beer.

"How is it possible that you don't know? Either he crossed or he didn't. You must know!"

"I don't."

"Why?"

After a long pause, in which Coyote had his eyes fixed on Cesar, he said quietly, "Porro stayed behind."

Sweat appeared on Cesar's forehead. "What does that mean?"

"It was a big group, and when one of the guys got sick and delayed us, I decided to make up for lost time and continue the march. There was no time to make a count of the group, and when I realized Porro was missing, it was too late to go back for him. That kid should have known better."

Cesar considered what Coyote was saying. Something

didn't fit the story. He knew Porro, and he knew he had a good heart. It was possible he would have stayed behind to help someone who was sick, but the fact that he was also running for his life would have made him think twice about it. He would have realized that he couldn't make it on his own.

"I don't believe you," said Cesar.

"You can believe it or not," said Coyote, spitting a piece of hot pepper he dislodged from his teeth. "It doesn't make a difference why he stayed behind, does it? At this point, all I can say is I didn't cross him. He stayed alone with a sick companion; chances are he didn't make it."

It was amazing how people gave away their innermost secrets by just slipping on one word. "It doesn't make a difference why he stayed behind," he had said, and the word that stood out like a lake in the desert was *why*. Cesar smiled. "Something tells me you're lying."

Coyote swallowed and remained quiet.

"I'm not leaving until you tell me." Cesar drummed his fingers on the table.

A whiff of rancid sweat rose from Coyote. His breathing quickened. "Look, I don't want any problems, Señor," said Coyote. "Here." He took a handful of bills from his pocket and gave them back to Cesar. "I told you all I know, but you can keep half the money." A faint smile formed under his black moustache.

Without touching it, Cesar asked point blank, "Is Porro alive?"

"How should I know?" Coyote shrugged his shoulders, the palms of his hands facing up in a gesture of utmost innocence.

"You're hiding something, Señor, and if Porro crossed,

you would have told me. So there are only two possibilities here: either he died in the desert or you killed him."

"I did not kill him," Coyote said convincingly.

"Prove it!" Cesar pounded on the table.

"I can't!"

Cesar got up from his chair, went around the table, and grabbed Coyote by the neck. Zulema, who had been watching from the kitchen door, covered her mouth, restraining a scream.

"Why should I believe you?" Cesar tried to suppress his mounting anger.

"Because I didn't kill Porro. I k...ki...killed his friend!" stuttered Coyote.

Cesar loosened the grip on Manuel Tejadas's neck. He stood motionless, digesting what he had just heard. His mind worked feverishly trying to reach some kind of conclusion. He replayed in his mind the conversation with Coyote. If Porro's friend had been killed, Porro would have stayed behind to save himself. He probably sensed he would be next. Alone in the desert, what chance did he have to make it to the other side? Would he know the route? Could he read the stars or find north with the movement of the sun? And what about the wild animals, lack of food and water, and relentless heat?

Releasing Coyote, he straightened his jacket and walked to the door. Coyote gathered all of the money and went after him. "Take your money, Señor! And let's call it even, eh?" he said hopefully.

Scoffing, Cesar snatched the money out of his hands, opened the door, and said, "If I don't find Porro Camorra, I'll come back to kill you." He put the money in his pocket with a nod.

As he got in his car and closed the door, he thought about all the people whose fate would be affected if Porro wasn't alive. Fuck!

It was three o'clock in the morning when he finally got home. All the lights were off except for the one in the study. He entered quietly and tiptoed toward his father, who sat on his leather chair in front of the fire. Don Francisco turned around.

"Son?"

Looking down, Cesar couldn't face his father. He shook his head instead. "Papá, I'm so sorry," he began.

"What did you find out?" asked Don Francisco.

"I'm afraid we've lost Porro. Coyote couldn't tell me much, but we know Porro got separated from the group at some point."

"What's that supposed to mean?" Don Francisco stood.

"He couldn't have possibly survived, Papá."

Don Francisco fixed his eyes on Cesar. For a moment, he lost all notion of time, and he traveled back to when he was twenty-eight years old. He thought about his late wife, Raquel, and a knot formed in his throat. He remembered the night Raquel's father had come to visit him, distraught and unannounced, to ask him if he would be willing to marry his daughter. Young Francisco had loved Raquel forever, having been childhood friends. But Raquel had fallen in love with the gardener instead and got pregnant. When her father found out, he was furious, but being the practical man that he was, he sought to cover it up. That union was out of the question, so after threatening the gardener and sending him away, Raquel's father set the stage for a more suitable husband for his daughter and made arrangements for the wedding to take place without her consent. Barely two months later, Francisco beamed as he walked down the aisle, arm in arm with the woman he had always loved. He hoped Raquel would eventually love him. Although she gave him two beautiful and healthy children of his own and was an exemplary wife, she never forgot the father of her first child. Living with a void she could never fill, yearning for her true love, she lost her will to live. After her diagnosis, she simply let herself go. Her legacy: Cesar, the son of the gardener, whose anger masked his own inadequacy within the family; Carlos, the bridge between them; and Azucena, now following in the steps of her own mother.

"There's no time to waste then," said Don Francisco, snapping back to the present. "We'll set a date for the wedding. Your sister will marry Pablo Calderón."

Cesar knew it would be futile to argue with him, but on the other hand, this seemed the best of all the alternatives. Pablo came from a good, respectable family and had always had a soft spot for Azucena. Feeling the burden of guilt and impotence on his shoulders, he excused himself. He couldn't imagine what awaited them all once Azucena found out.

Chapter 25

When they came back from the bakery that Sunday night, all Porro wanted to do was take a shower and settle in for the evening. He needed to wash away the conflicting thoughts that pullulated in his mind like bees buzzing incessantly with their obsessive perfection. Even though Azucena occupied his thoughts most of the time, the image of Gwen had begun to creep into his consciousness with more frequency. He had found her attractive, but she was married and therefore off limits. She was also older than he was, and to make matters worse, whenever he listened to the other voice, she was referred to as "the czarina," a concept he knew nothing about. He wished he could shut out the constant debate that went on between himself and his other self, that stranger who threatened his sanity and peace of mind. This invisible entity demanded constant attention, hurling inappropriate thoughts and uncontrollable desires at the most unexpected moments. He needed it to stop.

As if that wasn't enough, he was surprised to be thinking time and again about God, and it got more complicated when his confusion and anxiety turned into peace and serenity after a session of prayer. He couldn't explain why this worked, but he wasn't going to question that which brought relief to his torn spirit. No wonder his mother had turned to religion. He was beginning to understand life at a deeper level.

He went into the bathroom and turned on the water, got

undressed, and stepped into the tub. Hot water shot from the showerhead like little fingers against his body. The lemony lather of slippery foam worked its soothing effects, because he felt upbeat and invigorated as he rinsed the last bubbles from his skin.

Once dry and dressed in a clean cotton shirt and pants, he went to the kitchen, where Trixie was preparing dinner.

"Mmm," he said with dubious enthusiasm.

Trixie was flipping hamburgers in a pan. The grease sizzled, creating a cloud of smoke above the stove. He inhaled, but no trace of onions or garlic rose from the pan, not even the aroma of searing meat. Still, it was an upgrade from the food in the desert, and a little gratitude prayer sneaked up on him once more.

Trixie placed a sliced bun on each paper plate and squirted some ketchup inside each one. Then she put a burger on each bun and brought the plates to the living room, placing them on the coffee table right in front of the TV, which blared with the catchy tune of a commercial.

Porro followed her, carrying paper napkins and two cans of American beer, which he regarded with disdain. Then he sat at the end of the sofa opposite her.

"Aren't you gonna eat?" she asked through a mouthful of chewed hamburger. A smear of ketchup remained on her upper lip.

He looked at his plate and sighed.

"Look," she went on, "tomorrow is Monday. The bakery is closed. I'll take you to the local school, and we'll register you in English classes."

Porro could only guess what she was saying, but he was getting used to her chatter. Reluctantly, he took a bite of the hamburger and tried to swallow. It tasted like cardboard. Resigned, he took a second bite before settling back, trying to guess what the TV show was about. His mind wandered from Azucena to Gwen and back, a soundless commotion that fought to get his attention. Twenty minutes passed, and Trixie was so engrossed in the TV show that she didn't notice when he slipped off to the bedroom.

He walked in and closed the door. A faint light peered through a crack in the closed blinds, enough for him to walk to the bed without tripping. He stretched the bottom sheet, tucking it under the mattress as his mother had taught him, and then pulled the top sheet straight, folding it back over the comforter. He took off his shirt, slipped off his pants, and crawled under the covers. The sheets smelled of sweat. He missed home, with its scent of sun and moon magic. He wondered what Azucena was doing right now. Was she thinking about him? Was she wondering where he was? And did she try to find out what happened to him? Now that endless miles separated them, it hurt too much to remember.

It's the here and now that counts, Porro. Look at the woman in the living room, waiting for you to make a move. Don't waste your time with the past. I guarantee you that Azucena is marrying somebody else. Her father will see to that.

Porro sat up and covered his ears to shut off the onslaught of unrelenting verbiage. Who the hell are you? he thought. Who do you want to turn me into? Is this what America does to people?

America, Russia...what's the difference?

It was 11 o'clock when Trixie turned off the TV, stretched like a cat, and yawned. She brought the plates back to the kitchen and threw them away. Turning on the faucet, she watched as the cold water filled the pan, solidifying the fat into a white, crumbly layer like white chocolate. I'll deal with this mess tomorrow, she thought. Leaving the splattered grease on the stovetop and crumbs on the counter, she turned off the light and headed for the bathroom.

After flushing the toilet, she brushed her teeth and rinsed with mouthwash. She tinkered with her strawberry hair and played with different looks, lifting a strand here, tucking another one there. She leaned over the sink and examined her eyebrows. Little black hyphens resembling a Braille poem peeked above her eyelashes. She searched in the top drawer until she found the tweezers and began to pluck away the short, emerging hairs. Through the corner of her eye, she noticed the purple towel that Porro had used to dry himself. It hung neatly from the hook on the wall behind the door. She turned around and took it in her hands. It was still wet. She lifted it up to her nose and inhaled. The lingering scent of his skin filled her with excitement, a wild desire rising from deep inside her.

All of a sudden, a thought struck her. She opened the medicine cabinet and looked for the round plastic dial. Shit, fuck, she said to herself. I must have thrown them away when I broke up with Jared. Fuck, fuck, fuck! What am I going to do now? She considered her options for a moment and decided that it was okay. Porro had appeared in her life as a gift from heaven, and if she got pregnant, they'd be forever bound to each other. It worked like a charm.

His breath was deep and rhythmic, and he slept on his right side, arms crossed. With his back to the window, he moved imperceptibly as the door squeaked open. Trixie tip-toed around the bed and took off her clothes, her silhouette slim and flexible against the faint light that filtered through the blinds. She slithered under the covers. Her heart beat faster than usual, proof that Jared had not broken it after all. When Jared told her he was leaving her, she had laughed. "It's a bad joke, right?" she had said. But very soon she realized that he was leaving, and for good. First she cursed at him, then she begged him to stay, and finally she overdosed. It had been five months since he had made a clean exit from her life. The thought of being held again filled her with joy.

Putting her arm on Porro's back, she began to caress him. His skin was soft and fresh with the smell of citrus. He shifted as the curved fingers of her hand contoured the shape and length of his body, causing goose bumps to form on his back. She took that as a sign to go on and inched closer to him. When her cold skin touched his, she felt as if the night sky burst open with fireworks, making her alive with desire. A sudden warmth sailed downstream to that place where two souls connect in the most intimate way. Imbued with a sense of urgency, her body began to respond with a pulsating force. Instinctively, her hands traced the arch of his buttocks. He was pure muscle.

Porro stirred. Rubbing his eyes, he turned on his back and squinted. Her sweet breath rested on his shoulder, and for a moment, he thought he was with Azucena.

"Hey," Trixie whispered.

Porro frowned at the sound of her raspy voice. "No, no," he protested when he realized it wasn't Azucena. Still on his back, he propped himself up on his elbows.

"Yes, yes," said Trixie, her hand resting on his hardening member.

No puedo hacer esto, he thought. I can't do this. It's not right! I'm going to be a father; I can't do this to Azucena!

Don't be stupid, Porro; it's here and now, remember? You can always go back to Azucena, but this girl needs you. You can make her happy. Don't disappoint her.

I thought you loved Gwen! You're asking me to be unfaithful to her. I thought she was your "queen."

There's a time for everything, Porro. We'll deal with Gwen later.

Unable to ignore his growing lust, he turned toward Trixie, trying to contain himself. She begged.

He rubbed the tip of his male organ in a circular motion against her swollen vulva, sensing her ecstasy. "Is this what you want?" he asked in Spanish.

She writhed underneath him, trying to bond with him at some level, any level, while he continued to taunt her. "Do you feel that?" he asked as she moaned. He continued to prolong her agony in this manner. Desperate, she raised her hips, starting the slow dance of give and take, tentative and bold at the same time. As her breathing quickened, he reveled in her helplessness. He laughed, enjoying the power he had over her, while a primitive rhythm cradled her fire. Panting, she begged him to enter, but he withheld. Just when she thought she was going to lose her mind, he thrust forcefully inside of her, breaking the barrier of pride that had overtaken him.

They bounced with rhythmic movements, their bodies connecting where each craved it the most, both unable to contain the mounting pressure that built up before exploding in a sea of pleasure. Their excitement oozed like bubbles on the sand after the waves recede back into the ocean. This can't be real, she thought, complete and fulfilled.

She drifted into a heavy stupor, but soon he was ready for more. He got on his hands and knees and climbed over her again.

"*Otra vez, gringa*," he said, forcing his way in again before she was even ready.

"No, let me be," she mumbled.

"*Vamos!*"

"Please, no more!" she said. But soon the wings of desire transported her again to that new place where only pleasure of the flesh existed. She climaxed once, then twice more, eventually losing count and feeling the intensity of his manhood as it unleashed mercilessly inside her.

Chapter 26

"María," Azucena whispered at the door of the housekeeper's room. "It's me, Azucena. Open the door!"

María scampered across the room, cracking the door open.

"*Qué pasa, m'hija?*" asked María. "What are you doing up this late?"

"I need you to help me pack."

"Where are you going, Señorita?"

"To my Aunt Sofía. *Vamos!* Hurry! And don't make noise. Nobody knows about this."

María followed Azucena into her room and closed the door behind her. Azucena's suitcase already sat on her bed.

"Don't stand there! Hurry!" she demanded, opening the drawers and handing María her clothes.

"I don't know if I should be helping you, Señorita Azucena," said María. "El Señor Francisco is going to be upset when he finds out. I feel like I'm betraying him. Please don't go, Señorita."

"He wants me to marry Pablo Calderón, and there's no way I'm doing that."

"But Señor Calderón is a good man, Señorita. Perhaps you should consider it."

Azucena looked at her. "Whose side are you on, theirs or mine?"

"Nobody's. I just want you to be safe and happy. That's all. It seems to me he can give you the life you are accustomed to."

"But I don't love him." She snapped the big suitcase closed and started filling the smaller one. María folded the clothes lovingly, nice and neat, as she had done since Azucena was a baby.

A half hour later, they were finished packing enough clothes to last Azucena a few months, although in a few weeks they wouldn't even fit her. She took them anyway, quickly threw a few toiletries in an overnight bag, and went to the door.

"Now, call a taxi so I can go to the station."

"But, Señorita—"

"Do it!"

It was just after lunchtime. All the daily chores had been completed—breakfast dishes washed and stacked away, floors swept and polished, and rooms dusted and aired. Sofía tied her apron behind her back and pinned the sides of her black hair behind her ears to keep the breeze from playing with it. She picked up the basket that carried a pair of scissors, a spade, and gardening gloves, and then stepped out into her garden. Yellow clusters of marigolds and orange gladiolus greeted her. Bees and butterflies fluttered about, helping themselves to generous servings of lavender and jasmine nectar. A wisteria inched its way up the wrought iron fence that separated Sofia's sanctuary from the rest of the world, a garden of dreams waiting to bloom, season after season, before withering again in the natural cycle of life.

EXCHANGE AT THE BORDER

This ritual had sustained her over the years. It started when her neighbor next door had knocked on her door the day after she moved in. "Here's a welcome gift for you," she had said, offering a blue velvet pouch to Sofía. "It contains seeds," she whispered and nodded. Sofía had wondered why this gift was treated like a secret, but she soon found out that the seeds in that pouch contained more than potential gardens in bloom. Skeptical at first, she scattered them in the barren, grassless piece of land that was her backyard at the time. That afternoon, fat clouds gathered from the four directions of the wind, pushing and shoving each other until it rained. It poured long and hard for two days, a phenomenon that the residents of the quaint little town still talked about to this day. And true to the circular nature of things, the sun came out, drying out the clouds and warming up the earth. A few days later, Sofía came out to the backyard to find a fuzzy carpet of little green shoots emerging from the soil. In the end, those became the seeds of comfort, of new beginnings, of promise, of a new life. She found herself thanking the invisible spirit that pushed each plant to life and soon discovered they in turn responded with blooms and fragrance. It was the beginning of a ritual that sustained her in times of sorrow and taught her that while there's life, there's always hope. Taking care of her plants also taught her how to care for herself, how to grow new roots in a foreign soil and blossom despite the grief of deception. Her loneliness soon turned into solitude, a skill she mastered gracefully.

Dandy, her Collie, fanned the gnats with his bushy tail as he lounged in the shade under the fig tree. Betún, the black Scottish terrier, chased butterflies. A soft breeze skated inland from the Pacific nearby. Sofía brushed away some pollen that had flown in her face as she cut violets and baby's breath and collected them in her basket. Just then Betún pricked his ears. Dandy followed suit. Both ran barking around the cottage to the front yard. Sofía ignored them. Probably somebody on his afternoon walk, she thought. But the dogs insisted, and Dandy came back and stood a few feet away from Sofía, wagging his tail. Sofía turned around, wondering what was going on. Dandy twirled playfully in place and ran back to the front, inviting her to follow him. When she didn't, Dandy came back, followed by Betún, and stood beside Sofía, tugging at her apron with his teeth. "What is it, Dandy?" The dog barked. "You want me to go up front, don't you?" Taking off her gardening gloves, Sofía put down her basket and followed the dogs. "Let's check it out," she said.

A six-foot brick wall surrounded the cottage. Poison ivy had climbed up and around the back and sides of the wall. Sofía squinted against the glare of the sun as she got closer to the gate. A young woman stood on the street holding a designer carryall, its expensive initials glinting in the sun. A suitcase rested on the ground next to her. For a moment, Sofía thought she saw her sister, Raquel. "It can't be," Sofía whispered. "Azucena?"

Azucena nodded.

"Oh my God! It is you!" Aunt Sofía hurried toward the gate, holding her hat in the breeze. She opened the gate, being careful not to let the dogs run out, and stepped outside, looking at her niece. "*Querida!*" she said, throwing her arms in an embrace. Azucena returned the affection, resting her head on her aunt's bosom.

"Look at you, all grown up!" she said, taking a few steps back to get a better look at her.

Azucena smiled feebly. "Hola, Tía," she said simply.

"That's it? That's all you have to say to your aunt after not seeing her for fifteen years?"

Azucena looked down as Aunt Sofía scrutinized her face. Azucena broke down sobbing.

"Shhh...," Sofía whispered, bringing Azucena to her chest. "*Ya, querida, ya.*" She caressed her niece's silky mane of hair. Despite all those years apart, the spiritual bond that had connected them still existed. They didn't need words. The circle had begun the process of closing, connecting the past with the present. They strolled along the path around the little house, arm in arm, followed by Dandy and Betún who frisked gaily behind.

They followed the flat stepping-stones flanked by beds of flowers. Tucked in the northeast corner of the garden, a wooden bench sat lonely under the shade of a golden shower tree, whose branches cascaded forward, heavy with yellow blooms. A hint of lemon, mint, and honeysuckle infused the air. A small pond on the left teemed with orange koi that skittered away whenever they perceived human presence. The waterfall gurgled crystalline songs as tiny drops spattered onto the buds of birds of paradise. Dragonflies, with their iridescent wings, kissed the water lilies that opened, white and generous, toward the sun. That was Sofía's garden. That was her world.

They sat down. Sofía waited. "So," she finally said, "what brings you here?" A cloud moved in front of the sun.

"I wish I didn't have to tell you, Tía."

"Can't be that bad."

"It's worse, I suppose."

Could anything be worse than what had happened to her twenty-eight years before? Could their destiny be so linked as to repeat itself in a pattern of unhappiness and unfulfilled dreams? More clouds moved in. Soon the breeze turned into a salty wind from the west. Dandy barked. A drop fell in the pond with a sinister, ominous plop. Then another.

"Let's go inside," said Sofía, picking up the big suitcase.

The dogs followed them, wagging their tails. The house smelled of furniture polish and wax, and the wood parquet floors shone with an amber luster.

"Make yourself comfortable, dear," Sofía said, leaving the big suitcase at the foot of the stairs.

Azucena put down her overnight bag by the French doors leading into the garden and walked toward the white sofa. Embroidered pillows were neatly spread across the back and sides, displaying colorful but simple Japanese motifs. One had the picture of a kokeshi doll holding a lotus flower.

"This is cute," said Azucena, picking up the pillow. "How come the doll doesn't have any arms or legs?"

"In Japanese culture, kokeshi dolls symbolize the infanticide of unwanted Japanese babies killed after birth; *ko* means child, and *keshi* means erasing, extinguishing."

Azucena's eyes filled with tears. Sofía waited.

"Why do you have this in your house?" Azucena finally asked.

"I simply liked them."

"It doesn't make sense."

Sofía didn't answer.

"There's a secret in our family, isn't there? How come you never come over for a visit?"

"It's not my place to tell you, Azucena." Tía Sofía looked around the room, fidgeting with her apron.

"Kokeshi dolls, a cottage by the sea far away from your beloved sister. I always wondered why you disappeared from our lives."

"How about some coffee?" Her aunt started for the kitchen, followed by Dandy. Betún had already claimed his place next to Azucena.

"Only if it's decaf."

Tía Sofía stopped. Decaf? She turned around, a demure look on her face. "Don't tell me..." she began.

Azucena nodded and started to sob, this time inconsolably. Sofía hurried to her side and put her arms around her. Twenty-eight years had passed since she had held her sister, Raquel, in the same way, after she had confided that she was pregnant with the child of the gardener. Sofía, being the eldest of the two sisters, spoke to their father on Raquel's behalf, but her act of selflessness backfired. Like the breath in a body buried alive, her shot at happiness was extinguished forever. Their father, in an effort to save Raquel's reputation, arranged for Francisco Gonzalez Barista to marry her. Francisco, whom Sofía had secretly loved all her life, was snatched from her forever, his future like little pieces of glass, inextricably enmeshed in the fabric of their family tapestry.

In a haze, Sofía released the grip she had on Azucena and sighed, "This calls for tea instead." Tea had been a family ritual instilled in both sisters by their mother, who, being the granddaughter of an Englishwoman, had inherited a stiff adherence to this aristocratic custom. In stark contrast, Fabiana, their maid, had humanized the ritual with ancient songs that invoked magical healing powers. Thus, tea had become the beverage of comfort that, according to Fabiana, cured everything from stomachaches to the tears stemming from the depths of the soul.

Tía Sofía put the kettle on and placed two porcelain cups and saucers on a silver tray. She arranged the matching sugar bowl in the center, together with two white linen napkins embroidered with a matching violet motif. Then she arranged slices of lemon in circular domino fashion on a small plate. She brought the tray to the living room and placed it on the coffee table.

When the kettle whistled, Sofía filled the strainer with a handful of tea leaves and poured the hot water through it into the porcelain teapot. The reddish-brown tea steamed up with a delicate herbal scent. She brought the teapot to the living room and filled Azucena's cup.

"I feel better already," said Azucena, inhaling.

"Told you." Tía Sofía smiled.

"So now you have to tell me the story behind these little dolls," Azucena said, patting the kokeshi doll pillow next to her.

Sofía dropped a lump of sugar into her tea. "First things first, dear. Does your father know you're here?"

"No," said Azucena, smashing a slice of lemon with her spoon. "I'm not talking to him."

"He's probably worried about you," said her aunt. "We'll have to tell him you're here sooner or later."

"I can't. He'll force me to marry."

"And what's wrong with that?"

"He wants me to marry Pablo Calderón. He's not the one I love."

"Oh my God." Tía Sofía put down her cup.

"Oh, Tía, what am I going to do?" cried Azucena.

I can't let the same thing happen to her, Sophia thought.

Back in the city of Hope, Trixie hummed "Girls Just Want to Have Fun" as she prepared breakfast for Porro and her. She didn't remember being in such a good mood in months. She felt complete, as if all the pieces of the puzzle had suddenly been put in place. Her life had meaning now, and she was grateful just for being alive.

As the coffee brewed, it permeated the kitchen with a bitter aroma. She served scrambled eggs on two plates and set them on the kitchen table, on two bamboo placemats. Dancing to the rhythm of the song, she put four slices of bread in the toaster, and arranged the butter and jelly nicely in the center of the table.

"Breakfast is ready!" she called.

Porro came out of the shower, wearing the purple towel around his waist. He was hungry, but the sight of Trixie wearing that sexy camisole and matching shorts, with her hair still tousled from sleep, ignited a renewed desire in him. He hesitated whether to go back to the bedroom and get dressed or give in to his growing desire. I have to have her, he thought. He swaggered down the hallway through the dining room and into the kitchen, stood in front of her, and casually let the purple towel drop onto the floor. A wanton smile formed on his lips as her face melted into helplessness. He came closer, causing her to lose the grip of her mug, coffee splashing all over the cabinet doors and floor, pieces of porcelain scattering in all directions.

"What do you think you're doing?" she giggled, ignoring the mess.

He drew her toward him and pulled down her shorts. He pushed her against the counter, thrusting with urgency, until they both came fast and violently in a quick, fiery climax. Still erect, he turned around and headed for the bedroom to get dressed. Then he walked to the front door and, without a word, left the apartment.

"Where are you going?" she asked, trying to catch her breath.

He looked at her with disdain and closed the door behind him.

⚜

"What brings you here, Porro?" asked Father O'Leary.

"I want to apologize for my behavior last Sunday. I was abrupt and disrespectful to you."

"Apology accepted, son. It's very commendable of you to recognize your mistakes."

A beam of sunlight shone through the stained glass window, highlighting a thin layer of dust on the carved cherry table. A coffeemaker and four glass mugs were arranged on a ceramic tile tray in a corner of the table. Walking toward it, the priest asked, "Coffee?"

"Sure, thank you," said Porro, reaching over for the mug.

The priest walked slowly back to his desk and slumped on

his chair. He fought his fatigue while the spoon in Porro's cup clicked rhythmically as he stirred his coffee. Father O'Leary waited patiently, but no words came from Porro. "Everything going okay?" he finally asked.

Porro nodded, blew on his coffee, and took a sip. He didn't look up.

The priest studied him. "How's it going with Trixie?"

"Good," he said, slurping.

Father O'Leary's piercing blue eyes rested on the young man in front of him. "Why are you really here, Porro?" he finally asked. He knew the apology was only an excuse.

Porro rehearsed the words in his mind before answering. "It's hard for me to explain what is happening to me. I feel uplifted like never before, as if there's a piece of heaven inside of me. It's so strange," he said with moist eyes.

"I think that's wonderful!" said Father O'Leary, suddenly interested.

"Do you think it's God acting through me?"

"Now easy, son. We don't go about talking like that. We need to have respect for the Lord."

Porro looked him straight in the eye. "How am I being disrespectful?" His vein began to swell.

"What do you exactly mean by 'God acting through you'?"

Porro shook his head. "It's difficult to explain. I feel like people are drawn to me, and I'm able to see through them. I know what they think; I know what they're feeling at the moment. I even know what will happen next in many instances. I want to take classes."

The priest slumped back in his chair. His life had been devoted to teaching, inspiring, and uplifting. Now a stranger who had come into his life out of nowhere was gathering the harvest of the seeds he had planted all these years. Who was Porro? he wondered. He had mixed feelings about this poor immigrant, but he knew better than to be judgmental. "Don't you have to work?" ventured the priest.

"The bakery is closed on Mondays. I can come every week and learn with you."

Father O'Leary was quiet. He crossed his fingers and rested his head on his hands. He took in a deep breath and sighed. "When do you want to start?"

"Now."

I should have known Azucena wouldn't go for it, Don Francisco thought. What made me think she would marry Pablo Calderón just because I said so? Now she's gone, Porro's nowhere to be found, and Pablo is not willing to marry her under the circumstances.

Don Francisco had tried so hard to make everyone's life happy, comfortable, and worthwhile. He worked hard to win Raquel's love, pampering her with all the comforts and love he knew she deserved, but in the end, he had to come to terms with his defeat. He realized she would never feel anything other than gratitude for him.

Now the same destiny lurked on the horizon for his daughter. The man she loved could be dead for all he knew or, in the best case scenario, was somewhere in the United States. How would they be able to find him? How would they know whether he was dead or alive? Not only would Azucena be scorned but the social repercussions would extend to the whole family too. For everybody's sake, she had to comply, even if that meant sacrificing her future by living with a man she didn't love. As a father, he knew what to do. But as a man who had lived through that, he was torn. To complicate things, although Pablo Calderón loved Azucena, he had made it clear he'd only marry her if she agreed. "She has a right to be happy, and if Porro is the one she loves, I don't want to marry her."

Pacing up and down the library, his hands tightly clasped behind his back, Don Francisco thought she couldn't have gone too far. Maybe she went to her friend Melisa's house, and she'd come back once she cooled off. He hoped her bond with Porro was weak, a temporary fever of the flesh, which once satisfied would die off into the embers of memory. That would make things easy if she could eventually forget him and move on with somebody else. He'd give Azucena one week to reflect, but in the meantime, he would have to find her.

"You can't hide here forever, Azucena," said Tía Sofía. "You're welcome to stay for as long as you need, but you must let your father know you're with me. I'm sure he's worried about you."

"I'm not going back, ever, Tía. If I can't marry Porro, then my life is not worth living."

"Don't talk nonsense," said Sofía, slightly raising her voice. "It's not about you now. You're responsible for the little life you carry in you."

"I'll stay here with you until the baby is born, but if Porro doesn't contact me before then, I'm giving the baby up for adoption. After that, what's the difference? I'll start a new life away from everybody I know. It'll be a fresh start without prejudice or judgment."

"Hmm…" Tía Sofía thought. "So Porro is nowhere to be found?" she asked.

"I think my father gave up hope of finding him. He says it's highly unlikely he could have made it through the crossing. Even Cesar tried to get as much information as he could, but Coyote wasn't that helpful. He claims not to know whether Porro crossed over or not, or at which point. We don't have a clue where to begin the search."

"But there's a possibility he might be alive."

"He would have contacted me already, and he didn't." Azucena started to cry again. "He must be dead."

"Maybe he's afraid. All he knows is Cesar and the police are looking for him."

"That's true," Azucena conceded. "But then again, what good is it if he doesn't contact me? He might as well be dead. It seems I'm destined to live my life without him."

"You give up so easily."

Tía Sofía got up from the couch slowly, rubbing her knees. She stood in front of the window, looking out into the front yard. An orange butterfly with black and yellow spots rested on a cluster of purple heathers in a corner. A whiff of lavender floated into the room. "I know if you give up the baby, you'll regret it for the rest of your life," she said. Her mind trailed off to when her own sister struggled with the same conflict. In the end, she decided to keep the baby as a reminder of the man she truly loved. "Even if you marry Pablo and grow to love him, your life will never be the same. You need to fight for what you want. Fight!"

Azucena was quiet. Where was the sweet woman who gathered gardenias and served tea on a silver tray? "Why are you telling me all this?"

"A heavy heart will drag you down and drown you in your own tears."

"Is that what happened to you?"

"No, not me." Sofía turned away from the window, the creamy voile curtains swaying like ghosts. The breeze picked up. Gray clouds cast their shadow on the room. She stood in front of Azucena, her arms folded. "I could have had a chance at happiness, but another woman ended up marrying the man I loved. In the end, she never loved him the way I did. Both her life and mine were ruined because of it. What was the point of that?"

"That's terrible, Tía. I didn't know this. Why do adults always keep secrets from the kids?"

Sofía nodded. "Take it from me. Go after what you want."

"I need to find out if he's alive first. And if he is, I'll have to find him."

"I think if Porro is alive, he will contact you. I'm sure."

"Do you think so, Auntie?"

"Life is full of surprises, my dear, and it always comes full circle. You should rest now, but before dinner, call your father and let him know you're with me, so he doesn't worry."

"You call him."

I haven't heard his voice in so long, Sofía thought. How on earth am I going to pull that off?

Chapter 27

Trixie was busy all day Monday, catching up on things she never had time to do. She shaved her legs, painted her nails purple, and went grocery shopping for the week. In the afternoon, she watched MTV while a cake baked in the oven. She wondered where Porro could have gone all day after making love to her on the kitchen counter, but she was in such a good mood that she ignored the nagging feeling that something might be wrong. Maybe he wants to explore the town, she thought, and that was fine with her.

When Porro finally came back that evening, Trixie decided not to confront him. "I'll take you to the community high school tonight, if you want," she said. "I'll help you enroll in English classes." They went and found out that he could start that same day, so he attended class while Trixie waited for him in the lobby.

"How was your first day of school?" she asked him as they walked to the bus stop.

"Good!" he answered. He was thrilled he could understand that question and was able to answer it in English.

"What did you learn?"

"One, two, three," he said, unfolding his fingers as he counted.

"What are those numbers?" she pointed at the sign on the bus stop.

"Three, eight."

"Very good! That's bus thirty-eight, and that will take you back home from school," said Trixie.

"Zir-tee ate," he repeated, beaming.

"You're cute," she said, giving him a sideways glance.

"You're cute," he repeated, pecking her cheek.

After a night of lovemaking and cuddling, they woke up Tuesday morning with renewed energy. Trixie sang all the way to the bakery, but Porro was quiet. The vivid image of Gwen kept popping up in his head, and every time with more frequency. He couldn't understand the source of these thoughts. Why Gwen? She was a married woman, and he really knew nothing about her, except for the fact that she was Marco's sister. And being married really put her in a class all its own. You don't go there; she's off limits to you, he said to himself. Simultaneously, the memory of Azucena kept fading away with every thought of Gwen.

"Hello? Come back to Earth, you!" Trixie said, waving a hand in front of Porro's lost look.

Momentarily snatched away from Gwen's image, he went to the kitchen, tied his apron around his waist, and began to clean the counters. Trixie started two pots of regular and de-caffeinated coffee and then opened the fridge.

"Would you like to help me?" she asked, taking out the eggs, milk, and butter.

"No." He needed to be alone. He needed quiet to think, to put the conflicting words the voices were hurling at him in some kind of order so he could make sense of them.

"Oh, c'mon! I'll teach you how to make a cake," she said,

tying her own apron around her waist. "Look." She took a bowl and cracked twelve eggs in it. "Give me the egg beaters," she said, beating an imaginary bowl with her hands.

Porro looked around. Ladles, spoons, and knives of all sizes hung from several hooks on the wall. He looked on the shelves under the counter, and there they were, inside a bowl. He gave them to Trixie.

"*Muy bien!*" she said, impressed.

Porro watched her beat the eggs. "Sugar," she said, pointing at the container to the right.

"Shoogar…," he repeated, getting into it. He passed the sugar to Trixie.

"Vanilla extract."

"Vainisha extract…"

Trixie laughed. "Flour," she said, pointing again.

"Flauer…"

"Now, we pour this inside the cake pans. See?"

"*Sí!*"

"And then we bring it to the oven to bake for forty-five minutes. We set the timer and get to the next task."

As time went by, Porro settled into the city of Hope like a crow in a red robin's nest. Like an uninvited guest, he developed an unjustified sense of entitlement. Although Trixie had gotten used to bossing him around at the bakery, at night she was his puppet, surrendering to his every whim. Still the thought of Gwen now inhabited his mind permanently. It was like a migraine: intense, invasive, and persistent. Somehow Porro knew that she was going through a difficult time in her marriage. He felt compelled to rescue her emotionally and in every other way.

As far as Azucena was concerned, she became a foggy remnant of a not-so-distant past, and every now and then, he felt the need to call his mother. But the memory of Cesar's rifle pointing at him always slapped him back into the present, burying his past life deeper and deeper into the hole of oblivion.

It was five o'clock in the afternoon. A song blared through the speakers on the TV. Unable to sit still, Trixie sang along and danced. At that moment, Porro walked in. He crossed the living room toward the bedroom. She decided to confront him. Making an effort to sound indifferent, she asked him, "Where have you been all day?"

Porro began to whistle. He picked up his school bag from the closet in the bedroom and walked back out. She intercepted him.

"I said, where have you been all day?" she asked again, her arms crossed.

A sliver of a smile formed on his face like a half moon. He spit disdainfully on the floor.

"Excuse me?" Her eyebrows arched as if somebody had suddenly blown air in them, only to deflate, all wrinkled and twisted in a frown above her nose.

He brushed past her on his way to the kitchen, picked up an apple, and took a bite. Then he took milk from the fridge and poured some in a glass. She watched in disbelief. "What's with you?" she said, her hands on her hips. The familiar feeling of inadequacy resurfaced as she recalled how Jared's respect for her had gradually faded away. How could men change like that? Was it an act then when they showed pleasure in bed? She considered the fact that Porro depended on her for everything. How dare he disappear all day without an explanation? And why didn't he include her in his plans? What gave him the right to come home and ignore her like this?

He opened his mouth to take another bite, but she slapped the apple away from his hand. It fell on the floor with a solid *pflopf*. The vein in his forehead began to swell.

"I'm talking to you," she said.

Slowly, he placed the milk on the counter and bent down. Lint and hair stuck to the juicy flesh of the apple, which had started to yellow by now. Without dusting it off, he turned to Trixie and squeezed her jaws, forcing her mouth to open. Then calm but forceful, he shoved the apple in her mouth, and pushed it in deeper. She gagged. Struggling to free herself from his grip, she opened her eyes wide, desperate.

Holding the apple in her mouth with one hand, Porro grabbed the glass of milk in the other and poured it slowly on the floor, watching it flow. He threw the empty glass in the sink and headed toward the door, his new shoes sloshing and splashing on the white puddle.

Shuddering, Trixie pulled the apple from her mouth. She gagged again as the hair and lint tickled her throat and stuck to her palate. A wave of vomit rose from her stomach, hot and acrid, scraping her insides on its way out. She bent down letting the vomit mix with the spilled milk on the floor. Then she crawled to the living room, tears streaming down her face, while the song still played in the background.

"Shut up!" Trixie yelled. The music went on. She grabbed the peace lily that sat quietly by the window and smashed it against the TV. Who is this guy? she thought. How could he do this to me? I thought he loved me. What did I do to deserve this? I gave him everything. Of course! That's the problem. There's nothing left for him to conquer, no challenge. He has it all. The pills. Where are my pills? She turned her face to the right and then to the left, as if the pills would have been there waiting for her. I wish I had the fucking pills, she said to herself. That bastard made me throw them out. I shouldn't have listened to him. Fucking Jared! She started kicking and punching the sofa, picked up the pillows and hurled them across the room. The lamp on the side table tumbled down, glass shattering all over the floor. She pulled a poster off the wall and shredded it, and flung the magazines on the shelves across the living room. Then she sat in the middle of the chaos and cried.

At first she felt sorry for herself, then angry toward Jared and Porro, and then ashamed for allowing people to use her. Finally, when there were no more tears left in her, she dragged herself to the bathroom. She stood in front of the mirror. Her hair, smooth and silky, complied with each stroke of her brush, framing her oval face. Her eyes were red and puffy, her nose stuffed. "Why do I let people treat me like this?" she said aloud. All of a sudden, she felt the urge to be kind to herself. "How could I allow myself to go so low? I don't deserve this."

She stripped, turned on the shower, and let the cold water wash away the leftovers of an anger that no longer served her. She had found that place inside where she could hold her own hand and walk away from shame and sadness, and step into a more peaceful and beautiful place. Then she put on her red silk nightgown and sprayed on her favorite cologne, the Japanese cherry blossom that Porro despised. When she finally went to bed, she was in a blissful mood, satisfied at having recovered that part of herself she thought had been lost forever.

"Trixie," Porro whispered, caressing her cheek. "Trixie, wake up!"

She pushed her hair away from her face and half opened her eyes.

"Hmm? What time is it?" she mumbled, squinting at the alarm clock.

"Time to get up. Here," he said, pushing a tray toward her, "I brought you breakfast." The tray held huevos rancheros, toast, and strong black coffee. "I made this for you." His voice was soft and sweet.

Trixie sat up, allowing him to prop the pillows behind her so she would be more comfortable. Slowly, scenes of the previous day began to assault her. Was this a dream?

"Wait. Why are you doing this?" she asked, confused.

"Shhh," he said, touching his lips with his finger. "Eat."

It did smell good.

Should she lower her guard? When was the last time somebody had given her breakfast in bed? Maybe she had over-reacted. This must mean he loved her after all. But as she recalled the calculated anger with which he had treated her, she dismissed the thought. No, he didn't love her, she decided. There was scorn in his eyes, and that mocking half smile that made him look so disgusted irked her. He treated her with disrespect, and his only interest seemed to be sexual. This breakfast in bed was—well, it didn't matter what it meant. She was not going to forget what had happened the night before so quickly. She was determined to find out what this was all about. She had a plan.

Chapter 28

That day at the bakery, despite breakfast in bed, Trixie kept her distance. She needed space and time to think, but with Porro fluttering all over her—being solicitous and trying to make up for the nastiness of the day before—she found it difficult. Still she kept to herself at work, and by the end of the day, he seemed to get the hint and left her alone.

The rest of the week transpired in the same way, each doing their own thing and respecting each other's space, until the following Monday. Porro got up at seven. While he was taking a shower, Trixie got up quietly and dressed quickly. Then she went back to bed and pretended to be asleep. After the shower, Porro finished getting dressed, and without having breakfast, he tiptoed out. As soon as she heard the lock, she jumped out of bed, put on her boots, and went out after him.

Staying a hundred feet behind him, she followed him, his cocky gait unmistakable among the passersby. He went three blocks straight on Dulcinea Street before turning east on Lamotte Street, finally arriving at the church. He went in.

So that's where he goes on Mondays. She waited outside, wrapping herself in her felt jacket and pulling her gray crochet hat all the way down to her ears against the chill that insisted on staying. She waited, thinking he would be out soon. He'd probably forgotten something the day before. After two hours, however, she knew something more serious was holding him there. Realizing she might have to stand in the cold for some time, she walked into the café across the street and ordered a cup of coffee.

An hour passed before someone in a black coat entered through the side door of the church. She didn't think much of it. Perhaps it was the cleaning crew. She got distracted with people coming into the café, but her attention always returned to the church across the street. Throughout the day, several people went in and out of the church, all of them through the side door. She didn't think anything of it until it struck her as odd that, although there was uninterrupted traffic, none of it was through the front door.

The waitress kept coming to her table and warming up her coffee. "Would you like something to eat?" she offered.

Trixie looked at her watch. It was close to five. Where had the time gone? She had been sitting there for close to seven hours and didn't even notice that she wasn't hungry at all. What was going on? And where was Porro? Could she have missed him when he slipped out? "Let me have a cheeseburger with pickles, no tomato," she said to the waitress.

"We don't serve burgers here, ma'am," the waitress said condescendingly.

"What do you have?"

"Let me bring you the menu."

Trixie rolled her eyes. How can they not have burgers? What kind of place is this? She brooded. She leafed through the menu, skipping the fancy stuff, and finally ordered scrambled eggs.

"I'm sorry, ma'am," said the waitress, "breakfast is over."

"Can't you make fucking eggs?" fumed Trixie.

"I'll ask the manager."

Bitch. Haven't had my breakfast yet.

Suddenly, the double doors of the church opened, and the stout silhouette of Porro emerged. He seemed poised and well rested by the way he made his way to the bus stop. She knew he was going to school, so there was no need to follow him there. She took a five-dollar bill and left it on the table. She crossed the street and entered the church.

"Trixie, what a nice surprise!" said Father O'Leary. "You just missed Porro."

"I know."

The priest gave her a quizzical look.

"What did he do all day?" she finally asked.

"He took Bible classes with me, like every Monday."

"All day?"

"No, we study for a couple hours and then he stays in the chapel, praying and meditating." The priest hesitated and then went on. "People come to see him, too."

"What do you mean?"

"He heals. Last Monday, a homeless man came in asking for food. He was so drunk that he tripped and fell, cutting his lip on the floor. Blood poured out. Porro was in the chapel praying, but he heard the commotion and came running. He put his hand over the man's mouth, and the blood stopped flowing! Barely a few moments later, it coagulated, covering the opening completely. The man said it didn't hurt anymore."

"I mean, maybe it just stopped on its own?"

"That's what I thought at first, but then one of our members was very sick and was discharged from the hospital. The doctors said there was nothing else they could for her, so they sent her home. She came to discuss her funeral arrangements with me last week, but while she spoke, her semblance changed from grayish pale to a healthy, rosy appearance. Her voice gained strength, her shoulders straightened. She revived like a flower. She told me she couldn't explain the change in her, just by talking to me."

"So, like...what's that got to do with Porro?"

"Porro was in the room, finishing his homework."

"Like...I don't understand."

"Trixie, he can heal."

"Um...yeah, okay."

"You have to believe me. I saw it with my own eyes."

All her conjectures, suspicions, and plans for revenge, all of it came to a halt. How could she have judged him so harshly? What kind of person had she become to suspect him so unfairly? And could he be so holy that he had been gifted with the ability to heal? How could she have known?

"To be perfectly honest with you, Trixie," continued the priest, "I don't know who this guy really is. He's in awe, as if he just had a spiritual awakening. Although I've witnessed the changes, not only on the man and woman but also on dozens of others who have flocked to the church since then, I still have my doubts." He scratched his chin and the back of his neck, looking down. "Tell me"—he walked slowly around her—"how does he treat you at home?"

The question took her by surprise. How could she equate the seemingly pure soul the priest was describing with the monster she had witnessed at home? Could he have a double personality? Or was it she who brought the worst out in him? Trixie could blame herself as she had always done, but a tiny voice told her this had nothing to do with her. He was who he was, although she hadn't figured him out yet. "Well…" Her voice trailed off and tears welled in her eyes as she remembered. Should she tell the priest that the week before he had stuffed an apple into her mouth, or that he sloshed through the milk he had spilled? Or better yet, that he took her on the ride of her life when he made love to her? How could the priest understand that? Trixie stared down at the floor, her eyelashes flapping like the wings of an injured butterfly.

"Something about him isn't quite right, is it?" continued Father O'Leary. "He has this magnetism that makes people like him. But then those eyes pull you in deep, and you fall into a whirlpool of darkness, making you feel confused and exhilarated at the same time."

Trixie nodded. She understood all too well. His mere presence mesmerized her, but she had also seen his dark side. Sometimes she liked giving him the benefit of the doubt. Perhaps he had had a bad day. But how bad could it have been if he had spent it in church? How could she justify his behavior? She desperately wanted to believe he was good.

"I think we should be careful. He possesses special powers," said the priest.

"Maybe he's holy?" She wanted to believe that so bad.

"He's not holy."

"How do you know?"

"Trixie," he said, holding her by the shoulders, "look at me."

She averted her eyes and looked away. Suddenly, she felt defeated. She had started to believe that she had finally found balance in her life, but the mask she had worked so hard to wear suddenly fell off her face, leaving her once more naked and vulnerable in front of the priest. She couldn't hide from him anymore. The truth hurt like a broken mirror glaring at her under the sun. She sighed and shook her head. A teardrop, light and crystalline at first, made its way down her cheek, leaving a trail of black mascara on her skin. Her diamond stud stopped glittering.

"Come," said the priest, putting one arm around her shoulders. "It's time you begin to pray."

Porro was imbued with such a heightened sense of awareness that, as the students left the room, he was able to perceive the acrid smell of bodies and breath mixed with the faint and delicate perfume that wafted from Ms. Taylor whenever she moved. He could hear the creak of the janitor's closet door as it opened down the hall, despite the shuffling of feet from the outgoing students. The classroom, once gray and dull, became vibrant and well-defined. Overall he experienced a sense of well-being that was new to him. He wondered if prayer was the cause.

At the same time, he felt like an alien in his own body, as if a separate person had settled under his skin and shared the space. He recognized that although he had always harbored love and compassion for people in general, this new vibration came from the other entity, the same one that had been encouraging him to misbehave.

He remembered how his healing abilities had increased over the weeks, and now he was able to see through situations and people at an even deeper level with unmistakable accuracy.

He waited for the last student to leave the classroom, and then he approached Ms. Taylor while she gathered her papers into a brown leather tote.

"*Dónde está* hospital?" he asked.

"What's the matter? Are you ill?"

Ill, ill, what does that mean? he wondered. In an effort to make her understand, he joined his hands in prayer.

"I'm sorry. I'm not sure I understand what you mean, Porro," she said. "Pray? Hospital? Hmm…"

He took a sheet of paper and drew a triangle on top of a square. Then he drew a cross on the tip of the triangle.

"Church?" She smiled.

He nodded and waited. It took a few minutes for Ms. Taylor to connect the dots. "I get it. You pray for people in the hospital on behalf of your church, is that right?"

Although he wasn't sure he understood what she said, he nodded nonetheless. She was on the right track, anyway. All he needed to know was how to get there.

"That's very nice! Come with me." They walked out to the street. "See that post?" She pointed to the bus stop a block and a half away. "Wait there for bus forty-five. Four, five." She flashed four fingers, then five. "It will take you directly to the hospital. It's only a ten-minute ride."

"Gracias, Miss Taylor! Good-bye!"

Just as Ms. Taylor had said, Hope Mercy Hospital appeared in bright red letters against the dark sky of the night. He got out. Bracing himself against the wind, he walked up to the entrance.

"Sign in," said the security guard, sliding a clipboard across the desk.

Porro's heart beat faster. What if they recognized his name? They probably were looking for him, and the authorities had more than likely issued an alert about him. He started to sweat. *Write 'Gregory,'* the voice said. Immediately, a sense of confidence came over him. His breathing slowed down, and he even asked for the pen. He scribbled the name as best as he could spell it, a smirk on his face. He handed back the clipboard and started for the elevators.

"Excuse me!"

Porro froze.

"Who are you visiting?"

Easy now. Have faith.

This time his vein swelled. Why couldn't things go smoothly? Why was everything such a struggle? As he approached the front desk, a young woman glided her svelte figure across the hall, her blond hair bouncing.

"Good night, ma'am," the guard greeted her as she waved.

Smiling, Porro took the clipboard and wrote *Linda Chica*. The guard nodded. "Thank you, sir."

Porro walked to the elevators and waited. The doors opened, he pushed number two, and leaned on the wall, relieved. Once on the second floor, the smell of disinfectant hit him straight in the face. The hallway floor was scrubbed to a shine, and the nurses' station buzzed with phones ringing. He stepped out.

"Porro? Is that you?" He recognized Ellen, the nurse who had lost her composure when she saw him naked.

He turned toward her and his face lit up. "Hello!" he said, his white teeth glaring.

Ellen came closer and hugged him. "I was so worried about you," she whispered. "How've you been?"

"Good!"

Ellen felt his stare undress her as it went from her eyes down to her feet and up again, resting briefly on her generous bosom. Little butterflies swarmed in her belly. "You look good. So...why are you here?" She hoped he wouldn't notice the quiver in her voice.

But he did. He relished the effect he had on her and dwelled on it as he prolonged his response. "People ill," he said, pointing to a patient's room, "I pray."

"You came to pray for a patient?"

"Yes."

"Is that right?" She narrowed her eyes.

"I pray." He joined his hands in prayer. "Patient good."

The ants began dancing again. Gosh, is he cute! "So who are you visiting?" she asked.

Porro shrugged. What did she mean?

"Do you know," she said, raising her voice, "the name of the patient? N-a-m-e?"

"Oh! Yes, yes!" Porro nodded. "No," he frowned. How could he get away with writing a fake name every time? Eventually, it would catch up with him.

"I can help you with that," she whispered. Together they walked to her desk. Looking around to make sure nobody was watching, she tapped a few keys in the computer, waited a moment, and scribbled something on a piece of paper: Oliver Kindle, room 28B; Nancy Petakiss, room 30A. "These people have no visitors. You can write their names on the sign-up sheet next time. Then you can go to their rooms and pray for them." She handed him the paper.

Porro identified the few words he had learned in school:

people, no visitors, room, pray. He nodded, folded the paper, and put it in his pocket. Then he flashed another one of his smiles at her.

"Oh, wait. This is another one who could use some of that angel dust prayers are made of," she said, shifting the cheeks of her butt on the narrow chair. "It's a baby, and he's very sick. Doctors don't think he has much of a chance."

"Baby?"

"Oh," she mumbled, getting up, "sometimes I forget you don't understand English. Come with me."

They walked together to the elevators and went up to the fourth floor. They passed doors and corridors that turned right, left, straight, and left again like a labyrinth. Finally, they were in front of a room with a wide window. A baby the size of a shoebox lay inside a glass crib with tubes attached to his wrinkled chest and arms. His skin had dark spots and was pale rather than red like most newborns. A lamp warmed the body, and his swollen belly rose up and down with each labored breath.

Immediately, Porro felt drawn to him, letting a sense of connection permeate his consciousness.

"Why baby here?" he asked Ellen.

"Baby has a rare disease."

Porro looked at her, his eyebrows raised.

"I don't know how else to tell you, Porro. I'm sorry you don't understand English, but baby"—she began gesturing with her hands, mimicking a game of charades—"his blood no good."

"Blaad?" repeated Porro in his strong Spanish accent.

Ellen looked around. "Come," she said. Together they

walked to Room 29, where a nurse was drawing blood from a patient. Ellen pointed to the red vial and said, "Blood."

"Ah, sí!" A big smile framed his white teeth.

"See?" she nodded, satisfied that he had finally understood.

"Sí!" he repeated, although he meant yes. "Me," he said, pointing a finger on his chest, "pray for baby. Baby okay."

"I have to go back to my floor, but you can stay here and start praying."

Seeing that Porro didn't move, she went on. "Anything else?"

"Yes!" he said.

"Well?" She bit her lip.

"You, me, friends."

"Yes, Porro, we are friends," she said, laughing.

"No! You girlfriend!"

"Mmm...maybe." Ellen blushed.

"Yes, you my girlfriend." And with that, he turned and walked across the hall toward the nursery while Ellen followed him with her eyes fixed on his tight, rock-solid butt.

Chapter 29

Gwen was removing the silver-edged, white porcelain plates from the dining room china hutch. They were a wedding present from a distant but wealthy relative and were only used on special occasions.

"Who's coming?" Tony asked. He walked back from the kitchen table, where he was helping his wife set the table for dinner.

"Nobody."

"Somebody important must be on his way here."

"Not tonight, but soon."

"Not tonight, not tonight...," Tony repeated, pacing the hall between the dining room and the kitchen. "What's that supposed to mean?"

"It means exactly that: not tonight." She leaned on a chair, her left hand on her hip.

"Then why are you taking out the china today?"

"Do you have to know everything?"

Tony put down the last fork on the table. "Excuse me for trying to make conversation."

"About the china?"

"What else are we going to talk about?"

"Perhaps we could continue the conversation we started last week and which you so abruptly put an end to."

"I told you. He's not welcome. We don't know anything about him. How can we bring him into our family, expose our kids to a total stranger?"

"For the hundredth time, he's not a total stranger, Tony! He was my brother's friend!"

"And for the hundredth time, the answer is *no*. N-o. He has no business mixing with people like us."

"Maybe people like you. I should have known when I married you that eventually you would see our differences."

"Why do you always think it's about you, Gwen?"

"Because his culture is my culture and if you don't want to mix 'with people like him'…" She gestured quote-unquote with her fingers, her mouth contorted, mocking him.

"I'm going for a walk," he said, grabbing his jacket on his way out.

She followed him. "I hope you know I won't bend this time. This is my house, too, and I will have him over, with your permission or not."

"We'll see about that." He slammed the door behind him.

Later on that night, when Tony came back, he felt like leaving again. Dirty dishes were piled up in the kitchen sink, burnt food stuck to the stove, and the leftovers hadn't even been put away in the fridge. This was not characteristic of his wife, who was obsessive about leaving everything spotless before going to bed. The house was dark and quiet, and at this moment he preferred it that way. Reluctantly, he rolled up his sleeves and looked for the plastic containers. He put all the food away, turned on the hot water faucet, and began washing the dishes. As he piled them up in the dish rack, one of the pots fell, making a loud noise on the floor. The light upstairs went on.

Gwen ran down the stairs, tying her robe around her waist. "Can't you be more careful? Did you *have* to make all this noise?"

"I figured I'd help."

"I don't need your help, only your support."

"You're really acting up. I'm calling the doctor tomorrow, and I'll tell him to check your hormones."

"Again with the hormones?" She turned around and went back up, shaking her head. It was impossible to reason with him. Once an idea got into his head, it stuck like a tongue to ice.

She recalled Porro's dark skin against his bright white teeth when he smiled, and chills went down her spine. She hugged her robe and lay down on her bed. Images kept popping up in her mind, one after another, without interruption. Porro looking at her in the street the day they met invaded her consciousness. She imagined his eyes peering through her innermost realm.

"What happened today?" Tony said, entering the bedroom. She hadn't heard him come up.

How could she tell him? How could she explain, even to herself, what was going through her mind every waking hour of the day? What did it mean for her? She knew she loved Tony, but the fact that she thought of Porro assiduously confused her. Had she fallen in love with Porro? And if she had, what would the consequences be? What would become of her children, her life, her future? What kind of future awaited her with Porro? Was she prepared to go back to Mexico?

"You would never understand; please leave me alone."

Tony unbuttoned his shirt, then his pants, and went to the

bathroom. A few more minutes of peace before he comes back and grills me with his questions, she thought.

"How about taking a few days off and going somewhere? We could leave the kids with my mother."

"You want to go away while our baby fights for his life in the hospital?"

"This is taking a toll on your nerves. You're of no use to Little Marco in this state of mind. He is safe at the hospital, and two or three days away won't make a difference to him. We can go camping, away from everything and forget our problems."

"I can't forget our problems. The baby is sick, and you think hiking and cooking in the woods will make me forget that? The only thing I can think of right now is my baby," she lied.

Porro's image appeared again in her mind. She couldn't stop thinking about him. She realized with horror that she was obsessed. Porro was competing for attention in her mind with her own son, whose life depended on a miracle. She felt like a lousy mother and was torn between the urge to reach out to Porro and protect him, and concentrating all her energy on Little Marco, who needed as many prayers as he could get. To complicate matters, the fact that the authorities were after Porro enhanced her maternal instincts toward him. How could she expect Tony to understand that if she didn't understand it herself? Would he eventually accept her need to help Porro? Perhaps Tony was right. If they went away somewhere remote, she could probably put her thoughts back in order. Her obsession had taken over her ability to function.

All of a sudden Melody began to cry in her room. Gwen

raised her hands and pressed them hard against her head, trying to shut out the noise. She inhaled deeply, trying to swallow her anxiety, before going to Melody's room. Now Daniel woke and was crying as well, scared.

"Why? Why is this happening to me?" she cried.

Gently, Tony approached her and surrounded her in his arms.

Feeling defeated, she allowed herself to find comfort in the fresh smell of his bare chest. She wept.

Tony caressed her hair and then her back, all the time kissing her head and saying, "Shhh, shhh. Everything will be okay. You'll see." He walked her to the bed, pulled the sheets back, and helped her lie down. The children were still crying in their rooms.

"But...," she protested.

"I'll take care of it," he said, walking out of the room.

⚜

Once alone, Gwen kept her eyes open, fighting the surrounding darkness. I wonder what Porro's doing right now. I need to see him again. Ask him about my brother. And about him, too. I want to know everything about him. I can't stand this!

"You and I need a date," Tony said, slipping inside the bed. The rest of the house was already quiet. He lifted her chin up to his lips.

I don't want a date! I want to see Porro, she said to herself.

Tony's hands began caressing her breasts, his lips planting kisses all over her skin.

I *need* to see Porro.

"Not in the mood tonight?"

"I'm sorry, Tony. I had a long day." She brushed him off.

"How about breakfast at the little bakery on Sunday? After that, we can go together to the church around the corner and talk to the priest."

"Breakfast?" she said absentmindedly.

"Unless you have a better suggestion," he said.

After pondering it for a few minutes, she sat up on the bed. "Actually," she said suddenly in a perky manner, "that would be lovely."

Chapter 30

Back in Mexico, Don Francisco paced in his library, his hands clasped together behind his back. "Why didn't you tell me before, Maria? You've seen me agonize with worry about Azucena, and you knew all along where she was?" Don Francisco was tired, but his voice still thundered across the library.

"*Lo siento*, Señor. I promised Señorita Azucena I wouldn't tell."

"Yes, but your loyalty is to me, and it was very irresponsible of you to keep it to yourself."

Maria lowered her head and headed to the door.

"And one more thing," he said, lifting his index finger. "All the wedding plans will continue full force. Nothing has changed. We're going to have a big wedding, and you are responsible for making sure everything gets done."

"Yes, sir."

The rice was almost cooked. All she needed now was to add the hot peppers to the pot that already simmered with garlic and tomatoes. A pungent aroma wafted from the stove, drenching the cottage with a homey feeling. Outside, the moon cast its veil on the garden, which shimmered in the ghostlike glow. The sprinklers popped up, spraying a soft mist on the freshly cut grass.

Sofía hopped constantly from the counter to the fridge to the stove and back to the counter, stirring and tasting. She had spent most of the afternoon cooking. In between, she took out the china that belonged to her mother and set the table with the embroidered tablecloth reserved for special occasions. She didn't know how much longer she would have Azucena in her life. It was only a matter of time before Francisco would come to claim his daughter. The bell rang. She wiped her hands and went to open the front door.

He had aged. A faint smile peeked uncertainly under his twirled-up moustache, the creases on his face like the grooves of a country dirt road.

"Hello, Sofía," he said. His voice was still sensual, just as she remembered it.

She had rehearsed a thousand times how she would re-act the day she would be face-to-face with him again. When Raquel died, she hadn't had the courage to show up at the funeral, but after everyone had gone, and every day thereaf-ter, she cried on Raquel's grave, grieving for her and for lost chances. Sofía always knew someday they would meet again, but she could have never imagined it would be this way. Where was the young, robust man she had loved? Recalling him in his youth, clothed in designer suits, with his aura of authority, she was sad to see the transformation. His eyes had lost their spark; his frame had shrunk. Did age do this to people? Or was it disillusionment? Did he see the same decline in her?

"Hello, Francisco," she said, letting him in.

"It's been a long time," he said, holding her hands in his. She blushed. Should she break the ice and kiss him on the cheek as was the custom among Spanish people, or should she

EXCHANGE AT THE BORDER

let him take the initiative? As if he'd read her mind, he with-
drew his hands quickly, and she led him into the living room.
He waited for her to sit down and then sat at the opposite end
of the sofa.

"You look good." Except for a few silver threads in her
black hair, she looked youthful. The lace at the sleeves and
collar of her white cotton dress emphasized her appearance as
a carefree spirit.

"Thank you." Her heart skipped slightly.

"Where's Azucena?"

"She's taking a bath."

"How is she?"

"She's doing well. Azucena is a brave girl, you know. You
should be proud of her."

"I am," he said curtly.

"Something to drink?"

"Whiskey, please."

She laughed. "No whiskey in this house. How about some
tea instead?" she offered.

"That was Raquel's favorite beverage."

"It's good for the soul," said Sofía, heading to the kitchen.

He looked around the room. It was small and cozy, the
yellow pastel walls setting off a soft glow against the white
sofa. Unlike his big house in the hacienda, the cottage abounded with warmth and personality. A sense of peace infused the
place, sealing out the rest of the world.

"Raquel loved you very much," he said from the living
room. "But I don't think I can ever forgive you for leaving her.
You never kept in touch."

Sofía came up to the doorway that separated the kitchen from the living room and leaned on the frame, speechless. She opened her mouth to say something, but he went on. "I'm impressed that my daughter chose to come to you after all these years."

"She can stay here for as long as she wants."

"What about my grandchild?"

"She's considering giving him up for adoption."

"No grandchild of mine will be floating around the world. That won't happen!"

"She doesn't want to be a single mom."

"She doesn't have to be. It's all set."

"You'll ruin her life, Francisco."

"How dare you," he frowned, standing up.

"You're doing what my father did. You must give them a chance! I know you can find Porro. You must find him," she said, slapping her hand on the coffee table.

"I tried, but we're at a dead end. It's very possible he might not even be alive." He began his characteristic pacing up and down, his hands always clasped behind him like the wings of a stork. "We don't even know if he made it to the border."

"There's one way to find out."

"How?"

"If he's alive, sooner or later he'll contact his mother. I guarantee it."

Don Francisco thought about it. "How much longer can we wait?"

"He knows when the baby is due. He'll call around that time."

"By then, it will be too late, and if he doesn't call, she will have had a baby out of wedlock. No, I won't allow it. Anyway, what do you care if she marries Porro?"

"Because they are bound to each other with this child."

"Nonsense. Pablo will make a fine husband."

"And she'll die of a broken heart."

Don Francisco didn't respond. Of course he wanted the best for his daughter, but the shame of being a single mother was more than he was willing to bear. And how would she live happily without knowing the fate of her child? Would it be fair to Pablo Calderón? But then again, just because Raquel had never learned to love him, didn't mean Azucena wouldn't love Pablo.

"I'm not waiting for Porro to show up," he said, lifting his index finger toward the sky, "and I expect you to be at the wedding, too."

Chapter 31

A few congregants lingered in the almost empty parking lot, clustered in small groups of three, talking to each other. Tony and Gwen walked through the sanctuary out to the courtyard, where a couple of homeless men were still enjoying their meal.

"Is that Porro?" asked Tony, pointing in the direction of the table where the soup was being served.

Gwen walked closer to take a better look. "Oh my God, I can't believe he's here."

"Go up there and talk to him," prodded Tony in a scornful tone.

"I might just do that," she answered defiantly. But before she could take a single step, the priest approached them.

"Hey, Tony! It's been such a long time! How have you been?" Father O'Leary had seen them from his study and came to greet them.

"Father, it's such a pleasure. We get busy, and we forget the real important things. Or I should say, we remember God during tough times, right?"

"I see," he said, caressing his goatee. "How can I be of help?"

"We'd like to have a talk with you in private, if it's possible."

"Well, I'm expecting someone soon for counseling. I prefer you make an appointment," he said, looking at his watch.

Tony thought for a moment. If Gwen didn't meet with the priest now, he might not be able to drag her back to the church. He decided not to take a chance.

"I'd rather see you now; it will only take a minute."

The priest led the way, while Gwen, taken by the arm, followed Porro with her eyes. Once in the study, they sat on the black leather sofa by the fire as the priest indicated with his hand.

"So what's going on?"

"I don't see the point of all this, Tony," Gwen said, frowning.

"Honey," he said, smiling apologetically at the priest, "Father O'Leary might be able to help us."

"Fine," she said, a tinge of exasperation in her voice. She turned to the priest and said, "We just had a baby, and he was diagnosed with leukemia. It's rare for neonates to have it, but he's that one in a million." She shook her head. "He's in intensive care."

"I'm sorry to hear that, Mrs. Romano. God's paths are inscrutable. We don't know why he does things the way he does. Perhaps he tests us with difficulties to see if we still believe in him. We'll add your baby to our prayer list," he said, looking away. He seemed distracted.

"What is it, Father?" Tony asked.

"Like I said, we'll pray for your son. Now, is there anything else I can do for you?" he asked, rising from his chair.

"I guess that will do it," Tony said, catching the cue. He helped his wife up.

"Of course," Gwen said, relieved. "We can find our way back to the courtyard, Father. No need to show us out." She started for the door but then hesitated. "That young man serving the soup, who is he?"

"I…I'm afraid I can't give you the details of his presence here at the church, but—"

"You don't have to be so secretive about him, Father. In fact, I know his name."

"You know Porro?" asked the priest, surprised.

"Yes. He knew my brother, and I made his acquaintance by chance. I am curious to know why he's here, in this church."

The priest shook his head. "Again, that's God's will. He brought him here, and I'm sure there's a reason for it. I just don't know yet what that reason is. Now," he said, looking at his watch, "if you'll excuse me—"

"Sure, we'll let ourselves out."

Walking through the hallway, Tony stopped at the men's room. "You go on without me. I'll meet you outside in a few minutes."

She continued alone until she stepped out into the brightly lit courtyard. The afternoon sun shone down on the white stone floor. She looked for Porro but didn't find him. A renewed sense of loss gnawed at her.

"Hi," a deep male voice said.

She turned around, startled. "Oh! Hi!" she said, blushing. He was watching her with those eyes that pulled her in so intensely. They both stared at each other, not knowing what to say. Immediately, Porro identified the source of her embarrassment and, sensing her insecurity, knew he had gained control over her.

"What are you doing here?" he asked in Spanish.

She fidgeted with her hands, exhilarated. In fact, she couldn't believe the coincidence. It must be meant to be, she thought. But where is Tony? Although her obsession with Porro was assuaged now that she knew he was around, she realized how much she relied on Tony. She was confused. "We came to see the priest," she said cautiously. "What about you?"

"I help in the soup kitchen every Sunday, and I also study religion on Mondays since the bakery is closed."

"The bakery?" She held her breath.

"Yes. I work there every day, except Sundays and Mondays."

"So you gave my brother's locket to the girl in the bakery. Why?"

"I wanted to pay her for the food she gave me that day. I didn't have any money."

"But the locket wasn't yours to give."

"What's eating you?"

Gwen looked away and remained silent, feeling the weight of his eyes on her. What was he trying to pull? Where is Tony? she wondered. Then she imagined Porro and the girl in the bakery, working side by side. Had they become friends? Would they end up in a relationship? What difference did it make to her, a married woman? The assaulting thoughts upset her. She had no business prying into the lives of others. Desperate, she looked around for signs of Tony.

"I live with her," Porro said, jolting her.

Gwen was startled. How did he know what she had been thinking?

"Her name is Trixie. She offered me a place to stay."

She felt a pang in her stomach. Was it jealousy? "I don't

really know why you're telling me all this. I didn't ask you," she said.

"Sure you did. It's written all over your face." His voice was almost a whisper.

A chill ran up her spine. "Who are you?"

"C'mon, Marena, why don't you tell me what's bothering you?" He took a step toward her.

She backed off quickly. "My name is Gwen," she said. "Don't call me Marena anymore; do you understand?"

"Whatever. But something is making you sad, frustrated. Who are you crying for?"

"Who's crying?" she said, annoyed.

"Your voice is filled with tears. You need to let them out."

"Who the hell are you?"

"Having your brother back in your life wouldn't have worked out," he went on, ignoring her question. "He wasn't the same boy you left when he was five. You need to let him go. Bury your past and start living in the present."

"You don't know anything about me or my family." Her voice cracked.

He waited patiently, his eyes fixed on her. A long silence followed as she let his attention fill her with calm.

"My baby is sick," she finally said.

Porro nodded. "But he's making progress."

"What? How do you know?"

"Marena," he said, shaking his head. "I know a lot of things. As I was saying, Little Marco is actually doing very well."

The floor under her moved. She tried to steady herself, but Porro, noticing she was going to faint, grabbed her just in time. "Breathe," he said gently as his arms surrounded her.

She inhaled, long and deep.

"Now let it go," he said, still holding her.

At that moment Tony appeared. "Hey!"

Porro loosened his grip, and Gwen hurried to explain. "It's okay, honey. I felt queasy and almost fainted. It's better now. We need to see Father O'Leary." She looked up at her husband, who was still frowning at Porro. "C'mon," she said, tugging at his shirt.

"What was he doing holding you?" he asked.

"I told you! I almost fainted!"

"Why?"

"That's why we need to go back to the priest," she whispered.

"I don't like this. I don't like it one bit." He put his arm around her waist and walked her back inside. Porro's icy eyes followed them.

"Forget something?" asked the priest when he saw Tony and Gwen at the door of his office.

"What do you know about that man? You need to tell me," Gwen said and frowned.

The priest walked around his desk in silence. "Gwen, I've known you for a while, but I am bound by confidentiality. I will show you, though, something that may give you the answers you're looking for. Then you'll draw your own conclusions, okay?" He walked out of the studio and motioned them to follow him.

In the kitchen, the priest took a knife and made a small incision in his left thumb. Blood streamed down his wrist.

Cupping his right hand under it, he walked out to the court-yard, with Tony and Gwen following close behind.

"Porro!" he called. When Porro saw the priest holding his hand, he immediately approached him and took charge of the situation. He lifted his eyes, concentrating on an imaginary point in the distance.

"Holy one," he began, "listen to my prayer. Show your mercy to your faithful servant." He closed his eyes, lifted his arms toward the sky, and began uttering unintelligible words. His body shook and trembled for a few seconds and then suddenly stopped. The incision was gone.

Father O'Leary kept his eyes on Gwen, who watched transfixed. Porro walked slowly to a corner of the courtyard. He sat on the tile, his legs pulled up to his chest. Then he rested his head between his legs, looking down.

"I don't know what you're after, but I strongly suggest you stay away from him," said the priest.

"I knew there was something weird about that guy," said Tony.

"The only thing I can say is that God works through him, but that doesn't mean he's entirely good. There's something about him I can't quite explain. It's very unsettling."

"We better listen to the priest, Gwen. I don't like what I see." He put his arm around her shoulders and started for the parking lot.

But Gwen's thoughts were far from the church, her husband, or the priest. Only one thing occupied her mind. What if Porro could heal Little Marco?

Tony pulled onto the main road, made a U-turn heading south, and continued toward Mercy Drive for about three miles. He parked in front of the entrance and looked at his wife. She had been quiet all the way, and she seemed lethargic.

"Our daily visit," he said, opening the passenger door. Gwen got out. They walked arm in arm toward the lobby, signed in, and went to the fourth floor to the Neonatology Intensive Care Unit.

They stood in front of the window. Little Marco lay in a glass capsule, red and blue tubes connected to his tiny body like spider legs. A nurse was sitting next to him writing on a chart and checking the numbers on the monitors surrounding him. She looked up. A smile formed on her young face as she motioned for them to come in.

"Hey there, little champ," said Tony.

The nurse opened the glass crib. "You may caress him if you want, Dad," she said, beaming. "He's ready to be transferred downstairs to a regular room. He's out of danger."

"Are you serious?" Tony asked.

"You just missed the doctor. He's probably calling you as we speak," she said, looking approvingly at the baby.

"Is he on the floor?"

"Yes, let me page him." The nurse went to the station and dialed a number. She came back a few minutes later. "The doctor is on his way. Have a seat."

Gwen sat quietly in the armchair by the window, still in shock. Thoughts flooded her mind, and all she managed to do when the doctor came in was nod in silence, her hands folded on her lap.

"Mr. and Mrs. Romano," he said, "we have good news.

You may be able to take your baby home sooner than we expected. Little Marco has made a remarkable but unexplainable improvement. We haven't started treatment yet, but the numbers on his blood count are exceptional. It's a miracle."

"You must have done something," said Tony.

"No, we were actually reluctant. Treatment is harsh on the body, and being so tiny, we didn't think he'd survive. Also, his prognosis was not good."

Gwen approached the crib. She patted Little Marco's arm with her index finger. Her features softened as she noticed the healthy color in the baby's skin. "Did an angel visit you?" she whispered.

"As a matter of fact," said the nurse, "somebody has been coming here every evening. He stands by the window and stares."

"Who?" asked Tony.

"I don't know. I never asked him his name. He just stands outside the hallway and looks as if he's lost in thought for ten minutes. Then he leaves."

"What does he look like?"

"He's short, pitch-black hair, and a deliciously reddish-brown skin."

Gwen looked up at Tony before collapsing on the floor.

Chapter 32

The apartment was dark and quiet, and it smelled of burnt toast from the morning's breakfast. Just the way I like it, Trixie thought as she let herself in. She took off her jacket, crocheted hat, and mittens; hung them in the entrance closet; and went straight to the kitchen. She took an apple from the fruit basket on the counter. Mmm...I don't think so. She put it back. She opened the fridge and took a beer. A brand-new feeling came over her. She didn't want beer either, or alcohol. Anything that reminded her of her past, and especially the past few weeks, she suddenly rejected. She emptied the beer in the sink, watching the white foam as it fizzled away on the stainless steel.

She went to the living room and slid a finger over one of the shelves. Look at this mess, she thought. Overcome with renewed energy, she rolled up her sleeves and began taking down the old magazines and random brochures that cluttered the bookcase, filling up a trash bag. She dusted and polished the shelves, and placed on them, sparingly, a few items that had been scattered throughout the room. Right away she felt lighter, as if a big burden had been lifted off her shoulders. She shook off the mattress on the black futon and fluffed up the pillows. Content, she sat down. Porro would probably be home late tonight, she thought. She didn't know what kept him out so late after his English class, but she assumed he had met somebody at school. It was fine with her.

Trixie leaned back, closed her eyes, and tried to put all the events of the past weeks in perspective, trying to understand how her relationship with Porro had unraveled so quickly. She acknowledged he had been acting aloof in the bakery as well. But now that she was listening to her thoughts in the silence of the cool night, she discovered, to her surprise, that she really didn't care. All the hype about this stranger who suddenly appeared in her life—his uniqueness, his exotic presence, everything—had evaporated as soon as he had become abusive.

She had been so good to him. Who did he think he was to come uninvited, take what he wanted, and bully her? Being alone all these nights had given her the opportunity to get in touch with that part of herself, the one that had been silenced all her life and which was now reaching out, trying to be heard. She was finally listening, and she loved the sound of it. A door had opened, inviting her into a new dimension. Not even drugs had had that effect, she noted. For the first time, she tasted the freedom that comes with self-love, and she vowed never to let it go again.

The clock struck eleven. Enjoying her solitude, she went to the bathroom, closed the bathtub drain, and turned on the hot water. She poured in shampoo for lack of bath salts and whipped the rising water with her hand, making a layer of white foam and bubbles. She took off her clothes and immersed herself completely. She felt the healing effects of the bath and wondered what had taken her so long to be good to herself.

She inhaled and her lungs filled with the smell of cherry blossoms. She lingered in the warm water for another fifteen minutes, her eyes closed, and cherished the simple happiness of being at peace with herself.

After rinsing off, she unplugged the tub and got out, watching the water recede into the drain. She had the strong sensation that her old self was going down with it, never to return. She wrapped herself in the towel and tiptoed barefoot to the living room, still dripping on the floor. She lit a candle, and immediately the room became infused with the scent of cinnamon apples.

Just then, the front door opened. Porro walked in, his chin up high, and threw the keys on the kitchen counter, making a loud clanging noise. Instinctively, she hugged herself.

"What's with the candle?" he said. He wasn't smiling.

"Do you have a problem with it?" she asked, water dripping from her hair. Without waiting for a response, she turned around and walked to the bedroom.

Porro blew out the candle.

"Hey!" she said, coming back. Without looking at him, she took the matches and lit it again.

He blew on it once more, a cold stare hardening his features.

Motherfucker. She considered at that moment whether she should rekindle it. Unable to foresee his reaction, she opted for going to her bedroom instead and closed the door. From there, she heard the clickety-clack of silverware against a plate, and smiled to herself as she pictured Porro serving himself dinner. She put on a pair of sweatpants and an oversized sweatshirt, towel-dried her hair, and combed it backward, sleek and flat against her head. On her way to the kitchen, she stopped at the corner table and lit the candle again for the third time. Porro sat chewing his food carelessly with his mouth open, mashed potatoes spilling over and resting on the corners of his full mouth. Before he could realize it, she had taken the plate away from him. The garbage disposal roared as it gobbled up the food.

"What do you think you're doing?" he said, grabbing her by the neck.

"Let go," she said, her purple eyes flickering in the candlelight.

"*Puta*," he said.

It was like a switch. "What did you say?" her voice a measured whisper. Freeing herself from his grip, she stared at him, slicing through his confidence. For the first time he saw the determination in her demeanor. The two sides of him that had merged into one personality suddenly came apart. He was now able to see his old self, the one that would never dare to treat a woman like that. Horrified, Porro faced the violent, despicable being that he could be at times, the one that constantly pushed to take over and influence him to do bad things. Who was this entity, this voice? Could this be a side of him that had been buried in the politeness of his Spanish manners? Was it possible that he had accepted freedom as something he was inherently entitled to and decided to express himself once safe on the other side of the fence? What kind of monster had he become since setting foot in the United States? The image of Azucena flashed for the first time in a long time in his mind. How could he have entertained a relationship with Trixie while his own child was on its way? Wasn't the whole point of him being here to remain alive so one day he could return to Azucena?

He opened his mouth to apologize, but no words came out. Like a blob regrouping into his body, he felt the effect of the feared voice coursing through his veins again.

Don't waste your energy, Porro. You will not prevail! I am too powerful for you to even try. Let her be. She was just a link in the chain of your journey, our journey. Remember, you made a deal, and we are getting closer to our goal. Do not disappoint me.

"Fucking bitch," Porro said instead.

She slapped him so hard, he didn't see it coming. "Get out of my house."

Rubbing his cheek with his hand, he did as he was told. In a haze, he dragged himself to the bedroom and sat at the foot of the bed. It was as if the slap had temporarily buried Rasputin's voice deeper, giving his good side a rare moment of glory. He realized his days with Trixie were over. Either she brought out the worst in him or he had allowed his bad side to take over. Whatever the cause, his relationship with her couldn't continue. What if he hurt her one day? No, he couldn't stay in her house. The time to keep running had come again. He would have to leave.

He opened the closet and took out the two backpacks. He quickly packed the few clothes he had, wondering where he would spend the night. It seemed his only option was to sleep in the street, under the stars, and then he would wait for things to happen naturally, trusting the process. His fate seemed to be predestined anyway, no matter what he did.

Without a second thought, he walked out of Trixie's life without even slamming the door.

Chapter 33

Gwen pulled into the driveway and turned off the radio. It was ten o'clock on Tuesday morning, and she had gone grocery shopping after Tony offered to take the kids to school. Little Marco was being discharged that day, and she wanted to get all her chores out of the way before picking him up from the hospital.

After bringing everything in from the car, she hung her scarf and jacket on the coat rack by the door and headed to the kitchen. The dishes from breakfast remained on the table, an empty milk carton sat on the counter, while spilled sugar formed sticky bumps. The coffeemaker was on, but no coffee was in the carafe. Why can't he clean up after himself? she thought. Everything always falls on me! She decided to leave everything the way it was. This time Tony would have to do it when he came back from work.

She put the groceries away and went upstairs to her bedroom. At least he had made the bed. The plan was to meet Tony for lunch and then go to the hospital. He had made reservations at the French Quarter Restaurant for 1:00 p.m. to celebrate Little Marco's recovery and subsequent discharge from the hospital.

She kicked off her sneakers, slid off her sweatpants, and put on a pair of pantyhose and a royal-blue pencil skirt. She changed into a cream blouse, which she accessorized with a red silk scarf. The mirror reflected her slim, sexy figure.

It hadn't been difficult to lose all the extra weight after the baby's birth, because the stress and the everyday trips to the hospital had kept her appetite to a minimum. She climbed into a pair of cream pumps and untied the hair band from her ponytail. Her black hair cascaded in bouncy waves onto her shoulders. The phone rang.

"Hello?" she said.

"Marena," said a voice.

Gwen froze.

"Marena, I need help," he whispered in Spanish.

"Who is this?" She didn't even know why she asked.

"It's me, Porro. I'm hurt."

"Where are you?"

She scribbled the directions on a piece of paper. "I'll be right there." She hung up the phone and ran to her car.

Pulling into the Dreamtown train station, she saw a short figure walking slowly in the direction of the parking lot. Porro was bent over, holding his stomach. She parked the car and ran toward him.

"What happened to you?" she said, bending a little. She tried to stand him upright but couldn't. "Let me see," she said, kneeling down on the asphalt. Her pantyhose snagged. Ignoring it, she moved his hand away from his stomach. He groaned in pain.

"Somebody beat me up," he mumbled.

"Who? Where?"

He was about to answer when he realized that fate might finally have caught up with him. Could this be punishment for abandoning Azucena? What if God had decided to let him have the beating he had avoided from Cesar back in Mexico? You can run, he thought, but you can't hide. There would always be something to remind him of that. Cesar. Was he still looking for Porro? Could he have gone to his mother and harassed her? How likely was it that he gave up the search? Suddenly, he felt like calling his mother. He needed to know that she was okay. He made a mental count of all the events that had taken place from the time he left Mexico and considered the possibility of going back. What would happen if he stopped running?

"Porro, did you hear me? I need to know what happened to you."

Escaping his deep thoughts, he made an effort to answer. He felt awkward, vulnerable, and in a haze, and he barely remembered how he had ended up in the street to begin with.

"I was sleeping when all of a sudden somebody started shaking me. I opened my eyes and saw two men standing in front of me. One kneeled down, and for a moment, I thought he would bring me to a shelter. Instead he began searching my pockets and my backpack, and when he didn't find any money, he and the other guy started to beat me."

"Where were you?"

"Under the bridge by the train station," he said, pointing in the direction of the overpass.

"What on earth were you doing there?"

"I told you. I was sleeping."

"I thought you had a place to stay."

"I did, until last night."

Her immediate reaction was to cuddle him. He seemed so

harmless, so defenseless. She felt the innate need to protect him. What could have happened that made him leave Trixie's place? Who could be so cruel as to harm someone like Porro? Had she kicked him out of her house, or had he left on his own? She decided not to ask him any questions for the time being. A flag went up in her head, though. He was hurt, yet he was able to heal. Was this gift only good if applied to others? Or was he a fraud, a liar? She recalled the episode at the church and the fact that Little Marco had made an almost complete recovery, so why wasn't he able to heal himself? Whatever the reason, it was important that she bring him home and let him recover. Eventually, she would find the answers to her questions.

When they got home, she fumbled with the keys and un-locked the door. She helped him into the house, brought him to the sofa, and helped him lie down. Then she went to the kitchen and picked up the phone. It was already noon.

"Tony," she said. "I won't be able to meet you for lunch."

"How come?"

She hesitated.

"Are you picking up Marco first?" There was a slight change in the pitch of his voice.

Marco! How could I possibly forget? she thought. What kind of mother am I?

"Gwen, are you there?"

"No. I mean, yes."

"What's going on? Is everything okay?"

How am I going to tell him this? "It's Porro," she finally blurted.

"Where's the baby?" Tony's voice became louder.

"Honey, Porro got hurt and—"

"I asked you about the baby!"

"I didn't pick up the baby!" she yelled back.

"Is Porro there with you?"

"Yes, I had to pick him up from the station and—"

"Number one: you get rid of him right now. I don't want him in the house."

"But he's got nowhere to go!"

"Number two: I'm picking up Little Marco and bringing him home. Porro better not be there."

Tony was home by 1:30 p.m. He brought the baby directly to the nursery upstairs and laid him in his crib. Little Marco slept peacefully, and Tony watched him as he covered him with the blanket. Tony felt complete. He could exhale now. All the stress of the past few weeks had come to a close, and he hoped they would soon settle into a happy routine. "Daddy is here now, little champ," he said, caressing Marco's little hand. "Everything will be fine." The baby squirmed, a healthy glow emanating from his peaceful face. Tony raised the volume on the monitor before tiptoeing out of the room.

He checked Daniel's and Melody's rooms, opening closets and looking under their beds and behind doors. On his way down, he passed Gwen on the stairs; she was coming up to see the baby. He had not greeted her when he came in the house. He continued to ignore her and proceeded to search the rest of the house.

"What are you doing?" she asked, after she came down again.

"Making sure Porro's not here."

"You told me to get rid of him, and I did."

Satisfied with the search, he felt better. His wife was too naive and good hearted, and he felt vulnerable with her in charge of the kids. Things had been rough for her the past few weeks, especially when she learned about the fate of her brother, Marco.

"Are you going back to the office?" she asked.

"No. I'm staying right here. I took the rest of the day off."

"Oooh…well…that's nice…" her voice trailed off.

"You bet," he said, settling down on the couch in front of the window, overlooking the backyard.

"I mean," she started, "I got it. I have everything under control." She wrung her hands.

"I'm sure you do. But Porro might be lingering some-where in the neighborhood. It's safer if I stay. These are my kids you're talking about." He looked away.

"You have a lot of nerve, you know that? Are you implying I'm incapable of handling the situation?"

"I believe you need to get yourself centered. You've been acting strange lately."

"Would you have done any better? My brother is dead, and my baby could have died, and then an incredible miracle—"

"Don't even go there, Gwen. This conversation is over."

Without answering, she turned around and went upstairs. It's just as well, she said to herself. This will give me a chance to think.

Later on that afternoon, the neighbor brought Daniel and Melody home from school. After thanking her, Gwen gave the children milk and cookies while she put a load of laundry in the washing machine. Tony had been on the phone with his office most of the afternoon, giving instructions to his secretary on the many issues that arose during his absence. He and Gwen each checked on Marco every twenty minutes but had not spoken to each other again.

At five, Gwen began preparing dinner. She admitted to herself that her behavior was not that of a balanced person. She was embarrassed that she had put Porro's needs ahead of her baby's. She felt guilty for not meeting her husband for lunch. He had taken time out of his busy schedule to take her out in style so they could enjoy some special time together. She would never admit to Tony that he was right. She resolved to make it up to him.

She opened her *French Dining for Fine Occasions* cookbook and followed the directions for Chicken Fricassee. While Daniel and Melody colored with crayons at the kitchen table, she went to look for Tony. He was on the couch writing some notes on a yellow legal pad. He didn't even look up. She went back to the kitchen.

"Mommy will be right back," she whispered to the kids, taking off her apron and lowering the heat on the sauce to let it simmer.

"Where are you going, Mommy?" asked Daniel, as she opened the door to the backyard.

"Shhh. I have to check on the chinchillas," she said, putting one finger on her lips. "Now you and your sister stay here and help Daddy with Little Marco if he needs you, yes?"

Melody jumped down from her chair and clutched at her legs. "I wanna go with you, Mommy!" she cried.

"No, honey, you need to stay in. I'll be right back." She gave Daniel one of her looks.

"Come here, Melody," Daniel said. "Help me color this heart. Let me have a red crayon." He filled the image with red.

"I want to do that," she said, pushing him away.

"Here you go," said Daniel, taking a yellow crayon and giving it to her. "You can color the sun."

Gwen sneaked out quietly and crossed the yard. She glanced at the house before fixing her hair and opened the door. Porro was sitting on the floor in a corner, his head between his legs, just as she had seen him do at the church.

"How are you?" she asked, closing the door behind her.

He shrugged.

She approached the first cage where she kept the sick chinchilla. The chinchilla was up and perky.

"I knew you could heal her!" she said, taking a step back. "Just like you did with my son."

"The chinchilla will be fine now. You don't have to worry about it anymore."

She kneeled down next to him and put a hand on his shoulder. "How do you do it?" she whispered.

"You shouldn't ask me those questions. I just can, that's all."

"Do you think my Little Marco is out of danger?"

Don't tell her he's fine. We need a reason to stay here.

Is that why you didn't let me heal myself when those two guys beat me up? Porro said to himself.

You're beginning to understand, Porro. I'm impressed.

You're disgusting. I wish I didn't have to listen to you at all. And I wish I didn't have to fight with you.

You don't have to fight me. You can choose to go along with every-thing I do and enjoy the ride.

"Porro," she repeated, "did you hear what I said?"

"I'm sorry, what was the question?"

"Is the baby going to be okay?"

Be careful, now.

"Well, I don't know. I'm not a doctor." His eyes were fixed on hers.

Something stirred inside of her. She wanted to believe that Little Marco would be fine, but the doctors had not given him any treatment. His recovery could have been a coincidence. Maybe it wasn't a recovery at all. What if his numbers went down again? What would they do then? "We have to find a way for you to stay with us," she said suddenly. "I would feel so much safer with you around."

Porro nodded. He perceived her anguish and her need for reassurance. He could appreciate having a place to stay, and being close to Gwen was an added bonus.

After putting the kids to bed that night, Gwen sneaked to her bedroom while Tony read the newspaper in the family room. She fluffed her hair and sprayed perfume behind her ears and on her wrists. She took off her clothes and put on the silk nightgown with Chinese designs that Tony had given her for one of their anniversaries. The design flattered her fig-ure, making her look taller and more slender as she buttoned the Mao collar. It felt soft and luxurious on her skin, and she relished the freedom of her body under it. Full of anticipa-tion, she reviewed the plan in her head and said a silent prayer.

When she felt ready, she went downstairs to the kitchen and started the coffeemaker.

She lined two dessert plates with white paper doilies, placing a slice of chocolate cake on each one. Then she arranged them around a sugar bowl with two linen napkins on the silver tray Tony's mother had given them and brought it to the coffee table by the fireplace. A whiff of her French perfume trailed behind her. Tony raised his eyebrows.

"I'd like to make it up to you," she said, sitting next to him and swinging her leg.

"Well, you can certainly try." He reached for his coffee cup, but she jumped in.

"Allow me," she said, stirring in a teaspoon of sugar. Then she offered him a slice of cake. "How was your day?" She sat back and played with her hair.

"It could have been better." There was still resentment in his voice.

"I know; I'm sorry. It's just that Porro has nowhere to go and—"

"Well, at least he's not here," he said.

She bit her lip. "Hear me out, please?" she said.

"We know nothing about him. Even the priest doesn't want him around. He's not our problem."

"Well, see…if we hire him to help with the chinchillas—"

"There's no end to this!"

"Well, now with Little Marco home, I can use help cleaning the cages, feeding the chinchillas, and monitoring their reproduction cycle."

"You keep missing the point. We should listen to Father O'Leary. Porro might be dangerous—"

"Dangerous! He saved our baby! How can you call him dangerous?"

"He could use his powers to do harm."

"Why would he do that?" she retorted.

"How far are you willing to go for this guy?" He put down his cup.

She secretly admitted Tony was right. Doctors couldn't explain the reversal of Little Marco's condition. It was clearly a case of some powerful but obscure force that somehow had been used to do good. However, how could she explain what she felt and expect Tony to understand? Now that Porro was back, she felt complete, as if all the members of her family had gathered in one big reunion. It had always been so easy to get her way with Tony. All he ever wanted was to please her. Except now. "Porro saved our baby, not the doctors. I want him around for our son's sake. I won't let anything happen to him. I promise."

"The answer is no. I won't allow it."

Gwen sighed. Her heart ached for Porro. She thought about how her brother had died in the desert, and she hadn't been there for him. Perhaps helping Porro was a way to heal that part of her. Tears streamed down her face.

Tony took a deep breath. "There's something about him that doesn't sit well with me. You need to understand that," he said softly.

"But we can try for a week or two," she said between sobs.

He hated seeing her cry. He actually couldn't stand it. "Suppose we hire him," he began.

"Oh, you're an angel!" She planted a kiss on his cheek. "We'll pay him minimum wage, plus room and board, of course."

"I hope we're not making a mistake."

"I'll prepare the den. He can sleep on the sofa for now until we get him a bed."

"No, he will sleep on the sofa until we find him another place to stay."

"You're the best!" She jumped on his lap. She figured Tony would eventually come around, once he warmed up to Porro. She wiped her face with the back of her hand.

Tony put his cup down and held his wife in his arms. He slid his hands under her silk gown, exploring her back while his fingers lingered softly around the hooks of her bra.

"Here?" she whispered.

"Why not?"

"Wait," she said, wiggling herself free of his embrace. "Let me check the door of the chinchilla house one more time. I don't remember if I locked it."

"I'll be upstairs waiting for you," he said, getting up. "Don't be long."

"I won't," she said.

As she turned to go to the backyard, Porro dashed back to the chinchilla house. He'd been under the window, watching them all along.

It took Trixie a good night's sleep to realize the magnitude of what had happened the day before. As she washed the breakfast dishes, she smiled at how easy it had been to stand up for herself. He had left without even putting up a fight, she thought, pleased. She had been good, giving, and generous. And that's how he repaid her? I'm not going to let him get away with this, she thought. She dried her hands and opened the kitchen drawer under the telephone. She picked up the business card that was face up on top and flicked it with her fingers, hesitating. Then she picked up the phone and dialed. When the voice on the other end answered, she took a deep breath.

Porro locked the door of the chinchilla house after Gwen left, and lay on the floor, still savoring the dinner—and the news—she had brought him. She was so considerate, he thought. He wrapped himself in the blanket to process all the information.

He closed his eyes. Now that he was going to be working, he envisioned the coveted dollars pouring out of his pockets by the hundreds and thousands in a steady flow. What would his friends at home think? It was the dream of many: to come to the United States, find a job, and live with dignity; to send money home and still have some left over to splurge. If he played it smart and saved, soon he'd be able to buy a bicycle, rent a room, and eventually have enough for an airplane ticket back to Mexico. There, he would buy a piece of land and become a landowner. Dollars meant Azucena was tangible; it meant fulfilled dreams, and it meant power. But was that what he still wanted?

Each time he tried to think about her and the baby, the image of Tony and Gwen loving and caressing each other interfered. It left a sour taste in his mouth. Was it jealousy? Envy? Loneliness, perhaps? When he imagined Gwen, his heart beat faster. When he saw her, his stomach jumped up to his throat.

When he was near her, his heart soared in awe, as if he'd seen an angel.

He suspected that he might be in love with her, but he refused to admit it. She was a married woman and had become his benefactor. As for her husband, he sensed Tony's only motive was to please his wife. The fact that he might not want to help Porro opened a breach between them, even if in the end and for whatever reason, he came around. The old resentment crept into his heart.

As much as he tried to put all his contradictory feelings in order, he failed. His feelings for Gwen were gaining strength like a tropical storm before landfall. The more he tried to avoid thinking of her, the stronger his desire. Fear for what might happen if he wasn't able to control himself, especially now that he was going to stay in her house, took hold of him. Could he trust himself not to seduce her? And what about Tony? It was ludicrous to fight him. A random thought flared in his mind: should he try to get rid of him?

Aware, he recognized the shift in perspective, that foreign but already familiar force inside of him that had plagued him since the crossing. He didn't trust it. He couldn't. He suddenly felt like grabbing his backpack and disappearing; perhaps this was a sign that he should go back, face the fate that awaited him with Cesar and Don Francisco, and hope for the best.

You give up too easily, Porro.

You again? Porro said to himself.

She could be yours...

She's married! Leave her alone!

That's what you say, but you have a chance, I mean we.

How do you figure?

Tony's warming up to you. He'll end up trusting you.

I don't follow you.

You're so simpleminded. Do I have to do all the thinking here?

Whatever you have in mind won't work.

I didn't come down to Earth for nothing. It will happen my way, sooner or later.

Why do we have to struggle all the time? Why can't you listen to me for a change? Why do I always have to argue with you?

Because that was the deal you made, my friend.

What deal?

You're supposed to steer me on the right path, but I'm stronger than you. In the end, I will prevail.

She had brought food and water to Porro and then left the chinchilla house after a few minutes of chitchat. Although she worried about Tony wondering where she was, she decided to linger in the backyard before going to the main house. She needed to put her thoughts in order.

She looked up to her bedroom window. The light was on. She imagined Tony undressing on his way to the shower, putting on fresh pajamas, and checking on the children before settling in bed with his book. She could feel his thirst as he stumbled down the stairs to fetch a glass of water and checked on the kids again on his way back up.

She definitely needed time alone. Tony had been her guide, the light to follow as she transitioned from orphan to adopted child to the pampered queen she had become. Although the Parkers had been good to her, they had failed to let her keep her ties to her native Mexican culture. Perhaps because they loved her so much and wanted to protect her, they had obliterated any expression of the cultural idiosyncrasies that characterized her. But when she met Tony, he had captured the essence of who she was and encouraged her to embrace it. He loved her volcanic temper and the sweetness that came after the storm. Under his guidance, she had been able to uncover the layers of personality that she had suppressed over the years.

With Porro in the picture, that peace had been shattered. Who was this individual who appeared in her life bringing the bad news about her brother and turmoil to her heart? Was she willing to submit to her desires and risk it all for him? Was she capable of destroying the security under which her whole family functioned? How would Tony react if she told him she couldn't stop thinking about Porro and his well-being? What consequences would that have on their marriage? On their children? Would Tony fall apart without her or would he pick up the pieces of his broken heart and move on with somebody else?

The moon was sinister this night. Sporadic clouds partially covered it and a soft breeze presaged an atypical shower. The light in her bedroom finally went off. Had Tony gotten tired of waiting for her? Had he given up on their little adventure for tonight? Each question brought to the surface one more tear that she fought to suppress. When she looked up, the moon was completely covered. Not even the stars shone. It was safe to cry in the silence and solitude of the night. She allowed the first tear to trickle down her cheek, landing on her lips. The salty taste of it embittered her even more, making her feel desolate and lost. She looked behind her toward the chinchilla house and wondered whether Porro had gone to sleep. She could go to the house, toward her security, toward the sincere love of Tony, or she could go back to the frigid chinchilla house, where a stranger lay on the floor wrapped in the blankets that she had provided for him. What would it be? Would she dare do the unthinkable and simply abandon herself to her impulses, risking it all? Or would she find strength in her role as a mother and wife? She was torn.

Unable to control the opposite emotions that struggled with each other, she stood up and started for the chinchilla house. Stumbling in the darkness, she guessed every step with hesitation. She raised her hand and was about to knock when the clouds swiftly moved away from the moon, exposing her hand just above the doorknob. What am I doing? she asked herself, horrified. How far am I willing to go for this guy? Am I willing to risk it all for him? What do you think your life would be like without Tony? You know nothing about Porro. You simply get entangled in the depth of his eyes. She heard movement on the other side of the door. Did he know she was there, waiting for the door to open? And if he did open the door, would he pull her in and sweep her up in a passionate embrace? She felt weak in her knees, unsure of what to do next. All she had to do was turn around and walk away, but she didn't find the will to do it. She broke down and fell on her knees. On the verge of making the biggest mistake of her life, she joined her hands in prayer and raised her eyes toward heaven.

Porro felt his vein grow in size. This time it pounded in his head, hammering away the little grip he had left on his sanity. He held his head with his hands. Please stop! What do I have to do to shut you up?

How are you going to stop me?

I'll kill you if I have to.

Rasputin's laugh was so loud, it echoed across the atmosphere. Lightning crossed the sky like a jagged sword, the roar of thunder following shortly afterward. Heaven shook with the force of an earthquake. *We are two souls in one body, imbecile; I'd like to see you try.*

Chapter 34

The peace in Heaven flowed from the inside out like a fountain of boundless energy, continuous and unending. Blessings, love, and harmony abounded. The angels went about their tasks saturated in the otherworldly light that surrounded them.

All of a sudden, the sound of windy chimes tolled across Heaven. A breeze opened doors and windows letting in a parade of prayers. Like soldier ants on a summer morning, they marched into the Receiving Chamber, where hundreds of angels had been waiting to welcome them in their midst. Holding hands, the angels formed a circle, and as their fluid bodies blended with each other like ethereal dancers, they merged into a circular vessel that embraced the chorus of wishes and petitions conveyed by the prayers. Although each prayer had its own sound, it mingled with the others in a symphony of twinkling echoes.

Heaven glittered. Satisfying the dreams and hopes of humans was the highlight of every angel's life. Searching for reasons to deliver people's wishes, looking for ways to embellish the fulfillment of a dream was what angels lived for. It meant gaining access to the Supreme Power, God's gate. But, by far, the best part was basking in the happiness of the receivers and getting drenched in their tears of joy. Nothing compared to that.

Main Elder sat across from Julius Elder, a chessboard

between them. "It was a good move to send Porro back," said Main Elder, moving a pawn forward.

Julius Elder advanced his knight and knocked the pawn out of the game. "I suppose. He seems to be managing." He pursed his lips.

"Maybe we'll set a precedent. Imagine if good prevails; then we can try sending Hitler, Perón, or the Ayatollah Khomeini on future missions to Earth to repair their past misdeeds," said Main Elder against the melodious background coming from the Receiving Chamber.

"Wishful thinking. The truth is if there's no evil, there's no need for us angels!" Julius Elder moved the queen in front of Main Elder's king. He opened his mouth, but before he could announce his victory, a lament trickled into their studio followed by a dissonant flash.

"What's that?" asked Main Elder.

Julius Elder tensed up. Recognizing Porro's plea for help enmeshed with the macabre jangle of Rasputin's laugh, he breathed out his tension and smiled.

"Is it my imagination or is Porro in trouble?" Main Elder's voice trailed off as he leaned back on his chair, his hand on his chest.

"It's not your imagination, and Porro is in trouble, indeed. The game is over." Julius Elder grinned. "Checkmate."

"It's unprecedented! Unconscionable! How could we let him fool us like that?" Main Elder paced around his desk.

"It was worth trying."

"Hear him laugh now!"

"Well, Porro's time was up, and he challenged it. You were kind enough to give him a second chance by extending his life on Earth."

"I set him up for failure is what I did."

"Too late for regrets now. We need to let this run its natural course."

"But you see where this is going, Julius. We can't let Rasputin have his way."

"Why not?"

"Because if he does, he'll do harm now that he has a body from which to work."

"This is not your struggle, Main Elder, nor mine. It is up to Porro to fight it. If Rasputin wins, it's because he's the stronger of the two, and you'll just have to accept it," said Julius Elder. A smirk formed on his lips.

"Not if we step in and help Porro."

"Why should we help him? Everyone has to fight his or her own demons. Porro should be no different."

"Rasputin is quite a force to contend with. I can't see us sitting idly while Porro battles him on his own."

"That was the deal, but if you insist, there is a way we can move things along," said Julius.

"I'm glad you feel that way. We may have to intercept his prayer to purify it from Rasputin's influence."

"That's not really what I meant...at all." Julius's jaws formed a square, the muscles in his face like marble slabs under two ice-blue eyes.

"What else could we possibly do? Are you suggesting we put Porro out of his misery by staging his death?"

"A deal is a deal."

"A deal is a deal? Whose side are you on?"

"I admit it was unfair to put Porro in this predicament. We gave him an impossible mission."

"You mean *you* gave him an impossible mission."

As the fog that veiled Julius Elder's true intentions began to lift, Main Elder wavered. Short of breath, he struggled for air. He leaned on the windowsill watching the dance of the prayers on their way to the Acceptance Chamber, where the Dome was. Suddenly, it was all clear. How could he not have seen it before? He, Main Elder, had allowed Julius to persuade him. Dismayed, he realized, too late perhaps, that Julius Elder had been motivated by an insatiable hunger for power that twenty centuries in Heaven had not been able to diminish. He needed Rasputin on Earth to help him become emperor of the world, a dream that was snatched away from him in his past lifetime when he had been assassinated. With Rasputin's powers and influence, his dream still could become a reality.

"I never imagined you would turn on me like this. Don't you have it good here? What do you need to go back for?" Main Elder's lower lip quivered; he pressed his chest with his right hand.

"There's no need to hyperventilate." Julius Elder motioned to the two angels who kept watch at the door of the studio. Immediately, they hovered outside and came back laden with red clouds. In no time, they had formed a fluffy throne for Main Elder, who plopped on it, oblivious to the trap he was settling into. He wiped golden pearls of sweat from his face. Julius Elder continued, "I won't let you interfere with the natural development of Porro's struggle. His prayer is contaminated and will have to be disqualified, just like everybody else's."

"I will grant him what he's asking for."

"And how do you plan to do that?" Julius Elder laughed.

"I can send it to the lab and have Rasputin's influence removed."

"If you're able to intercept it before it gets discarded, that is. But once again, you need to stay out of it."

"I won't. I will hunt down Porro's prayer and do whatever is in my power to grant it."

Julius Elder shook his head. "You leave me no choice, Main Elder." He glanced at the angels who kept guard at the studio and gave them a nod. Their mouths opened and blew fire on the majestic seat of red clouds. The throne melted into a mushy and sticky mess, trapping Main Elder.

"I can't believe this is happening," he muttered.

"Believe it," Julius Elder smirked. "Earth is a reflection of Heaven. As above, so below."

All the petitions and prayers basked in each other's energy inside the basin formed by the Receiving Angels. Before they could be answered, they had to be scanned for contamination. A prayer was considered contaminated if it contained the slightest wish to harm another soul. In that case, it would be automatically disposed of without further consideration. But if its purity was verified, the prayer had a chance of being fulfilled. The ushers led them up toward the Dome.

The Dome was a crystal sphere, as big as Mars, but transparent and pristine. It turned continuously on its axis, fueled by the incoming prayers. The energy generated by this movement caused the prayers to open up like jasmines in bloom, exposing their messages for the heavenly angels to hear. Each petition then was brought to the petitioner's file to determine whether it could be fulfilled or not. The Approving Angels studied the petitioner's personal history, and if they decided the petition should not be answered, it was taken to the Ice Palace, where it stayed frozen indefinitely or until Heaven deemed it propitious to grant. If the prayer was to be granted, it would go into a tunnel that led to the exit of the Dome, where it emerged glittering like an emerald. The accepted prayer would spring upward into a half-moon vessel made of ivory, with carved images of cherubim holding a net of gold and silver threads. The word *Granted* shimmered across its length and width. As the vessel filled up, it tilted downward, causing all the answered prayers to rain down materialized, making room for new ones.

Gwen's prayer had made it to the Dome. Because it was so pure, it draped a blanket of protection over Porro's prayer, making it possible for Porro's prayer to enter the Dome as well, outshining even Rasputin's laugh. But once there, he needed to keep his laugh barely audible so the dissonant sound of his wish couldn't be heard. He had invoked one of his magic formulas so that Porro's prayer would appear pure and the dark side of his own energy would be invisible to the Accepting Angels. What he didn't know was that Main Elder and Julius Elder possessed the ability to hear even silence. They were able to pinpoint the intentions engraved in people's hearts, which manifested into a high frequency sound only audible to them.

However, the positive energy in the Dome was so overwhelming, that once there Rasputin abandoned himself to its beauty and let down his guard, becoming intoxicated in the goodness that surrounded him.

"Stop the Dome!" said the Guardian Angel to one of the Approving Angels. "One of these prayers is contaminated."

The Approving Angel pressed a button in his forearm. The Dome slowed down until it stopped. In the stillness that followed, the unmistakable distortion of sound pierced through the silence. The angel tried to grasp it, but the prayer slipped through his hands like used-up soap in a bucket of engine oil. The Guardian Angel saw no other recourse than to take out his weapon. He opened his cloak and removed a spray can with a narrow straw in the nozzle from one of the inside pockets. He aimed it at Porro's prayer, which wiggled like a worm to avoid being caught, and shot. A black net sprung out and opened up like a parachute, trapping Porro's prayer.

"I got it!" said the Guardian Angel, locking the prayer inside a flask. "This is one wicked influence. We must dispose of it immediately."

A procession of Guardian Angels appeared as soon as these words were uttered, and they formed a horseshoe around the Approving Angel who, glad to be escorted, rushed to the Eternal Dump.

In the meantime, Main Elder never thought he would have to use the secret weapon he hid under his gauzy clothes. But when he had accepted his post as Main Elder, he had been provided with what the Supreme Power called an insurance policy against poisonous interactions and toxic angels. Main Elder had been naive and too trusting, and if people didn't learn their lessons on Earth, they would learn them in Heaven.

He waited until Julius Elder left the studio and began his own rescue. Wiggling through the sticky substance that kept him captive, Main Elder proffered a few secret and unintelligible utterings, summoning the Ice Sword. The sword came to be and, at Main Elder's command, began releasing ice needles, which gnawed at the red glue. On contact, they multiplied into an army of frozen icicles, allowing Main Elder's body to separate from the glue. Main Elder closed his eyes and waited for the sword to disintegrate into a rain of oily drops that poured over him and dissolved what little remained of the sticky throne.

Meanwhile Julius Elder was too indulgent in his confidence that Rasputin would prevail. Too sure that the Approving Angels would intercept Porro's contaminated prayer and dispose of it, he went to his quarters and sat at his desk already savoring the glory of his future position as emperor. Drawing from his long-ago experience, he decided that this time he would not trust anybody, not even his closest friend. In order to rule, and rule the way he wanted to, he needed to be alone, isolated in the high echelons of authority.

Everything in the lab was blue: floor, walls, ceiling, and tables. The teachers' job was to enhance the life of every human in the universe. To that end, one of the ongoing projects that kept them busy—and had failed across the ages—was to eradicate the forces of evil that disturbed the balance of the universe. For this task, the teachers picked apprentices based on the experiences they'd had in previous lifetimes.

"We need you to isolate the dissonance in this prayer and destroy it," said Main Elder to the Apprentice, after capturing the flask from the Guardian Angels on their way to the Eternal Dump.

"That is not my job," the Apprentice said dryly.

"Your job is to do what I tell you."

The Apprentice looked up from the cauldron he was stirring. His eyes flashed like two onyx stones pressed against his cappuccino face. He had been working on a syrup that would create the ability to forgive in people who held a grudge. He had been experimenting with several recipes and combinations, but his frustration grew as time went by and forgiveness eluded him. As Main Elder waited for a response, the Apprentice reviewed the rules to which he had agreed before taking this job. "Get in line," he said, frowning.

"Don't you talk to me like that. Stop what you're doing and get to it. We have a dangerous situation on our hands," said Main Elder. The prayer was jumping inside the net, struggling to get out. Lightning emanated from it.

The Apprentice resented being interrupted; now he had to set aside what he was working on and apply his newly acquired knowledge to something completely unrelated to his mission.

"Wait outside," he said to Main Elder who, knowing the rules, turned around and left.

Once the door was safely closed, the Apprentice grabbed the jar. The prayer immediately stopped its frantic movement and huddled in a corner, eerily silent. The Apprentice felt a spooky connection to it. He perceived a faint familiarity that drew him to it but repelled him at the same time. When had he been exposed to the energy that was now trapped in the jar in his hands? What sensations did this prayer awaken in him? Following the advice of his counselor when he had first arrived in Heaven, he turned his attention inward. "Identify what you feel," the counselor had said, "and then you'll be able to deal with it." The Apprentice waded through the murky landscape of his emotions, trying to avoid identifying what he really felt. It was too painful to relive the experiences that had landed him in Heaven. But his curiosity was greater than his fear, and he was puzzled that the prayer repulsed him and mesmerized him at the same time.

Now intrigued, he placed the prayer under the microscope. A magnified image appeared on a holographic screen. Carefully, the face of that odious Mexican emerged, distorted by its desperate need to shut out the alien voice in him, begging for mercy. His features were disfigured by his lack of inner peace, and the arrogance that had accompanied him in the desert had been subdued by his plea. Simultaneously, a sinister laugh, piercing and jagged like lightning, drowned out his cries for help. Apprentice Marco couldn't believe his eyes, but now he understood where his repulsion came from. Trying to keep his composure, he called Ariadna, the head teacher, through the intercom. "I need your help."

"Can this wait? I'm in class, training," she responded.

Apprentice Marco slammed down the intercom. It was imperative now to find the syrup for forgiveness. The resentment was literally eating him alive. He took a pair of tweezers and approached the screen. He tried to grab the crackling sound that flashed on the screen. Just like lightning, the sound emitted an electric shot. Launched by the force of the sound, he flew across the lab, and the tweezers went flying out of his hands. He tried to get up, but the sound congealed into a red serrated line that nailed his foot to the floor. The air creaked.

Writhing with pain, Apprentice Marco was trapped. If he could only reach the bookshelf behind him, he'd be able to find out first how to get himself free and then how to deal with the negative force once and for all. He stretched his arm backward in the direction of the books. Trying to remember which books were on each shelf, he wiggled his fingers, pulling one of the books toward him until it fell with a crash. He slid it forward and opened it. The title read *Colors, Sounds, and Their Influence on Inner Balance.* Following the lines with his index finger, he went down the contents page. "Here we go," he whispered. He opened the book to page 1,916 and read, "Once in a while, a dissonant sound will infiltrate a prayer and attach itself to it. The elements of distortion are many and have various meanings. Please refer to the *Book of Distortions*, which is arranged alphabetically according to its description. One of the distortions, though, is mentioned in this book as well as in the other because the consequences it carries are severe." His heart leaped. He read on, "If a prayer is contaminated with a red jagged line or distorted sound, it indicates a malefic spirit is attached to it. In that case, it must be reported to the elders immediately, bypassing the teachers, even the head teacher. It is charged with a much stronger force that weakens the good energy in the rest of the prayer. Heaven must act immediately to avoid the malefic energy from spreading like an epidemic of evil."

Apprentice Marco put the book aside. Why should he obey? After all, his whole life had been dedicated to the service of those in higher positions. He was always relegated to

doing what somebody else told him to do. His immediate su-
perior, Ariadna, was busy training newcomers, and although
the book said the elders needed to be notified, he decided to
take matters in his own hands.

He reached back, picked up a can of neutralizer from the
cabinet next to the bookshelf, and sprayed the red lightning.
He didn't know if this would work, but he had to try something. A few minutes later, the grip the lightning had on his
foot became loose. He was able to free himself, and jumping
toward it, he grabbed it. He placed the lightning on the counter next to the microscope and made an incision in its center. Immediately, a drop of thick red liquid oozed out, which
he placed under the microscope. Then he leaned back on his
chair.

So that's how it worked, he thought. What goes around
comes around. He recalled how Porro had avoided helping
him in the desert, how he had taken the locket and his belongings from him before he had even had a chance to breathe
one last time. Apprentice Marco relived with horror how the
crows had picked at his eyes until he could only see darkness,
how the fear of being alone under the merciless sun in the
desert had lodged in his bones. Porro had never looked back.
By the time Marco's life had expired, his body was a mangled
mess of shredded flesh, blood, and broken bones.

Now Porro's life was on the verge of being taken over by
the malevolent spirit. His energy was waning with each passing second as the interference became stronger. Eventually, it
would obliterate Porro's voice. Heaven needed to act quickly
on his behalf. But the key was in his hands.

Apprentice Marco took the red lightning and put it back

in the flask, where Porro's prayer was. "Let it rot," he said to himself. "Just the way he let me rot in the desert."

The knock on the door was imperceptible at first. The caller knocked again, this time louder.

"Who is it?" Apprentice Marco woke up. Nobody answered. Frustrated, he pulled the sheets off and floated toward the door.

At first he thought he was dreaming. He hadn't seen her since he could remember. In fact, the last time he had set eyes on his mother was when he was five, clinging to her skirt and begging her not to leave. But she had ignored his pleas, his tears, his desolation. With the empty promise that she would send for him one day, she left anyway. As he cried and screamed, she tried to calm him by promising to send him cars with remote control, blocks to build the most spectacular castles, and Atari games that could be played from any TV set. But he didn't want the toys. He wanted his life to stay the same as it had always been, pleasant and safe under his parents' and older sister's love. Worst of all, his parents had picked her to go with them, so he felt doubly betrayed. Now his mother stood in front of him, peaceful and ethereal, waiting for him to invite her in.

"Are you going to let your mother stay outside all night?" she asked.

He stepped aside, still in shock. What in heaven could she be doing here now?

"I don't have much time. I came to talk to you about your sister."

"What do you want from me, and what right do you have to ask me for favors now?"

"You were able to isolate the malefic influence in that prayer you're working on. Now you need to dispose of it, son."

Marco laughed. "That prayer is going straight to Hell, just the way it is."

"Have you considered the possibility that Porro might want to do the right thing?"

"That lowlife left me for dead. This is my chance to pay him back."

"Always so resentful, Marco. You haven't changed one bit, have you, son?"

"I have every right to be resentful. But who knows," he sneered, "one day I might get cured with the syrup for forgiveness."

"Forgiveness requires hard work, dear, not sweet concoctions."

"I follow instructions from my superiors, as I always have."

"Then do what I say. I am your mother."

"What's the urge anyway?"

"If you don't help Porro, your sister will fall prey to Rasputin's charms, and her marriage will be destroyed; then she'll trek the road to perdition, since Rasputin will not love her forever. Once he has her, he'll lose interest, just like he did with all the women in his previous lifetime."

"My sister, my sister, always my sister!" he yelled. "You never came back for me. You left me with that greedy sister of yours, and then, just when I begin to taste the hope of seeing Marena again, the Mexican leaves me to die in the desert. You know why?"

"Son, please, don't be so resentful."

"Because I was too weak to let him know I was still alive. So he abandoned me, taking with him the locket and all my things. And that's why I'm here instead of enjoying life with my sister in the United States. Now, by a twist of destiny, Porro's life is in my hands. Can you believe it?" He started laughing. "In my hands! I love the way things work out."

"But it's not about Marena or you, or even Porro. It's about the universal struggle between good and evil. Sometimes Heaven must step in to prevent a disaster. Believe me, we don't want Rasputin to take over. For goodness' sake, Marco, you must help Porro."

"I need my sleep," said Apprentice Marco. "You said your piece, now go."

When his mother left his chamber, he noticed he had been holding the flask with Porro's prayer so tightly in his hand that the glass had begun to melt into a gel. The prayer became sticky, clinging to the palm of his hand. As he shook it to set it free, it became warm and then hot, until it burned through his skin, seeping through his pores, coursing through his veins. He tried to stop it but couldn't. Under the heat of his anger, Porro's prayer had managed to reach the innermost chamber of Marco's heart.

Chapter 35

The next morning, Ariadna, the head teacher, went to the lab and was surprised to see that Marco was not there. She wondered what the reason could be. True, she had failed to come to the lab at his request the day before, but he had not insisted that she come, and she never heard back from him after that. Could his absence be related to the cause of his call, or was he so resentful because she didn't come to help him that he decided to take the day off without permission?

She approached Marco's work area and noticed that the holographic screen was still on, although no image was visible due to the screen saver. It wasn't like Marco to be that careless, she thought. She snapped her fingers and the screen brightened. A saved image of Porro's prayer was displayed. She saw clearly the different parts: Porro's plea for help and the crackling noise from the jagged, red lightning that competed with his voice. Immediately, she went to the library and found the book, *Colors, Sounds, and Their Influence on Inner Balance*, on the floor. Her hands trembled. She picked it up and read page 1,916, where it had been left open. When she finished reading, she closed the book and rushed to Main Elder's chamber.

"Main Elder," she said, "have you seen Apprentice Marco?"

"I saw him yesterday at the lab. Why?"

"He didn't show up for work today, and he was supposed to report to you about the prayer he was working on."

Main Elder stiffened. "I brought him the prayer in a flask. I warned him to be careful with it. Where is it now?"

"It's not in the lab. I'm afraid you'll have to come with me," said Ariadna.

When they reached Marco's chamber, they saw smoke coming out of it. They peeked through the windows but didn't see any fire, so they pushed open the door. Inside, they found Marco cross-legged in front of the mirror, smoke flowing out of his pores. He was in a trance.

"Marco!" Ariadna flew to his side and held his face in her hands. "Look at me!"

Marco lifted his eyes to her. They sparkled. "I feel so good," he said, a beatific smile on his face.

"Where is the flask?" asked Main Elder.

Marco nodded in the direction of the kitchen.

Main Elder flew toward it, followed by Ariadna. The flask was in the sink, empty. "Where is the prayer?" he asked.

"Inside me."

"You ate it?" Ariadna shook him by the shoulders.

"Relax, I did not eat the prayer," he scoffed. "It's a long story."

"You need to purge it right away. It has Rasputin's energy," Main Elder said.

"I know. I feel it getting to me all right," said Marco, his voice sweet and pleasant, "but this is what I must go through. I'm burning inside, and it's okay."

"He's hallucinating," Ariadna whispered.

"No, this is real. I am simply elated."

"Then you found the syrup of forgiveness?" she asked.

"Better yet. I swallowed my anger and tasted its bitterness

when I dared to face it. Then, as if by magic, the prayer, which I was holding in my hand, melted and got under my skin, swimming through my veins all the way to my heart. And that's where it's been ever since." He nodded as Main Elder and Ariadna exchanged looks. Marco continued, "Porro's voice has been having a conversation with each cell in my heart. Listening to his side of the story made me understand what really happened in the desert, and now I am so free of the burden of my resentments that I feel great. I wish I had been less judgmental in my life. I would have been a lot happier."

"But what about Rasputin's voice?"

"That's the best part. Rasputin's wish to overpower Porro's became weaker as my forgiveness took over. My own healing became the transforming force for Rasputin to see that doing good is so much more satisfying than just following a base tendency to do harm. I was able to have a conversation with him as well, in which his transformation became evident through a review of his past deeds, both good and bad."

"What did he say?"

Marco pointed across the room, and the mirror in front of him expanded, covering the walls of his small chamber. The reflection showed an X-ray image of Marco's body. He stretched his hand and touched his heart on the mirror. The image grew. Marco pressed a button on the remote control, and the mirror image of his heart seemed to move toward them, engulfing them all in a dizzying ride to the center of his heart, which beat with the sound of a soft drum, lulling them into a dreamy state of love and comfort.

From the deepest point at the core of Marco's heart, Rasputin's voice emerged.

"I was born a simple peasant in Siberia. As crude and il-literate as I was, one day I felt the urge to leave my village. I couldn't tell what force pushed me to do it, but I set off on foot leaving my wife and daughter to fend for themselves. Following a calling only I could hear, I covered thousands of frozen miles one step at a time, alone in the wilderness of the Russian steppes. For months, my only companion was the sound of my own breathing against the crush-crush of my feet, crunching on the snow below. No bird or flower dared to show signs of life, except for the night owl who spooked me countless times with its guttural hoot while I tried to sleep in the forest. I was alone with the Divine and felt closer to the truth I was searching for. In my pilgrimage, I met priests who shared their wisdom with me and came across sages who taught me the secrets of the universe. I studied, prayed, and learned. Soon the physical world had no meaning to me, and I learned to survive on very little, mostly on the charity of good souls who lived in the spread-out villages I stumbled upon. Through deep meditation and self-sacrifice, I reached a level of spirituality that enabled me to commune with the Higher Spirit, and I received the gift of the power to heal.

"Word got around that I could perform miracles. At the time, the royal family was desperate to find someone who could heal their son Alexei, who suffered from hemophilia. Having succeeded where doctors and other healers had failed, I was able to penetrate the high society of Petrograd, and I began moving in circles that would normally be off limits to a peasant like me. I frequented secret meetings held at the

homes of aristocrats, where we discussed the occult and prac-
ticed magic rituals. Stana Montenegro was one of the women
who took me under her wing, and eventually she introduced
me to the palace.

"It didn't take long for Czarina Alexandra to accept me
unconditionally after I rescued her son Alexei from immi-
nent death while they were vacationing at Spala. The czarina
loved her son the way only a mother does: fiercely, blindly,
and devotedly. Her anguish was such at seeing Alexei suffer
that when she finally met me and saw what I could do for him,
she transferred that devotion to me. Czarina Alexandra, or
Matiushka as I sometimes called her, invited me to be a part of
the court, and often consulted me on political issues. She became so dependent on my advice—and believed I had the gift
of clairvoyance—she thought I communicated directly with
God. My word became law for her. Soon she considered me
her friend and by extension, Czar Nicholas's. The deference
they bestowed on me, a lowly peasant from Siberia—in the
opinion of the aristocracy—caused a stir among the courtiers
and Nicholas's relatives. Since none of them knew the real reason that brought me to the palace—the royals kept their son's
hemophilia secret from everybody—they judged the czarina
for coming down to my level, while at the same time accusing
me of manipulating and exerting a negative influence on her.
Eventually rumors began to circulate that we were having an
affair."

"We know you didn't," said Main Elder.

"I never even touched her," Rasputin mused. "The truth is
Czarina Alexandra had never been fully accepted by Nicholas's
family, and because she was from Germany, they never trusted

her completely. The Romanoffs always suspected her of being a German spy. I believe she loved me in a special way, but not the way rumors have it. She was indebted to me for bringing relief to her son's pain, and because of that, she protected me ferociously. Whoever attacked me would end up exiled to Siberia by the czarina. That's how good I was to the royal family."

"But you also seduced married women. You destroyed families and marriages; you defiled the name of God with your base actions—"

"What are you referring to?"

"Excessive drinking, debauchery, pagan worship with the Khlysts, and the use of magic powers."

"Yes, but what about my good deeds? All day and all night, all kinds of visitors flocked to my apartment. Seekers of truth, ill people in need of healing, and the indigent looking for a morsel of bread or a warm place to spend the night knocked on my door. I welcomed them all, regardless of ability or willingness to pay. Those who could pay poured thousands of rubles into my fund, but I gave it all away. I didn't keep any of it. History books don't tell you that. Did you know that Jews were victims of pogroms and were subjected to all kinds of humiliations and discrimination? Many of them wanted to leave Russia, but Nicholas and Alexandra would not allow them. They needed special exit visas, which the royals refused to issue, so these Jews came to me, asking me to intercede before the palace on their behalf. I obtained those visas for them, and thanks to me, many Jews were able to escape to safety and build new lives in their adoptive countries. It's a mystery to me why history painted such an evil picture of me."

"You laughed at Porro while he argued with you about not seducing Gwen. Why?" asked Ariadna.

"Because of me, Matiushka lost the last shred of trust Nicholas's family had in her, and when the Parliament decided to do away with the monarchy altogether, they sentenced her to a convent for the rest of her life. But Nicholas wouldn't allow it. He loved her too much to let her end her days in seclusion away from him and the children, so instead he stood by her and accepted being exiled with the whole family, as long as they remained together, unaware that this would bring about the execution of the whole family. I knew that Matiushka lives in Gwen's body now, so I wanted to reconnect with her and tell her how much I regret what happened to them."

"But you laughed at Porro when he defied you," Main Elder pressed on.

"Despite my disheveled appearance, women seemed to lose their wits over me. I remember vividly when Lokhtina, the general's wife, abandoned him and their three children and became my concubine. After a while I got tired of her—I couldn't help it—and she became insane from my rejection. She wandered the streets with unfulfilled desire, begging for a meal and a place to stay. But the one woman who did not succumb to my charms and kept her place at all times was Czarina Alexandra. She may have revered me, but her husband was the one she loved. She was a woman of principles, virtuous and deeply religious. She kept her marital vows. So to answer your question, she was the one woman I couldn't have. Sitting in the fire pit in Purgatory, I watched as history books portrayed me as a despicable peasant, devious enough to have seduced the queen. And I figured, 'If I'm going to be remembered for having an affair with her, I might as well have it.' All I needed was a body so I could seduce her."

"And that's what brought you back to Heaven now in the form of a prayer, isn't it? Your prayer to get to Gwen against Porro's prayer to stay away from her."

"Yes. But being inside of Porro's prayer exposed me to all this goodness and holiness. It's overwhelming. I don't want to sin! I repent for my bad intentions, truly, from the deepest part of me. Please don't send me back into Porro's body. Let him have his way, and let me stay here. I want history to vindicate my image and remember me for the good I did, not the bad. I want my place in Heaven."

"Why should we believe you, Rasputin?"

"Because I understand for the first time what my role was in the history of Russia and acknowledge my contribution for what it was. You must give me credit for my good deeds. Here, in the most recondite corner of Marco's heart, I see Gwen for who she is now, a new entity, albeit a reincarnation of my beloved czarina but not her at all. Her prayer is being granted because of her purity of heart. She has succeeded once again to stay true to her husband. I see the love between Tony and her and regret the pain I put her through by trying to lure her into an affair with Porro. I see her for who she was as czarina and thank her for being good to me while so many others spurned me. Now I understand that I didn't need to go back and perpetuate my wrongdoings. Help me do good. Please grant Porro's wish to withstand his temptation."

Main Elder could not help it. He let a tear slide down his cheek. He looked at Ariadna who listened, too mesmerized to react. The personification of evil was actually asking to do good. He was interceding before him, Main Elder, and through him all the good souls of Heaven, to allow Porro's prayer to get through the right channels and be granted.

"I take it you succeeded in finding the syrup of forgiveness, Apprentice Marco," said Ariadna approvingly.

"No, my teacher. There's no such thing. Forgiveness already exists in all of us. We just need to learn how to allow it to reveal itself."

This was the ultimate victory of good versus evil in the history of the universe. Heaven had won the bet. Rasputin had come back, and he had returned a changed soul.

Chapter 36

Sunlight slipped underneath the door of the chinchilla house, a golden ray sliding between Porro's eyelids. When he opened them, it took him a while to realize he was in the chinchilla house. Something was different this morning. He felt like himself again, without the uptight sensation of being on guard. He waited for the voice to speak, pressing him to seduce Gwen, but no voice spoke. He remembered Trixie and how their relationship had gradually descended to the low echelons of abuse, and was horrified to realize that he had been the perpetrator of such behavior. At first, he thought it had all been a dream, a bad dream, but then he owned up to the fact that he was miraculously free from the voice and from the bad intentions it had been prompting him to carry out. His thoughts went immediately to Azucena and the child she was carrying. His child. Their child.

The smell of a decaying body hit his nostrils. He got up and walked over to the cages. One of the chinchillas was dead, stiff on her back. Many others were struggling to breathe. He recalled Gwen telling him that once a chinchilla gets sick, an epidemic is likely to occur. He approached one of the cages and took one out. The animal's chest heaved, trying to draw in air. Feeling the distress it was under, Porro caressed the tiny rodent in an attempt to soothe it. The chinchilla's breathing became more labored. Then it stiffened in his hands. She was dead. He rubbed his hands and laid them over the corpse, without touching it. He tried to utter words that had worked in the past, but nothing happened. The chinchilla remained dead. He had lost the power to heal too.

Although he regretted not being able to help, he felt relieved. It meant that whatever or whoever had possessed him was no longer in him, and that translated into the freedom to be himself again.

He had reached the end of his road. It was time to go back. It didn't matter what would happen. He needed to do the right thing, and that meant having an earnest talk with Gwen. He knew he had been the cause of anguish in her and hoped she would forgive him for it. He didn't know if she would understand what had happened between them, but then again, neither did he.

He washed up, groomed himself as best as he could, and stepped outside, heading toward the main house.

Tony came down the stairs, upbeat and refreshed from the previous night. It had been a long time since Gwen had been so sincere and warm in her lovemaking. He had fallen asleep waiting for her, but later on that night, she had woken him with tender caresses, whispering loving words in his ear. Then she had told him that Porro was sleeping in the chinchilla house, but that everything was clear now. She said she would drive Porro back to the church first thing in the morning and let Father O'Leary deal with him.

Tony accepted her explanation, grateful that whatever demons had possessed her in the past few weeks seemed to have vanished in last night's display of love. Although the doctors had warned him that the hormonal changes in a pregnant woman could cause erratic behavior, he never expected it to be so bad. However, after last night, he felt she was back from wherever she had been cast away.

"Coming! Coming!" he said running toward the kitchen door. He looked through the windowpanes and saw Porro standing there, holding the blankets and dirty dishes from the night before. Tony opened the door. "Good morning," he said.

"I need to go home," Porro said.

He looks so defenseless and small, Tony thought. How could I have thought him harmful? "Let's get you some breakfast first," said Tony, letting him in.

Porro called his mother. He told her that he was alive and well, but that he was going to be at the church until a collection could be gathered to buy him a plane ticket home. His mother told him it was safe to come back, and that he had nothing to worry about anymore.

After they ate and washed the dishes, they all got in the Suburban and headed to the church.

When Father O'Leary opened the door of his studio, he was not surprised. Face-to-face with the two men in green uniforms, he asked "May I help you?"

Officer Gallo flashed his badge. "INS," he said. "We have information that you have been harboring an illegal alien, Father. Do we have your permission to search the premises?"

"Be my guest," said Father O'Leary, opening the door of his studio to let them in. "There's nobody here except me."

Officer Gallo and Officer Striker walked in and searched every corner of the priest's office. When they didn't find even a clue of Porro's presence, they spread out throughout the church. They walked through, searching the kitchen, the guesthouse, the sanctuary, and the bathrooms. They found no sign of Porro.

"All right, Father, where is he?" asked Officer Striker.

At that moment, the door of the church opened, and Porro walked in, followed by Tony, Gwen, and the children.

"You are under arrest," said Officer Gallo, hurrying to Porro's side.

Porro smiled faintly. So this was it. The officer explained to him that he would be taken to a detention center where he would stay until the judge issued the order of deportation. "And that can take a few months," Officer Striker explained.

"I need to go home now," said Porro.

"I'm sorry, Mr. Camorra. You don't get to make that choice," he said.

Anastasia looked down from her vintage point in Heaven as the man in the green uniform locked the handcuffs around Porro's wrists. She watched him escort Porro to the patrol car, while her mother, straight and dignified, looked on until Porro became a dot in the distance.

Epilogue

The chairs were lined up over a carpet of golden shower blooms. The pond brimmed with fish, lush foliage surrounding it. The trickle of the water as it dropped from the rock and circulated back up reminded the attendees of the tears each one of them had shed at some point in their lives. Drop by drop, it meant water was needed to fertilize the seeds of the goodness to come. It was inevitable, and it was the way of the world.

The violins began to play Pachelbel's Canon in B minor. Sofía walked down the aisle, her arm wrapped around Cesar's. She beamed in her mature age, as her dream had finally become a reality. Cesar led her to where Francisco was standing, to the right of the priest, and gave her a kiss on the cheek before standing next to his father.

Sitting in the audience, in the first row, Carlos held his one-year-old niece, while Azucena sat next to him, her eight-month pregnant belly showing through her gauzy, cream-colored lace dress.

"Da-da," said the one-year-old, stretching her arms toward her father. Porro took her in his arms, smiling. Life was good. Now with Don Francisco retiring, he had assumed the responsibilities of a property owner and shared in the management of the estate with his brothers-in-law. He looked around the crowd, at his pregnant wife, and then at the sky, an immaculate blue canopy of goodness and bliss. He said a silent prayer and thanked the heavens for his luck. Against all odds, good had prevailed over evil.

About the Author

Alexandra Goodwin was born in Buenos Aires, Argentina. She came to the United States as a student and decided to stay when she met her soul mate. Now that her children are grown, and despite her full-time job as a bookkeeper, she finds time to write. She is the author of Whispers of the Soul, an illustrated book of poetry, and has published several articles, personal essays, poems, and short stories both in English and in Spanish in various print and online publications. She lives in Coral Springs, Florida, with her husband Craig and their two poodles.

www.ingramcontent.com/pod-product-compliance
Lightning Source LLC
Chambersburg PA
CBHW030350020726
47493CB00003B/761